Crying Wolf

Doug Joseph

FIRSTFLITE PUBLISHING

Copyright © 2024 by Doug Joseph

All rights reserved. No part of this publication may be reproduced, stored in a retrieval system, or transmitted in any form or by any means—electronic, mechanical, photocopy, recording, or any other—except for brief quotations in printed reviews without the author's prior written permission.

Paperback ISBN: 979-8-9917265-1-1

Ebook   ISBN: 979-8-9917265-2-8

LCCN Number: 2025931576

First Edition

This book is dedicated to a wonderful person
who inspired me to press on with writing:

To one of my biggest fans, my dad, George,
who always loved and believed in me.

I love you, Pop!

Table of Contents

CHAPTER ONE

The Blip Means Life

The quiet hum of the ship's engines made his room a welcoming place of solace. Captain Remy Eskar sat comfortably in his quarters, reading the latest International Planetary Federation News from his tablet. *This whole universe is falling apart faster than anyone could put it back together.* He guffawed and rolled his eyes at an absurd quotation from a senator caught bribing officials in his district.

The captain looked down at his tablet to see a low-priority request for his presence on the Command Deck. *No rest for the weary,* he thought as he slowly stood and headed out of the room.

The Bridge door slid open for the captain. He smiled as he walked onto the deck. Preferring a darker working area, he required the lights on the Command Deck of the advanced Corvette-Class warship IPFS *Gibraltar* to stay at half power during crew operation. As he walked onto the Bridge, the crew members' posture straightened, and they paid closer attention to their assigned tasks.

Eskar's frame was thin and athletic, though his stomach extended much more than he'd have liked. At 1.9 meters, he was tall for a Honduran, and his thinning salt-and-pepper black hair was mainly hidden beneath his hat. The forty-five-year-old's eyes had a charismatic twinkle, and his mild accent added to his attractiveness. The crew knew his pride in them, and he generously expressed it.

While on mission into interplanetary space, nearing the Jupiter side of the asteroid belt, scanners tracked a signal from a Federation cargo ship. The ship lay dormant under two hours from the *Gibraltar*'s current course and position.

Ensign Antoni Capalov called to the captain. "Sir, I'm getting a strange distress signal coming from inside the belt. Its signature is from one of our cargo ships but isn't through the usual communication channels. I've reached out multiple times, but there is no response."

Eskar walked over to see the signal. "How far off course would that take us?"

"It looks like ninety to one hundred minutes, sir."

"How close do we have to get to determine if there is still life onboard?"

"Maybe thirty minutes."

Eskar calculated the impact on his tasks. "Is there anyone else in the area?"

Capalov frowned. "No, sir. No other vessels are within days of our position."

Eskar rolled his eyes and sighed. "Let's head there."

"Yes, sir."

The ship diverted off its course to investigate. Eskar kept looking at his watch. He gazed over at the forward deflection shields, which already registered increased small-debris impacts. The captain's hands tapped the guardrail as he did his best to be patient.

"Captain? There it is. It's faint, but something's alive in that ship," Capalov said as he pointed to a small object on his display.

The captain squinted to study Capalov's control panel. *It's time to get those reading correction drops. My eyes are getting so bad,* he thought as he attempted to make sense of what the ensign was showing him.

An icon showed a medium-sized cargo ship drifting helplessly through Skeleton's Rift: a minor void within the Carlson asteroid belt. Every second, a tiny red blip emanated from the ship as he watched the pale icon on display.

Eskar's thoughts swirled. *We don't have time for this.* "I'll bet kreda to coconuts it's a damn rat or maybe a cat."

The comment drew a chuckle from the young ensign. "Maybe so, but the rules say we must explore if life is detected."

Eskar frowned as he took a sip from his coffee, knowing the ensign was spot on. "You think I don't know the rules, son?" Then he cursed under his breath as the black substance burnt his upper lip. "Why do they make the coffee up here so blasted hot?" He stared at the console again. "Is life support even running on that ship?"

Capalov highlighted the ship and clicked on 'information.' The system replied in a few seconds. "Okay, this is the IPFS *Hercules.* It should have docked six weeks ago. It appears that there's one room on the ship with atmo. It also looks like only short-range communication is working on the ship."

"That must be why we got such an unusual distress call on a lower-level channel. Just one room left? You've got to be joking." Eskar shook his head.

"No, sir, I'm not. It's the secondary mess hall in the aft end. The good news is that it's the nearest room to a docking portal."

Eskar rubbed his chin as he studied the console. "Can we attach to their comms?"

"There's not much power over there, but I can try." Capalov furrowed his brow as he began to type at a feverish pace. The intensity of his gaze caused Eskar to take a small step backward. Without notice, the typing stopped, and Capalov smiled. "You're patched in, Captain. The intercom should work as long as the volume is up in the room."

Eskar nodded and put on a headset. He tapped the blinking AUX icon on his command pad. "Um, hello? This is Captain Remy Eskar of the IPFS *Gibraltar*. If you can hear this, please respond."

The deck remained silent as everyone waited for a reply. Capalov tilted his head. "Captain? Do you hear that noise? It kinda sounds like shuffling."

Eskar looked up at the ceiling as he listened. "Yeah, it sounds a lot like a rodent. Let me try again." He tapped his AUX icon and began to express himself in a louder tone. "This is Captain Remy Eskar. If you're hearing this message, please respond in some way."

Capalov's eyes narrowed as he continued to make sense of what he had heard. "Can you hear that, Captain?"

"Hear what?" Eskar shook his head, pursing his lips in a slight scowl.

Capalov ignored the captain's body language. He rubbed his right thumb on his lower lip. "It sounds like someone's whispering."

"What the hell? Why would they be whispering? This is their one chance to live." The captain snatched his cap off and scratched his forehead in frustration. "Run it through LAM to see if it can figure out what's being said."

"Yes, sir." The Linguistics Analysis Module (LAM) was enabled in a couple klicks. "It should only take a few moments, sir."

Eskar nodded.

Words began appearing on the monitor:

Oh my god! Major Dillon Temkin here. Something's on here with us. I'm afraid to let it know where I am. Not human. Please be careful. It took out the crew. Even if those things don't get me, my life support isn't going to last too much longer. My acknowledge code is Bravo Bravo Foxtrot Alpha Four Niner Charlie.

Capalov typed the relayed information into the computer. "ID checks out. Major Dillon Temkin fought in both conflicts. Our boy is a badass. He was awarded a Navy Cross, Distinguished Service Medal, and a Combat Commendation Medal."

Eskar scratched his neck as he adjusted his headset. *Looks like we're on a rescue mission.* "What's the typical crew size for that ship, and what the hell is he doing on a cargo ship in the asteroid belt? Also, what does 'not human' mean?"

Capalov shrugged. "The charter says twenty-one people were on board. Can you imagine all that ship with only twenty-one people on it? That ship is over three hundred meters long. Maybe the IPF found *something* of military importance in the belt. Says here, he's Special Ops. What if it was an escaped animal? Remember that dude who tried to smuggle two lions onto the Kincade Hub?"

A lieutenant sitting behind Capalov chimed in with an enthusiastic confirmation, "I remember that. The guy's name was Porter, something or 'nother. One of the lions woke up when they were transferring it through the port hatch and nearly mauled the two workers on the station. Thirteen crew members were court-martialed, including the captain."

Capalov continued, "Yeah, that's some crazy crap. What was that bonehead thinking?"

Eskar put his hands in the air, and all conversation halted. "Hey, gentlemen, focus! This guy sounds like he's in up to his elbows, and it doesn't strike me like it's some circus animal doing it. Do you think renegades raided their ship?"

Capalov shook his head. "The guy said 'us,' but no other life forms are on the ship. Everything living on the ship's in that room, and I only detect one signature."

The captain pouted as he spoke. "What about weaponized droids? It wouldn't be the first time we've seen that. Cargo ships usually have construction droids on them. Those are ideal to be hacked."

Capalov checked. "Nope! There's no energy being used on that ship other than the life support system in that kitchen. All droids give a pretty sizable RF signature that I'd see a sector away. The only thing I can see is what appears to be some watches and minor electronics on the crew members who are presumed dead. The rest of the ship's been completely sucked of energy. It's amazing that the intercom works in that room, let alone the life support."

Eskar hailed Temkin again, "Hang in there, major. We're coming to get you." He quickly turned to his second in command. "Mason, take three teams over to that ship. Start with the drones, and let's assume this is an active and hostile situation. Bring medics and engineers to see if we can help any survivors and get the ship flyable again. Our priority is to extract Major Temkin, but not at the cost of our men. Make sure it's safe for us to enter, save our man, find any other survivors, then try to save the ship."

Capalov quickly interjected, "Sir, there's more to the message."

Eskar stopped immediately and looked at the ensign's terminal:

> **...the forward docking bays are compromised; be careful. I don't know if they can be repressurized. My hall is depressurizing, too. It's dropped twenty degrees in the last half hour. I'm in my suit but don't know how long I can last.**

Eskar let the words sink in before responding, "We're coming, son. Just hold on."

The captain turned to Capalov. "Do we have any more information from the scans on that damn ship? We need to know what we're getting into."

Capalov was already typing. "On it, sir."

Commander Jacob Mason waited in the preparation room. His hands shook from the adrenaline pumping through his veins. His deep, raspy voice garnered their attention as he stood before the twenty-four soldiers he commanded.

"Okay, troops. Captain wants us to break into three groups, launching our drones first and letting them do the dirty work. Parker? You're in the red group. I need you to head up the forward patrol. Wallace? Blue group. You're the satellite, and my group will go aft. There are possible hostiles, so stay on our game and keep communication open. There's at least one survivor. We need to find him, identify threats, and extract him with precision. Screw the lasers. Take real hardware and make sure to look out for each other. Are we clear?"

The crew replied in unison, "Sir, yes, sir."

"Okay, suit up. We leave in five. Dismissed."

Mason's com lit up, and Eskar spoke with some urgency. "Mason, there's little time to spare. We will let you know what the scan shows. Do not enter until we have inspected the whole blasted thing. Let the drones do their job."

Mason replied, "Yes, sir!" He quickly headed to his locker to take the necessary equipment for the mission. Slipping into his life suit, he zipped it up in one motion. The helmet hung on a hook above him, and his M27 rifle was safely stowed in the weapons box at the back. Holding the gun put a smile on his face. He reached back and pulled out a box of the sealed-hull ammo and shook it. "Okay, men, get to the Mantis ships. We need to go now!"

Eight troops entered each ship, and the pilots were already onboard doing pre-launch. Each soldier took his position and locked himself into place. The squad commander went down the line to ensure each man was secured in their seat and their helmets were fastened and energized. When the commander sat, the man beside him verified he was ready for launch.

After each commander indicated they were ready for launch, Mason called command. "Captain, we're launching now."

The Mantis ships closed their main doors, and the pressure change in the cabin was rapid. Mason wanted to adjust his ears, but the helmet had no way to do that. Instead, he sat back and closed his eyes, wanting this part of the journey to subside. Launching was his least favorite part of any mission.

The lights flashed and warning horns blared in the bay as the launch doors opened. A voice shouted through the intercom, "Launching in ten seconds."

Mason looked down and grabbed the metal handles on each side of his chair in preparation for what would occur next. He looked at the men around him and hoped they wouldn't notice as he closed his eyes for good measure. The chair Mason sat in rotated so that his feet faced the ship's rear. He grabbed the handles tighter as he heard his ship latch onto the launching catapult.

An automated voice came over the intercom, "Brace yourselves; launching in three, two, one. Go."

Mason could feel the compression of his suit squeezing his legs as the launching process began. He tried to take a deep breath to calm himself, but his heart raced at the moment. *It will all be fine in a matter of moments,* he repeated to himself like a mantra as his neck pain increased from the G-loading of the launch.

Ten seconds passed, and the forces on their bodies diminished. The chairs returned to their normal orientation. Mason immediately got on the com. "Red and Blue teams, when we're one klick from the target, launch the drones." He tapped the switch and said, "Captain, we're nearing the launching point for the drones."

Eskar immediately replied, "Great. Let's get as many eyes as we can on that ship."

"Yes, sir. We're on it." Mason looked down to see a blue group calling. "Wallace, what do you got?"

"Sir, we're in position and launching drones."

"Great work. Make it happen." Mason could see the red hailing him. "Parker?"

"Yes, sir. Launching drones."

As a voice came over the intercom, Mason could feel the ship slow down. "We're in position, sir. Should I launch the drones?"

Mason spoke with authority. "Affirmative launch!"

The pilot replied. "Launching."

The ship shuddered as eight drones departed to inspect the cargo ship. Mason looked out the starboard window and watched the drones speed off to the target. He calmly reached down to his communication device. "Sir, all twenty-four drones have been launched."

The screens in Mason's ships showed the searchlights on the drones illuminating the nearly dead cargo ship. One illuminated "IPFS *Hercules*" on the forward side of the hull. *Not a way to die. We better not add any names to that list.*

The drones finally made physical contact with the ship. Mason watched as the hexapods scurried about the ship's surface like massive man-sized insects. This style of drone creeped him out, but they were effective. The pilot called out to him. "Sir, most of the ship is unpressurized. The drones can enter without issue."

Mason watched their unnerving movement as he replied, "Let them enter."

Sometimes referred to as the Dragonfly, the DSV-17

Advanced Tactical Attack Drone (ATAD) was an invention effectively used in both conflicts. With its six appendages, nimble maneuverability, and a longer-than-normal body, the comparisons to the adeptly flying insect were unmistakable.

Mason wanted to unbuckle himself from his chair but knew it was against protocol. He tried to adjust his position, with little success. He quietly sat, waiting for the green clear signal and information from the *Gibraltar*. The clear light finally illuminated, and the troops all unbuckled and headed to their action stations on the Mantis.

Four crew members kept an eye on information coming from the drones, while two inventoried weapons and ammunition for the mission. Mason watched his team perform their duties with precision. He smiled with satisfaction.

Gibraltar's command channel burst into life. "Mason, do you copy?"

"Yes, sir. Loud and clear."

"Scans show that you won't be able to enter from the front. From what the scan can determine, there's something highly corrosive in the forward high bay. All the bulkhead doors are closed, but maybe the corrosion is working through the walls. Almost no power is left on the ship, and the batteries have been bled almost dry. This has become an extraction exercise. Focus all attention on saving Major Temkin. Make it fast, and we can send drones in to look for more survivors. The ship's hull looks compromised, so tread lightly."

"Affirmative, Captain. We'll focus on the known survivor. Sending in the drones first to ensure the coast is clear."

"Excellent. Carry on, Commander," Eskar responded.

Mason immediately shared the information with his team

leaders.

The intercom in Mason's ship came alive. "Commander, we've located the survivor at the aft end of the freighter. Scans show he's fully suited, but there's no pressure in the hallway leading to the room."

Mason reported back to the home base. "Captain, we've located Temkin. He's in a room towards the aft end of the ship, but the hallway to that room is depressurized."

"So that means you can just go in, right?"

"No, sir. We can't just open the interior door; everything will be decompressed too rapidly. The regulation of the suit can only accommodate so much decompression at a time. It'll balloon and possibly burst if we go too fast. Also, everything's going to be sucked to the door, so opening it is going to whip him around like a rag doll. I don't know if the target could survive that. I'd suggest cutting some holes in the door and letting the pressure equalize. We could probe the pressure and open the door when it has equalized."

There was a delay before Eskar responded. "How long will that take?"

Mason bluntly spoke. "Maybe fifteen minutes."

"That's a long time."

Thank you, Captain Obvious. Do you think we want to be out here that long? Mason thought as he suppressed his inner demons. "Yes, sir. But I don't see another option."

"Understood. I'll inform Temkin of our intentions. Get this done as fast as you can, but stay alert. We need to assume this is an active zone. Temkin insists there's still something on that ship."

"Roger that. I'm sending in two teams. Right now, the drones haven't detected any other life."

Eskar responded. "Copy that. We've looked at all the drone feeds, and there's no evidence of forceful entry onto the ship. The corrosion in the forward bay implies that whatever did this was brought on board."

Mason broke the momentary silence on the deck. "Sir, the drones have given us the green light. We're sending in two forward squads. Without power on the ship, we must manually open the docking hatch. Since no pressure exists on the other side, it should easily open. Captain, hold on, I'm getting an urgent message."

Mason flipped coms to the second incoming communication. "This had better be good, Parker."

"Sir, I'm looking at the drone feeds for the forward decks, and I'm just gonna send you the feed. I don't know what to say about this."

"Copy that, I'm ready."

Mason's Heads-Up Display (HUD) turned to a video feed from one of the drones scouting the forward deck. The image showed a half-opened door with a flickering light behind it. As the drone approached the door, the flashing light would give instances of the horror in the room. Blood spatter and human debris littered the floors, walls, and countertops.

As the drone looked in further, ten bodies were sprawled around the room, and a makeshift barricade dominated the feed. The gruesome deaths of the occupants struck Mason's heart, and the strobing light only added to the room's irreverence.

Mason's eyes became fixated on something else about the bodies. Most of the deaths he could see were headshots. *Holy crap, whoever did this was one hell of a shot,* Mason thought to himself. "That was one horrible fight, Parker."

Parker quickly responded, "Yeah, it made me sick to my stomach. I've seen some bad ones, but I think I'll be skipping dinner tonight."

"The mission just keeps getting better. No evidence of life, though, correct?"

"No, sir, not any."

"Roger that, let me get back to the captain."

The feed ended, and Mason reached down and returned to talking to Eskar. "Captain, I'm back. I looked at the drone feeds, and the front deck fight looked horrific. But it seems there is nothing else living on the *Hercules*."

"Understand, Mason, and again, be careful. The survivor sounds concerned that there's still something on the ship."

"Yes, sir. We still have drones hunting inside and outside the ship, and we've found no activity. Based on the images we're getting, it looks like it was one ugly fight, and someone in that fight was a killer shot. But we believe this Temkin guy is the last and only survivor."

Mason could hear the heaviness in Eskar's voice. "Understood. Keep the drones looking, but let's get our target to safety."

"Yes, sir. We'll do our best." Mason left the com on while he gave orders. "It's green to go in. Chester, take us in so we can open up the aft port. Let's move, but stay aware."

The Mantis ship closed in on the freighter. The pilot spoke again over the intercom. "Sir, we're near, and the freighter's gravity is pulling on us, but no electronics seem to be active. Nothing we can't compensate for."

"Okay, Chester. Could you bring us to the portal door? We need to do one more check to ensure a decent pressure balance. Then we need to open it manually."

"Affirmative. We should make contact in two minutes."

The Mantis slowly approached the portal. When it maneuvered close enough to the ship, an umbilical tunnel extended and attached itself to the portal. The connection caused the entire Mantis to shudder.

Chester spoke again, "Sir, we have made positive contact with the vessel. It's time to go to the depressurization chamber."

"Thanks, Chester. Okay, team. You heard the man... let's move."

The team fell in line and headed to the lower deck.

On the Command Deck of the *Gibraltar*, Capalov studied the transmissions with Temkin before speaking. "Sir, Temkin's words imply he might have been in contact with something foreign. The regulations state that he needs, at minimum, a ninety-six-hour quarantine."

Eskar acknowledged the observations, "Thanks, Ensign. You're right on all counts." He quickly turned to his com module and contacted Med Bay. "Jill? I need you to prepare a foreign substance Quarantine room for our arriving guest. The protocol recommends ninety-six hours."

Dr. Jill Kadon responded. "Yes, sir. We were already preparing it. It'll be ready for his visit."

Eskar smiled at the report. "Excellent news. Thanks, Jill."

Jill quickly responded. "You're welcome, Captain."

"Sir, can you take a look at this?" Capalov's comment startled the captain.

Eskar's eyes glared. "What's it now, Ensign?"

Capalov's ears turned a bright red. "Feed's coming up on the screen."

The six drone feeds were replaced with one. Capalov gestured towards the screen. "Look at the makeshift barricades. Do you notice anything?"

Eskar studied the screen. "Other than the dead bodies? Looks like they were set up for a fight that they lost badly."

"Yes, but look at the inside walls of the barricade."

The captain again walked close to the display. "Definitely a heated gunfight here."

"Yes, sir. All the damage is on the *inside* of the walls." Capalov stood up and pointed to the damaged fortifications. "Look here. There aren't any shots on the outer walls. See how the inner ones are scored."

Eskar put his face inches from the monitor and squinted, "What the hell? Were they fighting amongst themselves?"

Capalov shrugged. "Maybe the enemy somehow dropped into the middle of them."

Eskar kept studying the drone feed as he frowned. "Possibly." His eyes lit up as a thought came to him. "Can we get the drones to retrieve the ship logs?"

Capalov shook his head. "No, we can't access them without more power to the main computer and a full reboot sequence. I can get the drones to retrieve the black box. It won't have everything, but it will have CCTV and ship vitals."

Eskar deflated as he considered the circumstances. "Good. Maybe after we extract Temkin, we can try to revive the ship enough to get the logs."

"Yes, sir. I think that's possible."

"Very good. Carry on, Ensign." He quickly made contact. "Mason, what's your status?"

Mason stood at the entry port for the *Hercules*. He could feel his nervousness increasing as he went to respond to Captain Eskar. "We're opening the hatch now, sir."

Mason nodded to one of his subordinates, and they began the opening process. As the seal of the port broke, the familiar hissing of pressure matching caused Mason's ears to pop again. He held his gun in a ready position as the port door slowly turned inward.

The holding room for this port was only five meters deep, with a similar port-style door on the aft wall. Two soldiers cautiously entered the chamber and began to head to the back as the others followed.

Mason made his first personal assessment of the interior. "Captain, we're in the holding chamber. There is no power, but emergency lights are illuminated on the floor. Some gravity still exists, but I'd guess it's about a quarter of Earth's."

"Understood, Commander. Carry on."

Mason instinctively looked down to check the atmosphere in the chamber. The pressure-less room held steady at minus two hundred and fifty degrees. *It's colder here than on the dark side of the moon.* "Natty, open the inner door."

One of the officers obliged. At first, the handle wouldn't budge. He looked at one of the other soldiers, who walked over to help him open the hatch. After some physical exertion, the door finally began to move. When the seal broke, only a minor hissing and a small amount of dust scattered into the holding area.

The two soldiers moved into the adjacent hallway with their guns drawn. Mason followed cautiously behind them. The walkway extended to the aft bulkhead, nearly fifty meters from their position. One of the soldiers spoke. "Damn, Commander, this is a big-ass ship."

Mason looked down the unoccupied hallway. Small particles and debris floated lifelessly around the path as flickering track lights made it seem ominous. The door at the aft bulkhead was so far away that the particles resembled fog.

The hairs on the back of his neck stood at attention as he could feel sweat accumulating on his forehead. "This place is scary as crap. All we need is some mood music, and we'd have ourselves a horror movie."

The comment drew some uncomfortable laughs.

Mason continued, "Temkin should be in the room two doors down and on the left."

The crew wasted no time. Pulling out one of the multi-tools, they began their work on the door.

Mason took the moment to update HQ. "Hatch is open, and they're drilling holes as we speak. We've got a visual on the officer. No other reported activity on the ship. The holes keep icing over, so we must keep re-drilling them, but it's going as planned."

Eskar's smile could be heard through his reply, "Good work, Commander. Keep it up."

Mason looked down the corridor past the room where Temkin waited for rescue. The surreal landscape captured Mason's attention until a red icon lit on his communication module. "Parker, what have you got for me?"

Lieutenant Parker quickly replied, "Commander, we've been

studying the drone feeds and found two things that concern us."

"Go ahead, Parker. Did you find a possible enemy?"

"No, sir. Not exactly."

Mason could feel his blood pressure rising. "Well, don't leave me here guessing, Lieutenant. What'd you find?"

"Sir, the munitions room was stocked with Mark 109s."

"You're kidding me."

"No, sir. We counted twenty of them. But that corrosion we found is now in the munitions room. The 109s aren't that big of a problem, but the corrosion has reached asteroid tunnel carvers, and the drones saw evidence of leakage."

Mason could feel his stomach twisting in knots. "Oh, crap. Understand, Parker. Get your drones to retrieve the black box and pull out of the front."

"Yes, sir. Parker out."

Mason closed his eyes and took a deep breath before contacting Eskar, "Sir, we've found another problem."

There was a long pause before Eskar answered. "Go ahead, Mason."

"Something's eating away at the forward decks. Our drones can see it has visibly made a hole through one of the front Cargo Bays to the munitions room."

"We noticed that. Is there something we didn't catch?"

"Yes. Our drones indicated that the room was full of Mark 109s."

"109s? What's a cargo vessel doing with ship destroyers?"

"Yeah, we thought that too, but they're not the problem. They won't explode without help."

"Why are you talking about explosions?"

"Because there were asteroid tunnel carvers next to the 109s."

"Aren't they inert too?"

"Well, they don't explode if that's what you mean."

"Then what's the problem?"

"They implode."

"I don't get it."

How do I explain this quickly? Mason thought to himself. "They're designed to draw matter in for rapidly making tunnels in asteroids."

"But they're inert, right?"

"Yes, but it's a two-chamber design. It's like epoxy: the two substances are inert until mixed."

"So why would they mix?"

"Our drones noticed that the corrosion was on the carver canisters. The drone spotted some leakage. If the canister's other side leaks, it'll make short work of this ship."

Eskar barked, "Mason, get your men out of there."

Mason's men could be heard as indistinguishable chatter on the live microphone. Finally, Mason commented, "We're not that close to equalizing the pressure."

"Open the door now. Don't wait. We'll have to take our chances with Temkin."

"Yes, sir. Can you warn him?"

"Affirmative, I'll tell him now."

Mason could hear Eskar speak through the ship's intercom, "Temkin. We've got to get you out immediately. They'll open the door, and the pressure will drop rapidly. You need to brace yourself because it's going to get bumpy."

Mason looked in the window and saw the occupant with his thumb up.

Eskar spoke back through Mason's communicator. "Mason,

Temkin's ready. Open the door."

Mason shouted his reply, "We're on it. Go! Go! Go!"

Two soldiers placed crowbars in the door, forcing it to open despite its reluctancy. Small particles, wrappers, and other objects shot into the hallway like projectiles when the door seal was broken. As the door opened further, everything, including Temkin, began to be hurled toward the exit.

Mason had left his communication on. A loud thud could be heard on the intercom, and him giving orders. "There he is. Grab him, and let's get the hell out of here."

Three soldiers rushed into the room, clearing debris and picking up Temkin. In a matter of minutes, the team was back on the Mantis.

It took a few minutes for anything understandable to be said. "Sir. The target is captured. We're back on the Mantis."

Parker broke into the conversation. "Sir. We lost the feed of the drones in the munition room."

Eskar wasted no time. "Mason, get out of there. Now!"

"Yes, sir. We're heading back pronto!"

"How's the passenger?"

Mason looked over to see two soldiers strapping Temkin to a gurney and placing a 'quarantine tent' around him. "Unconscious, his visor must have cracked on the impact, but he's still with us."

The pilot came over the intercom, "Everybody, brace yourselves. We're in for a heck of a ride."

Mason instinctively grabbed the metal bar near him. Suddenly, the ship felt like it was launched out of a slingshot and was going in the wrong direction. He had expected the opposite and hit his helmet on the safety bar. The ship then began to unnaturally creak as rivets could be heard popping.

Mason shook his head as he watched the floor below him start to contort. He spoke on the intercom. "What in the hell was that?"

In a matter of seconds, all of the drone feeds terminated.

Eskar spoke. "I think the *Hercules* imploded... Mason, are you still there?"

Mason's ship spun wildly for what seemed like an eternity. All he could do was hold on, close his eyes, and think of happier times. It took thirty seconds for Mason to reply, "Sorry, Captain. Our ship was ripped back towards the freighter." He looked around the room and saw all the passengers were still with him. "We're all okay. No human casualties to report, but I think we lost most of the drones."

"Thank God. Drones are replaceable. Get your keister back here, Mason. Drinks are on me."

"Yes, sir. Mason out."

CHAPTER TWO

Wounded

M antis-7 approached the *Gibraltar*, and the pilot hailed the control tower. "Lieutenant Chester of Mantis-7. Requesting emergency landing status."

"Mantis-7, we're aware of your situation. We're setting up landing bay three for your entry."

"Roger that. I'm requesting a visual of my ship to verify damage on my aft end. She's not flying right."

"Understood, Lieutenant. We're sending out three drones to inspect. Please sit tight as they approach."

"Also requesting a med-bot for the survivor. Our initial scans show multiple fractures and some head trauma."

"Affirmative. I'm contacting Med Bay now."

Three new icons appeared on Chester's multi-purpose display. "I'm tracking the drones now."

Within thirty seconds, Chester could see the glitter of thrusters. "I've got a visual on the drones."

The control tower quickly replied. "Affirmative, Pilot. Just sit back while they do their job."

"Copy that." Chester sat back in his chair and watched the service droids scanning the Mantis. He took a moment to run through some checklists on the rest of his ship.

"Lieutenant Chester. The drones have verified significant damage on your port-side thrusters. We're calling out the tug to bring you in."

Dang it, Chester thought to himself, *I could have used the landing credit. I should quit complaining since it's better that I get to fly again.*

"Okay, Command. We'll prepare the ship for towing." The pilot entered a few items into his control panel. The inputs caused the mechanical subsystems of the ship to come to life.

Chester reached over and spoke into the ship's intercom, "Okay, folks. It looks like we're going to have to be towed in. Please secure everything, as well as yourselves, and keep your whining to a minimum as momma tug comes out to bring us in."

As the pilot spoke the words, he could see the hefty tug-bot launch from one of the bays. "Gentlemen, our tow truck has arrived. Prepare for attachment." Chester could hear laughter in the back and was pleased with himself.

The inter-ship com unit came to life. "Lieutenant Chester, please prepare for attachment in thirty seconds."

"Copy that, Lieutenant Driad. We're ready for the union."

Chester looked out his window to see the robotic arms expanding and reaching out to attach to his Mantis ship. The arms had flashing lights that refracted off the glare shield, but all motion was completely silent.

When the first arm secured itself to the Mantis, the ship shuddered. The latch of the robotic arm made a pleasing thud. The audible warnings and motion sirens could be heard throughout the ship. The noise echoed around the entire vessel.

Three more robotic attachments followed in quick succession.

Chester announced over the intercom. "We're about to move. Keep seated as we enter the landing bay."

Slowly, the tug took the wounded vessel inside the *Gibraltar*. When they finally touched down, the pressure normalized, the door opened, and two med-bots entered the ship to address the recovered soldier. One of them spoke, "Mantis personnel. It would be advised that no one is on the ship while we address the damage to Major Temkin. Please exit now so that we may tend to the wounded passenger."

Mason stood first. "You heard the med-bot: leave now, people."

No one had to be asked twice. All crew, including the pilots, left through the landing doors.

Mason was the last out. Captain Eskar greeted him, carrying two bottles in his hands. "Mason. Heck of a job out there."

"Thank you, sir."

"As promised, I brought you and your men something for the effort. Be sure to share them." He handed Mason the two bottles of rum.

Mason smiled as he graciously received the gift. He read one of the labels. "Wow! This really is the good stuff."

"Of course. I bought a case of it on our last furlough. It's the perfect stuff for an occasion like this."

Mason stopped reading to face Eskar. "Thank you again, sir."

Eskar was about to respond when the med-bots caught his attention. The two bots carried the near-lifeless body of Major Temkin off the Mantis. His arm and leg sported temporary casts that could be seen through the transparent fabric he was wrapped in. One of the med-bots held an oxygen mask over his face.

The captain tracked the bots to the door heading to Med Bay. He turned back to Mason. "I hope the guy is all right. That seems like one hell of an ordeal."

Mason nodded as he followed the bots. "Did you see the carnage in the front of the ship?"

Eskar patted Mason on the back. "Yeah, we saw the drone feeds. This guy was lucky."

Mason frowned as he stared down at the ground. "We'll see how lucky he feels having to live with that memory the rest of his life."

CHAPTER THREE

Rise And Shine

G ood morning, Mister Temkin." The advanced medical robot entered as the LED panels around the room slowly flooded with bright, warm light. The AMRV7 robot gracefully navigated around the small chamber. Its smooth, 1.5-meter frame and voice alluded to a feminine structure. The combination of chrome and a high-gloss white finish made the robot even more impressive.

The med-bot's top resembled a medical nurse's hood from the 19th-century American Civil War. The shroud covered the ventilation fans cooling the unit's core processors. A holographic facial projection on the front of the translucent plastic bezel was designed to calm patients. Still, DillonTemkin's body language indicated he found the tranquil design and speech unnerving. The primary difference between this version and the AMRV6 was that the eyes of the projection tracked who they were talking to better. This subtle improvement enhanced patient responses dramatically but did little to console him.

Temkin slowly started moving. He tried to rub his eyes, only to discover a cast on his left arm. The patient let out a small groan. He examined the room he was in for the first time. He lay on a hospital-type bed with a small table next to it. An IV was attached to his right arm, and there was a cast on his right leg. He pulled up the covers and saw that he was catheterized.

The bed seemed diminutive compared to Temkin's two-meter, one-hundred-and-twenty-five-kilogram frame. His shoulders and feet extended beyond the edge of the frame when he lay flat on his back. The young man's athletic build was only blemished by the numerous scars on his arms, legs, and back. Rugged looks and a humble persona assured him of potential company for most of his adult life.

The lighting revealed a room devoid of features. Two-tone, gray paint complemented the walls, and there was a single observation window next to an electronically controlled door. A small bathroom in the far corner would come in handy once he was without the catheter.

The soothing voice of the med-bot continued. "My name is Irena. Your left wrist was broken, Mister Temkin, as was your right tibia. I was able to set both of them properly, and the casts were made to fit perfectly. Based on your age, you should heal quickly. You made an audible noise, leading me to conclude that you are still in pain. Is that the case?"

Temkin tried to sit up in the bed. A flurry of grimaces and grunts followed the unsuccessful attempt. "Yes, Irena. I've got plenty of pain right now. Can you tell me how long I've been out?"

"Yes, Mister Temkin. If you mean how long you have been unconscious, it was almost forty-eight hours. Your contusions and other issues forced me to sedate you so I could set your bones and deal with the complications of your decompression. You have multiple fractures and organ bruising as well. There were minor issues because of the rapid decompression you experienced, but the worst of those have already been addressed. Would you like me to provide you with painkillers? I am going to take a blood sample, and then I can retrieve some medication."

Temkin rubbed his left eye with his right hand. "Yes, I'd like that. Thanks."

"You are most welcome, Mister Temkin. I would not recommend standing up. The pain alone will cause nausea. Now, please lie still while I draw your blood. This will require a needle prod, but I assure you there will be only minimal discomfort. If you do not mind, please clench your fist while I wrap this band around your upper arm."

Temkin complied with the med-bot's requests.

Irena cautiously reached out to grasp the patient's arm. It scanned for the best location for the blood draw and quickly inserted the needle. "You can relax your hand now." The willing arm provided three small vials of blood.

"Would you say you are in much pain, Mister Temkin?"

The young man shook his head. "Hard to say. Just sitting here, the pain is relatively low, but if I move at all, I'm getting very sharp pains."

The brief pause in Irena's reply caused Temkin to open his eyes and look at the med-bot. "At this point, movement is not recommended, Mister Temkin. I will give you a mild-to-moderate painkiller and suggest you sleep as much as possible. Because you were possibly exposed to foreign material, you will be confined to this room for the next few days. I apologize, but I must lock and seal the door behind me after I leave."

Temkin nodded slowly. "I understand. Would it be possible for me to get a tablet for reading? If I'm stuck in here, I might as well catch up on the news."

Irena began to turn toward the exit, answering his question on the way out. "I believe that is permissible, Mister Temkin. I will bring one back with me when I obtain your pain management medication."

The door slid open, and the med-bot left. The hissing of the decontamination chamber caught Temkin's attention, but it was too painful for him to turn his head fully. He sighed and waited for the good robot's return.

He was fast asleep within five minutes. "Mister Temkin, I apologize for disturbing you."

Irena's entry jarred Temkin's eyes open. He took a deep breath before speaking, "That's okay, Irena. It's not like I've anywhere to go."

"Yes, Mister Temkin. You are confined to this room for forty-eight more hours. I apologize, but I was prohibited from bringing you a tablet until you are formally debriefed about the incident."

"It's fine. Please inform your captain that I'm ready to be debriefed. I'd prefer to get this over with as soon as possible, while it's still fresh in my mind."

Irena stopped momentarily. "Thank you for your understanding, Mister Temkin. I have informed the captain of your wishes. I believe that it is also important that you begin eating solid foods. I have provided you with a list of possible options. The items on the list are small portions and liquids, but it is important not to overwhelm your body. My scans show that it has been at least four days since you have eaten solid food." Irena handed a paper to Temkin. It contained a menu of six items.

Temkin reached out his hand to accept the paper. The action

made him wince. "Whoa. That hurts. You're correct, Irena. I haven't had any real food for a few days. I ran out of food packs early last week. A nice pizza sounds wonderful, but I'm sure you're right about easing back into eating."

"We do have pizza, Mister Temkin, but based on comments from other patients, I cannot recommend it."

The comment made Temkin burst out laughing until the pain kicked in. "Either way, I'll take it. I feel like I could eat a horse right now."

"I would not recommend that either, Mister Temkin."

Temkin resisted laughing again, but the comment kept a smile on his face as he looked at the list of options. "Irena, I will have the chicken soup with crackers, and could I get some black coffee?"

"Outstanding, Mister Temkin. I will prepare that for you, and coffee is permitted. Would you like any cream or sugar?"

"No, thank you. Just black coffee, Irena. Thank you."

"You are welcome, Mister Temkin. Now, here is your pain medication and a small cup of water. There are controls on the side of your bed to aid in raising your body. I would recommend using them as much as possible right now. Audible commands control the lighting in the room so that you can dim the lighting at your discretion. As per protocol, I must watch you take these pills."

Temkin felt around with his one good arm until he reached the bed's controls. It allowed him to come to a sitting position. He slowly accepted the pills and water from Irena and consumed the tablets. "Thank you."

"You are welcome, Mister Temkin. I suspect that you should be feeling relief within ten minutes. The captain is coming down to speak to you while I prepare your meal."

"Thank you for all you have done, Irena." Temkin lost the fight to keep his eyes open as he spoke, closing them while still listening.

Without hesitation, the robot turned to exit and responded, "You are welcome, Mister Temkin. I will be back shortly."

The hissing of the decontamination chamber reopened Temkin's eyes.

CHAPTER FOUR

First Impressions

Because of the smooth surfaces in the Quarantine room, the intercom reverberated much more than normal. "Major Temkin? I'm Captain Eskar of the IPFS *Gibraltar*." Eskar's voice commanded attention, and the room's acoustics amplified this quality.

Temkin slowly turned to see Eskar standing at the observation window of his room. "Sir. Thank you for saving my life."

Eskar's head cocked as he smiled. The comment took him by surprise. "I just gave the orders. Some braver men did the dirty work."

"Yes, sir. I owe your whole ship and crew my appreciation."

Eskar examined the young man before him and took a moment to answer. "I know you're recovering, but I wanted you to tell me as much as you remember while it's still somewhat fresh in your head. I know there are cameras all around the room, but I like to keep a record for myself. If you don't mind, I want to record this, too."

Temkin didn't move but responded quickly, "I'm good to answer any questions you have, and I think recording is a great idea."

"Great, let me start the recorder. Just one moment." Eskar looked down at his control pad and fidgeted with it. "There, I think it's working now. For the record, this is Captain Remy Eskar's first interview with Major Dillon Temkin concerning the incident on the IPFS *Hercules*. The time is 0807, and the date is twelve March 2105."

Temkin looked away momentarily as his emotions got the best of him. After a brief pause, his composure returned, and he faced Eskar.

How old is this young man? Maybe thirty-five? "Can I call you Dillon, son?"

"Yes, but my friends call me Deke."

Maybe thirty. "Can I call you that, then?"

"Yes, I'd like that."

Eskar pulled up a stool to the window. He waited a moment before he spoke. "So, it seems so cliché as I say it, but how you holdin' up, son?"

Temkin looked up like he was trying to find the words. At first, he stuttered, "Captain, I can't explain how I feel. I'm thankful to be alive, but I can't shake the question: Why me? There were lots of good people on that ship. Why did I make it and not them?"

Eskar nodded, recalling the many battles of years gone by. He scratched his chin as he reflected on personal tragedies. "I've seen my share of death in both Martian conflicts and asked that question many times. All I can say is that it just wasn't your time, but that's neither comforting nor does it bring back our lost friends. I understand you fought in both, too."

Temkin frowned as he acknowledged the sentiment. "I don't know about you, but the Martian Secession was far worse for me. Maybe it was my rise in rank, but it really got to me. I dreaded every battle. Yallon's men never surrendered; they'd fought to the freakin' death."

Eskar exhaled as he put his hands on his knees. "Yeah. Those were horrible. Crystal Valley?"

Temkin's face turned pale. "I was there too. It's hard for me to trust Martians after that war crime was washed under the rug. As bad as that was, it was still better than this. At least we knew and understood who our enemy was. Something took over our ship, and we were helpless to do anything about it."

Eskar cocked his head. "What do you mean *took over*?" As he spoke the words, he noticed the numbers on Temkin's heart monitor continued to increase. *Tread lightly, old man,* he kept reminding himself.

Temkin's eyes widened. "It started with gremlins in the comm system."

"Gremlins?"

"Yeah, little problems. For instance, the intercoms would cut out. Then, an hour later, they'd play music all through the ship. Our techs buzzed out the entire system and couldn't find any reason for the anomaly. Eventually, we completely lost long-range communications."

Eskar removed his cap to scratch his forehead. "Was the antenna damaged?"

Temkin sat quietly, but his hands shook, and the heart monitor continued to race. "Nope... Not at all, and the wiring seemed intact. We re-flashed the computer, too, but we couldn't make any long-range contact. By the time this happened, the captain concluded we were under some kind of attack."

I'd be blaming lousy luck, but maybe the captain had seen more. Eskar leaned forward again. "Did anyone see anything?"

"Not exactly. More than once, I heard something shuffling down the halls from my bunk. When I went to investigate, nothing was there. This happened to a few of my buddies, too. It was like we were chasing ghosts."

Or chasing some Jack Daniel's. "Those older cargo ships make lots of weird noises."

Temkin frowned. "Captain? Come on. I've done plenty of tours. Do you think I don't know the many strange sounds of a ship?"

Eskar nodded as he put up one hand as if to say he surrendered. "Okay, okay. Sorry. I'm sure you could tell the difference."

Temkin continued, "One time, one of my buddies saw something, but by the time they got out of their bunk to chase it, they thought they watched something walk through a wall."

I'm telling you, son, check his person for a little whiskey. "...and you believed that?"

Temkin closed his eyes and shook his head. "What? Of course I did. Bigsby was a guy I'd fought with in both conflicts. He wouldn't make up stuff like that. The guy didn't have much sense of humor, but I'd trust him with my life."

Eskar adjusted himself on the stool. "I understand, Deke. Shifting gears just a little, can I ask why you and your men were on the *Hercules*?"

Temkin's hands stopped shaking. "I'm not at liberty to discuss that."

Crap, this is some sort of black op. "Umm... so you were on some type of mission, then?"

Temkin tried to turn to look at Eskar when he spoke, "I'm sorry, Captain, but I cannot discuss why we were on that ship. Suffice to say, we were there for data collection, but that's as far as I can comment on that."

"Was the data stick you were holding part of your mission?"

"You found it?"

"Yes, you were clasping it when we rescued you."

Temkin smiled. "That's at least some good news. I'd ask that you secure it. That data stick must be delivered to Command when we dock. I don't need it, but Command will."

The captain pressed further, "Can you comment on why there were Mark 109s in the munitions room?"

The patient's smile faded. "You know that answer too, Captain."

No surprise there. "Yeah. I figured, but I wanted to ask. I've been asking you a lot of things. Are you too tired or stressed? Do you want to stop for now?"

Temkin grimaced as he shook his head. "No, it's okay. I really think it's essential to get as much down as possible. This whole thing's a nightmare, and any detail I can provide now may help us for future encounters and investigations."

"Okay, son. Just let me know when we need to break. You're stuck in that room for two more days, so we've got plenty of time to kill."

The comment got a snicker from Temkin that he instantly regretted as he grimaced from the minor fractures in his chest. "I'll let you know."

"So, let's go back to the ship. You were telling me about hearing things and maybe seeing unexplainable things. What else happened?"

"Yeah... Umm... When the comm array died, Captain Haynes put us on high alert. We started armed patrols within the ship."

"Lasers or slugs?"

Temkin took a moment before answering. He slowly turned

and looked at the captain. "Only lasers, but I know I wasn't the only one carrying my Beretta on patrol."

Everyone wants to be a cowboy in space. Eskar shrugged as he nodded. "It wouldn't be the first time I've heard that. You own a nice one, by the way. Is that a vintage nine-millimeter? We found it on your person when we rescued you."

"Yes, it was a gift from my original CO… well… it wasn't as much a gift as a lost poker bet. But I'd like to think it was a gift."

Eskar puckered his lower lip and cocked his head at the explanation. He continued, "That must've been a heck of a hand. And that's why I won't play poker with my team. Sorry to get back, but did the patrols help?" Eskar looked up at the heart monitor and noticed his heart rate was increasing again.

"Not to find whatever this thing was, but it did help us find something else."

"Something else?"

"Yeah. Bigsby, the guy I mentioned earlier, noticed that the containers in the front high bay were corroding."

"From what?"

"No idea, but we think it might have been some kind of reaction with the containers themselves. By the time we recognized it, they had bonded with the floor. We sent construction bots to separate them, but those droids could neither move the containers nor open them. One of them tried cutting through them, and some highly toxic gases were released. We decided to open the bay to see if the cold could stop the reaction. It'd also help the toxic fumes to exit."

Eskar kept watching the heart monitor. "So what happened?"

Temkin let out an audible groan before talking. "The doors wouldn't open."

"Were they stuck?"

"No clue. But we could manually open the doors to port out the toxins. We thought we were good enough, but we had no idea how wrong we were."

Eskar watched the heart rate on the monitor race upward. He was about to make a call when the door to Temkin's room opened and Irena entered.

The robot glided to the patient's bedside. "Mister Temkin, I have been monitoring your vitals, and I believe I need to administer a sedative. Please relax while I add it to your IV."

Eskar spoke one last time, "Deke, I'm sorry to have upset you. We'll continue this at a later time."

Temkin raised his hand as he nodded. "Okay. Don't be a stranger."

Eskar laughed at the joke as he shut off his recording device. He waved and headed back to the Command Deck.

CHAPTER FIVE

I'm Fine

Temkin lay motionless on the bed. The combination of the sedative, warm food, and blankets assured his slumber. Eventually, his eyelids started to flutter as his heart started racing again. Suddenly, he sat up in bed and took a deep breath.

Rubbing his good hand through his hair, he looked around until he twitched in agony. He carefully laid back down. His eyes were slowly closing when the intercom came to life.

"Nightmare?" Doctor Jill Kadon asked through the intercom.

Temkin's eyes reopened at the interruption. "Umm... yeah... but it was more like a memory than a dream. Pardon me for asking, but who are you?"

Kadon's cheeks flushed. "I'm sorry. I'm Doctor Jill Kadon. I'm the closest thing we have to a counselor on this ship, so you're stuck talking with me, Major Temkin." Her black hair was back in a tight bun, and she wore an officer's shipboard uniform, which did nothing to hide her curvy figure. Her Filipino heritage gave her a skin tone that always looked tan, even in the middle of deep space. The only indication of her position was the words 'Chief Medic' on her chest pocket.

Temkin nodded as he lifted his hand like he was reaching out to shake hers. "Call me Deke."

Kadon played along and reached out her hand. "Okay, Deke. Dumb question number one: How are you feeling?"

Temkin tried to sit up on his own but could not overcome the pain. He opted to use the bed adjustment to rise to a sitting position. The motor reached the desired position and stopped, causing his head to wobble. He squinted as his head came back to a resting point. "Not dumb at all, but it's kind of rhetorical. I feel like crap, Doc. I'm in pain. I nearly died, I lost some good friends, and now I wrestle with their ghosts in my dreams. I'd say a general 'not good' would be accurate."

Kadon looked down at her tablet and made a note with her stylus. "That's fair. So, tell me a little about yourself." She looked up in time to notice the drawing of a dagger tip on the back of Temkin's neck. A regular shirt collar would have hidden it, but the medical gown showed the upper portion. The tattoo was well done, with vivid contrast and bright coloring.

Temkin's jaw clenched. "What?"

"Tell me about yourself. Where did you grow up? Why did you join the Navy? What sparked you to get that tattoo on the back of your neck? You know, what makes you, you?"

Temkin slowly raised his right hand to scratch his right eyebrow as he spoke. "Shouldn't you be asking me what I'm struggling with or what I dread in the coming days?"

Kadon's chuckle came out more like a snort. "We'll get to those eventually. Right now, I'd like some context. I mean, I don't know you. You don't know me. I figure we can start there and then move on."

Temkin's hand moved from his brow to scratching the top of his head. "Umm... okay. Well, I grew up mostly in the slums of

Pittsburgh but eventually ended up in Hoboken for high school. I lived with my mom and never saw my dad after I was ten."

"What happened to your dad?" Kadon wrote something on her tablet as she spoke.

Temkin watched her writing and slowly continued. "Well, one day, he went to work, and we never heard from him again. My mother was going to file a missing persons report when she found his letter. Six months later, we moved to Hoboken. When I was thirteen, I was informed that he was found dead not that far from our house in Pittsburgh. The police couldn't determine how long he had been there, and no foul play was suspected. It was labeled a suicide. That's about all I know."

The doctor nodded as she continued writing. "I'm so sorry. That must have been hard."

Temkin thought for a moment before answering, "My dad leaving? Yes, very — on me and Mom. Discovering my dad passed, not really. A part of me wanted to ask him many questions, and another part felt like he had it coming, you know?"

Kadon looked up from her tablet. "How was your relationship with your mother?"

"She's a saint. I don't know what she did to deserve a husband like that or a son like me." The young man's cheeks flushed as he spoke on this subject. "She worked two jobs to keep us afloat, and I decided I could do better on my own. I left home when I graduated from high school. I got in some trouble, and the Navy recruited me. My mother came to my graduation and deployments. I didn't talk to her for a few months, and then I realized what a crappy son I'd been to her. I started writing her every couple of days. She never made me feel bad. She continued loving me like she'd done her whole life."

Kadon leaned forward, resting her arms on the tops of her thighs while holding the tablet. "She sounds pretty amazing."

A slow, affirming nod preceded his answer. "She is. She'll be the first person I'll call when we get back."

"So, the Navy wasn't your choice?"

Temkin squinted. His head wobbled side to side as he answered, "Not exactly, but it was the best choice I ever made. What about you?"

The question took her by surprise. "What about me, what?"

He looked her in the eye. "Well... I've told you about my early life. What about yours?"

Kadon tipped her head slightly and began to speak. "Well, I was born in Guam. My parents were captains, and I rarely got to see them together, but they stayed happily married until my dad passed two years ago."

"Did they love each other?"

"Most definitely, and all five of the kids. We moved a lot, but they made everything fun. Choosing the Navy was a no-brainer for me and three of my siblings."

"What did the fourth one do?"

"Kerci? He's a physician in Guam."

"Are you all doctors?"

Kadon burst out laughing. "No. My younger brother is a mechanic, my other older brother is a pilot, and my sister is captain of the IPFS *Valkyrie*."

Temkin smiled. "Nice."

Kadon nodded with apparent pride for her siblings. "I think so... So, back to you. It's too early to talk much, but do you think you'll be okay? That nightmare looked pretty intense. I can prescribe you something."

Temkin frowned. "I really don't know. I feel awful but drugged, and I'm still fighting a lot of pain. I don't seem to be like myself, but I'm glad to be alive."

Kadon began writing in her tablet again. "That's good. Believe it or not, that's a big deal."

"I'll say this. It's nice to talk to any human right now. Until today, I haven't talked to anyone in about two weeks."

Kadon snorted again as she replied, "Don't worry. I'll be back many more times. You'll probably become quite sick of me."

Temkin started reclining his bed. "Well, so far, it has been most interesting. Oh, and Doc? The tattoo was a gift from one of my ex-girlfriends. I didn't want it, but she insisted."

Comparing Notes

Captain Eskar watched Doctor Kadon leave the Quarantine quarter. He quickly walked up to her, matching her brisk pace. "Doctor Kadon? Might I have a word?"

Eskar's words jarred her from some deep thought, but she recovered quickly. "Of course, Captain."

Eskar wasted no time. "I saw you leaving Major Temkin's quarters, and I was curious about your thoughts."

Kadon's lips pursed. "It's way too early to say, but my initial conversations indicate that he's friendly, highly intelligent, and somewhat evasive."

Yes! I noticed the same thing, Eskar thought as he stopped walking momentarily. "Evasive?"

Kadon continued walking. "Yes, he's good at deflecting conversations to avoid divulging too much."

"Do you think he has something to hide?" Eskar asked as he resumed walking.

Kadon looked up at the ceiling while walking slightly slower. "It's really hard to say, Captain. I think he's truthful, but I think with every answer, there's much more to the story. I get a sense that he has a past of hurts, even before this latest episode. I believe that his charisma has carried him through many tough conversations in the past."

Eskar realized asking the doctor these questions this early might seem presumptuous. He took a deep breath before speaking. "Sorry to bother you on this prematurely. I'm just trying to stay ahead of this. I've informed HQ of the situation and expect to hear back from them within forty-eight hours, but your words also confirm some of my initial thoughts."

Kadon nodded slowly. "I understand and appreciate that, Captain. That's one of the many reasons I enjoy being under your command. We can't judge this book just yet, but context is always helpful."

"I'll take that as a compliment, but we're both captains."

Kadon's eyes brightened at the comment as a dimple formed on her left cheek. "Technically, yes. But I'm on your ship, which means the buck stops with you. That's how it works."

Eskar cocked his head and squinted. "I don't know if I like the sound of that."

"Yeah. I'm pretty sure that's how the Navy makes it work."

Eskar's eyes turned towards Ensign Capalov walking in the other direction. "Jill, if you can excuse me, I need to talk to this young man."

"Of course, Captain." Kadon continued walking down the corridor.

Antoni Capalov's gangly figure was accentuated by his poor posture. His reddish-brown hair and freckles made him seem more like a young teenager than a man in his twenties. The ensign's contagious smile and clever comments made him popular and memorable among the incoming crew.

Eskar lifted his hand. "Ensign Capalov?"

Capalov stopped in attention. "Yes, sir."

Eskar gripped the folder he was holding tighter. "At ease, son. What is the status of the information package we requested?"

"Sir, a lot of it has already arrived. I have Temkin's military and most of his civilian background. We're waiting on some additional information concerning his parents. It appears that his childhood records were sealed."

"Sealed? What do you mean?"

"Well, usually it means that Temkin had run-ins with the law when he was a minor, sir. We won't know until we see the documents. It's a formality, but we needed an extra layer of approvals to obtain those records. I expect them to arrive in the next data dump in forty-five minutes."

"Excellent news. We need as much information as we can get. At some point soon, I must determine if it's safe to allow Temkin to walk around the ship. I want to make sure we aren't dropping the ball here. In fact, I think it's a good time to pay Major Temkin another visit. Carry on, Ensign."

"Yes, sir!" Capalov took a deep breath and continued down the corridor.

Eskar noticed Kadon had just finished talking to someone in the corridor. He quickly approached her again. "Oh, Doctor, one more thing. I think I need to get a prescription for some Presbyopia drops. My eyes have really been bothering me. Can you handle that for me?"

"I can. Please stop on by the Med Bay later today."

"Will do. Have a good day." Eskar turned around and headed back to the Medical Quarantine facility at a heightened pace.

CHAPTER SEVEN

Let Me Tell You a Story

Temkin sat in bed, eating a small cup of soup and crackers. His face was devoid of emotion, but he ate at a voracious pace. The low rumble of the aft engines drowned out the noises of the shuffling feet outside his quarters. A person standing at the observation window caught his attention.

"Captain Eskar. Two visits in one day. I must be doing something right."

Eskar smiled. "How are you, Deke?"

Temkin kept eating and replied between bites. "I've had better days, for sure. But I'm alive. I've had three human visits today, and mess hall soup never tasted so good."

"I apologize for stressing you so much earlier. I just know it's best to get as many details as possible while things are still fresh."

"No need to apologize. I understand and want to record all of this before it's forgotten. Thanks for being patient with me."

"Of course. Is this a good time to carry on?" Eskar assumed it was and started his personal recording device.

"Yes, sir. It's as good a time as any."

"I already turned the recorder back on. I think we left off with you manually opening the cargo doors to allow the toxins to exit."

"Yes, sir. I volunteered to do that. Because of the toxins, we were required to use external controls. I had the highest rating for that."

"Why didn't you send a drone?"

Temkin shook his head and snickered. "Drones aren't permitted to do something that would endanger the crew. Opening the Cargo Bay manually without a life-threatening incident in space is an example of what they aren't permitted to do."

"Oh, of course, but wouldn't the toxins constitute a life-threatening event?"

"You would like to think that, wouldn't you? But the toxin was sealed in the Cargo Bay, and the robots considered manually opening the bay doors life-threatening, or at least more dangerous..."

"You're kidding."

"Nope. So, I went out, made the walk, and opened the bay doors. I waited for fifteen minutes, then closed them again."

"That's crazy."

"Yeah, especially because we had to bring the ship to a full stop for me to walk." Temkin stopped for a moment and looked off into the distance. "That was the last time our engines ran."

"What?"

"When I returned from the walk, we went to restart the engines, and the reactor completely shut down. Our tech said it needed a core part we didn't have on the ship."

Yep, this is the ship of the damned. "Didn't you already tell me long-range communication was down?"

"Yes, and we were already on high alert. I don't know what

the part was, but the techs had never seen it fail. Normally, everything is spared, especially on deep space journeys like this, but this thing must've been overlooked. It's like this trip was cursed, and the captain was convinced we were under some sort of attack."

Eskar noticed that Temkin's heart rate was rising again. "Deke, I can see this is getting to you again. Let's talk about something else for a while."

Temkin winced as he put his empty bowl on the small table. "Okay, what else do you want to talk about?"

Eskar's eyes narrowed as he spoke. "I'm afraid you're stuck with us for the next three months. Your injuries aren't life-threatening, and we, too, have a mission to do. We've prepared a room for you after quarantine."

Temkin nodded in understanding. "Thank you. I can think of much worse places to be stuck for three months. I think I'm fine now if you want to continue with the debrief."

Eskar scrutinized the man before him. *This guy's a trooper.* "Okay, but if your heart rate keeps going up like that, we need to stop for the day."

"Understood. I was talking about the captain. Did you know Captain Haynes?"

Eskar shook his head. "No, I can't say that I did."

"A good and knowledgeable guy, but very much by the book. I liked working with him, and in this situation, there was no book he could go by. He broke the crew into three groups: one on patrol, one on finding a solution to the reactor, and one on fixing the communication array."

I can see where this is going. I've watched Scooby-Doo. Eskar chuckled to himself. "Let me guess. You were on security detail."

Temkin shook his head. "No. Because I've got an electronics background, they put me on the communication array. There were five of us, and we figured if the long array was down, maybe we could try boosting the short array and reach someone."

Heck of a good idea. Eskar's eyebrows raised. "That was the signal that brought us here."

Temkin slowly nodded. "We started sending that over three weeks ago."

Eskar understood. "We got that signal two days before we rescued you. You were lucky we saw it at all. We got here as quickly as possible."

"I get it, Captain. I'm just thinking about what happened next and how much of the crew could have been saved if anyone had heard it earlier."

"So, what happened to the crew?"

"The reactor group devised a possible way to bypass the broken part. It would require us to make a temporary replacement out of two other parts. It would also require us to expend a large amount of power to fabricate it."

"But you guys were already on batteries."

"Yes. We decided it was our best hope of surviving. We began shutting down non-essentials. One system that incorrectly got shut down was the forward-deck CO_2 monitor and scrubber. We also killed most of the lights on the ship and shut down atmo in the unused bays."

"All of that sounded reasonable, except the CO_2 monitor. That's pretty standard procedure when running on batts."

"The CO_2 monitor would have changed everything. We didn't realize it, but as the reactor team was working on the makeshift part, they were both taking the oxygen and creating large amounts of CO_2 that weren't being scrubbed."

"Oh no!"

Temkin stopped and sighed heavily. "Seven crewmates never woke up. I can only assume we were all suffering from hypoxia. One of the patrols discovered the dead bodies, while another found corrosion on the forward Cargo Bay door. The captain got two messages. One said there were seven bodies, and we needed a medic. The second message was that we had a breach in the forward Cargo Bay."

Eskar closed his eyes as he listened. "My God! This is a nightmare."

"The captain ordered us to barricade ourselves in the engine room and recalled the patrols. I think his thoughts weren't clear, either. I remember Bigsby and me working our tails off to barricade the room. About halfway through is when the two patrols arrived."

"Why didn't any of you notice the erratic behavior?"

Temkin grinned. "Erratic? Everything was crazy. Sorry, but the tension was so high we had no idea how others would respond."

Eskar gritted his teeth. "I'd say let's stop for now, but I can't. What happened next?"

A tear dropped from Temkin's eye as he spoke. "The patrols started helping with the barriers, and we got them about done when suddenly music blared from the intercom. The sound shocked two of the young cadets, and they began firing. Before you know it, most of the crew was firing their guns."

Eskar shook his head as his eyes closed tightly. "At what?"

"At each other. The captain called for us to stand down, and I think Bigsby and I were the only ones who listened. We stopped, but when the captain was hit, we decided to make a run for it. So

Bigsby and I jumped a barrier and tried to exit the door."

"Tried?"

"Yeah, the doors were no longer automatic. They had to be slid open. The captain shot Bigsby in the back as we tried to open the door. I squeezed through the door and ran as fast as I could. My bunk was in the aft, so I headed there and waited."

"Waited? For what?"

"I still wasn't thinking straight. I was waiting for the enemy to make a sweep of the ship, and this was my one last stand."

I can't even imagine being back there by myself. Eskar's mind was racing. "How long?"

"I stayed in my room for two days. I realized I needed to get to the mess hall because I was out of food. I made my way there and got some command equipment. When I ran diagnostics was when I realized that the CO_2 scrubber was off in the front. I checked the monitors to see lots of dead bodies. I also noticed that the pressure was dropping on the ship. I got a pair of life suits and sealed myself in the mess hall. I had atmo, food, and water until the batteries died."

Eskar's hands tightly clenched the rails of his chair. "I don't know how you did it, Deke."

"I lost track of time, and I'd lost all hope of being rescued. The intercom kept blasting music every so often, and I heard movement on the ship. Nothing would appear on the monitors, but I knew something was out there. I think it was about a week when I heard your message on the intercom."

The two men sat silently. Irena came into the quarantined room, breaking the tranquility. "Mister Temkin, is there anything you require?"

Temkin solemnly looked away. "No, I'm okay."

As Irena spoke, it took the tray with his emptied soup bowl and coffee cup. "I see you ate everything, Mister Temkin. That is a good indication that you are improving."

Eskar broke out of his silence, "I'm going to go now, Deke. I'm sorry to make you relive that."

Temkin tried to smile, but it looked forced. "If we go back, we could probably power the ship enough to download logs. I'd love to figure out what happened. I lost some close friends over there."

Eskar frowned. "I'm sorry, but the ship was completely destroyed shortly after rescuing you. One of the drones managed to secure the black box, but it was also damaged. We're in the process of pulling the drone apart to recover the item."

Temkin sighed. "Well, thanks for saving me. Hopefully, they can get that box intact. It can tell us a little about what happened."

"This is going to make one hell of a report. I'd love the corroboration. HQ will be chewing on this for years. Good day, Deke. I'll speak with you later."

As Eskar began to turn, Temkin interjected, "Sir, I've one last thing I need to tell you now, but you must stop your recording."

Eskar stopped moving and reached to suspend recording. "Speak freely, Major."

Eskar studied Temkin. It was clear to him that he struggled with conveying what he needed.

Temkin finally spoke. "Sir, I cannot tell you what I was here for, but I must tell you a phrase you might need if we encounter someone else out there."

"Someone else?" His left eyebrow raised.

"Yes, sir. Again, please don't ask me anything else, but the phrase is 'High tide is coming,' and the response will be,

'We should be prepared for that.' You can't write those down nor share them with anyone else here. Please note if this is considered a breach of security protocol, I will sign any paper to that effect, but I'd rather protect your crew."

"I'd say thank you, but I don't fully understand this."

"Just remember, 'High tide is coming.' It could avert a sticky situation."

Eskar closed his eyes as if it would help him to recall that phrase. "Okay, son. Get some rest."

chapter eight

Doing Research

Eskar sat at his desk, reading the limited reports on Major Temkin provided by HQ. The additional information that was supposed to be in the latest data cycle was suspiciously absent. *Why do they make this so hard?*

A knock at the door grabbed his attention. Eskar looked up and said, "Come in."

Ensign Capalov cautiously walked in. "Hello, sir."

"Ensign, thank you for getting as much of this information together as you could. I know HQ can drag their feet a little, but don't worry. It'll arrive sooner or later."

Capalov uttered a noticeable sigh. "Thank you for your understanding, Captain. Have you had a chance to look at any of it?"

Eskar studied the young man. He already admired his attention to detail and his quick thinking. "I just started looking at it. Can I make a request of you?"

"Of course, Captain. What do you require?"

"I need a second set of eyes on this investigation. I also need someone to bounce ideas off of. Would you be willing to participate in that capacity? Also, I'm asking you not to share any of this information with the crew."

The ensign started to salute, then abruptly put his hand to his side. "It'd be my honor, sir, and I will remain silent as a church mouse."

Eskar clapped his hands. "Great! Do you have time now?"

"Yes, sir, I do." Capalov grinned as he stepped further into the room.

"Okay, pull up a chair. Now, did you read my report on the two interviews?" Eskar pointed to the screen where the report was in plain sight.

"I did. This is one wild story, sir."

"Do you believe him?" Eskar cocked his head slightly as he spoke.

Capalov leaned back in his chair to study the captain. "I think it sounds too crazy to make up, sir."

Eskar nodded as he adjusted his cap and scratched his forehead. A bead of sweat caught him by surprise. He wiped it quickly and put his cap back on. "Yeah, I can see that. I don't know what it is, but something seems off in his account."

Capalov's brows furrowed. "Off? How so, Captain?"

"Let's talk about the most obvious. All military vehicles that fly the IPF flag keep all the parts to create a spare reactor. It's a requirement for any deep space mission. What are the chances that the one broken part on the ship's reactor is unavailable?"

Capalov thought about that for a minute. "Framing isn't spared, only the parts. Framing is assumed to be repairable. Could it be he meant that the frame somehow broke? In your report, he said something like he didn't know what the part was. Maybe he misunderstood what was broken, sir."

Eskar puckered his lower lip and nodded. "That's a real

possibility. See, Capalov? This is what I needed. Someone to think out of the box. I've got to find a way to ask him that without raising any red flags. And one more thing: We aren't on the Bridge, son. 'Sir' isn't required in this room."

The ensign relaxed visibly at Eskar's comment. "Thank you, sir... I mean, okay. That'll be a hard habit to break."

The comment made Eskar giggle.

Capalov continued. "Now that I'm sitting here thinking about it, I've got another thing that didn't make much sense."

"Okay, shoot."

"I remember looking at the blueprints of the ship. Temkin would have needed to reach the end of the aft hall to get a command console because that's where the tech room was. He seemed to say that he hid in his room for two days, then slipped over to the kitchen. So, he was terrified but managed to sneak up to the tech room to get the command console?"

This kid is sharp. "Could someone in the aft already have set up a console? Maybe they needed to work on the long-range communication problem and had it out?"

Capalov shrugged his shoulders. "That's possible. But if Captain Haynes is at all like you, you wouldn't have allowed it."

"True. But based on Temkin's report, I don't believe he was the sharpest crayon in the box."

Capalov chuckled as he considered the comment. "I've never heard that before, but that's pretty funny."

Eskar laughed. "My grandparents used to say it all the time."

"I will probably borrow that too. Hopefully it's not about you."

"Knock yourself out... And no, Nana didn't say it about me but often about a pair of my cousins."

Capalov recovered. "Back to Temkin. When you interviewed

him, was there anything else that struck you?"

Eskar paused for a moment as he considered the question. "You know, he was so comfortable. I really believed every word he said. All of his comments came off so naturally, and he gave no indications of exaggeration. I felt bad for him. It sounds like he lost some close friends. Maybe it's just the old captain in me, but I'm always worried when things are too easy."

Capalov leaned in closer. "Yes, sir. Let's make sure all of this checks out. Do you want to look at the records we got?"

The captain nodded and turned to his computer. He rotated the monitor so that both of them could look at it. "Maybe it would be better if you drove, Antoni." Eskar stood up, and the two men switched chairs.

Capalov quickly brought up the portions of the military record that were available. "I don't understand why they couldn't give us the whole thing. This bureaucracy is total BS." The ensign studied the captain, and his eyes widened as he remembered he was sitting with the ship's captain.

Eskar patted him on the back. "Don't worry, son. I've heard a lot worse. Plus, you're right. Dealing with HQ is always a pain in the ass. Let's just look at what we got, and we can go from there."

Capalov started reading out loud. "Major Dillon 'Deke' Temkin. Age thirty-one."

Eskar puckered his lower lip. *I knew he was around thirty.* "Look at those accomplishments. Not too shabby for a man his age."

"Yeah. He definitely was on the fast track up."

Dang, I forgot to stop by the Med Bay. Eskar leaned closer and squinted so he could see better. "You know, he talked about how tough the Martian Secession was. Let's look at what made it so tough for him."

Capalov's eyebrows raised. "Oh, wow! He fought at Hebes Chasma."

"Yikes. That was the bloodiest battle of the war. He also fought at Crystal Valley."

The ensign kept reading, "He was awarded the Navy Cross after Hebes Chasma."

Eskar nodded. "Not too shabby. Can you pull up the report on that?"

Capalov's eyes narrowed. "Okay. I found it. It says he was part of three units pinned down by heavy fire. Lieutenant Temkin jumped a dividing wall and ran at the enemy, holding two automatic weapons. He killed seventeen enemy soldiers and found an exit path for all three units."

Eskar adjusted his cap as he spoke. "Wow. That's one heck of a story. Look! There are some interviews on the right side."

Capalov moved the cursor over one of the interview files. "Major Lars Peliko's account."

"Yeah. Click on that."

It took a moment, but then the video started playing. Capalov interjected, "It looks like this was taken just after the battle. The major is still pulling a clump of dirt from his visor."

"Yeah. Let's see what he has to say."

The major's eyes were shifting left and right, and he could barely hold the microphone without shaking. The video quality was granular, and smoke from the battlefield could be seen in the background. When he spoke, he had a surprisingly deep voice.

"This is Major Lars Peliko of the advanced Echo division. On a routine sweep, our three units were ambushed by four enemy squadrons. We retreated to an abandoned warehouse at the end of Lux Avenue."

The major stopped for a minute to regain his composure. "We were already under heavy fire and could see the enemy bringing in heavier artillery. Getting to the warehouse, we lost four men, and at least six others were wounded. We were pinned in the building, and the gunfire was too intense for us to be able to leave. Lieutenant Temkin was lying on the ground, and it looked like he was crying. Suddenly, he rose and asked for two guns and a bunch of clips."

Peliko started shaking his head and chuckling. "In all my days, I've never seen anything like it. We all thought he was crazy, but Deke slipped out one of the side doors, and the next thing I heard were multiple gunshots on his position. Then, there would be a few moments of silence and more gunshots. This pattern went on for about ten minutes. The next thing we hear is Deke coming back in and explaining that he had cleared a path for us all to escape. We followed him to safety, and when we got back

over the line, Deke just passed out. All three squads made it out because of what he did. A short while after we escaped the warehouse, we looked back to see artillery destroy the building. We would have been in there if it weren't for him."

The video ended, and the screen went blank. Eskar and Capalov sat silently for a few moments.

Eskar was the first to speak, "Wow! That's pretty amazing."

"For sure. Hey, look at the link. They even have his helmet cam. There is an explicit advisory on it. Would you like to watch it?"

Eskar gritted his teeth as he nodded. "Yeah. Do it!"

The video began to play. A warning showed that the video contained violent and disturbing images of human death. The warning faded, and the feed began to play. In the right corner of the video was the name 'Temkin' with a date and time stamp. The feed began in a dark room as a hand reached out to open a door. The image flared as the camera automatically adjusted to the new light level.

Eskar watched intently. He looked down and realized he was gripping his pen so tightly that it snapped in two. He quickly threw the broken device into the trash and continued watching.

A somewhat muffled voice spoke up. "Let's

see what we have over here." The feed's eye point momentarily became obstructed behind a small concrete wall. Slowly, the camera moved and showed four enemy soldiers crawling on the ground toward the warehouse. The feed picked up four successive cracks of a gun as the camera shuddered with each recoil. The camera focused on four soldiers lying lifelessly on the ground. In the distance, a soldier could be heard barking orders and directing soldiers.

Capalov observed, "This is crazy! Those guys didn't even get a shot off."

Eskar couldn't turn away from the screen to reply.

The eye point quickly moved to another position as the shuffling of three sets of feet off-camera was heard. As the three men moved into view, running past the camera position, three shots were heard, and the three men fell to the ground. Temkin took the opportunity to load his gun. It also showed him looking for the clips on the fallen soldier's body.

A gunshot could be heard zipping by as the camera turned to see two men running toward the feed. Temkin's gun raised as he shot the first man in the forehead. The force of the shot caused the aggressor to fall onto his partner, who fired wildly into the air as he dropped to the ground. Temkin fired two more shots into the fallen soldier, who no longer moved.

Quickly, the camera moved again, and Temkin could be heard breathing heavily. As the feed stopped moving, the soldier's heaving was causing the view to rise and fall slowly.

In the distance, a voice could be heard saying, "I think he went over here."

The camera went completely still. The feed showed four more men approaching. Temkin raised his gun and began exchanging fire with the enemy units. Two of the four were neutralized before the sound of Temkin reloading could be heard. As he was reloading, a shot ricocheted off his helmet. The sound completely overwhelmed the camera's microphone with a high-pitched ring as Temkin swore loudly.

As the ringing stopped and the video stream steadied, Temkin's muffled voice could be heard, "Come on, Greg, stay calm!" He raised his gun and ran at the two remaining soldiers, catching them both by surprise. Firing three shots, one soldier slumped, leaving a clear shot for his partner. The camera feed showed

Temkin dropping to the ground and rolling. The unmistakable 'zing' of a bullet passed by the camera microphone. Two more shots were fired, and the remaining soldier fell to the ground.

Eskar blinked and raised his eyebrows. "What did he say?"

Capalov looked confused. "Come again, sir?"

Eskar leaned in. "Can you rewind the video a bit? I'm unsure, but want to hear what he said again."

"Yes, sir." Capalov started rewinding the feed.

Eskar pointed his finger at the screen. "There! Stop it and play."

The audio came to life. "Come on, Greg, stay calm."

Eskar pointed again at the monitor. "Yes, that! I'm not going crazy. Did you hear that?"

Capalov paused the video and scratched his head. "Who's Greg?"

Eskar nodded emphatically. "Exactly! Who's Greg?"

"Maybe he was saying 'Deke,' and it got garbled?"

Eskar contemplated the comment. "That's possible. Rewind it again, and let's take another listen."

"Come on, Greg, stay calm."

Capalov put his right ear closer to the monitor. "That sounds like 'Greg' to me."

"Me too. Antoni, can you look at Temkin's company and see if there were any Gregs in his unit? Maybe he took credit for someone else's actions?"

"I won't have that information now, but I will look it up

tonight."

"That would be great. I think we're at a good place to stop. I'll see you tomorrow, maybe at 0800? We can watch the end of this feed and look at some other material. Maybe we'll get more intel on his childhood in the next data dump."

"Yes, sir. At 0800." Capalov stood and exited the room, leaving Eskar to consider what they had just watched.

CHAPTER NINE

Tell Me Where It Hurts

Doctor Kadon looked around from the observation window. The bed was empty, but the IV lines led to the corner of the room. She saw Temkin lying on the floor in a curled-up position. "Mister Temkin? Are you okay?"

Temkin rose. "Me? Oh... umm... Yeah, I'm okay."

Kadon bit down on her lower lip, then spoke. "More bad dreams?"

Temkin stood up and hobbled back to the bed, his muscular frame pressed tightly against the hospital gown he wore. "Maybe a few, but I'm better now."

"Irena reports your wounds are healing quickly." Her eyebrows raised with the report of good news.

Temkin lay down with a heavy groan. "I wish it felt like they were. My leg and chest are killing me. Irena has given me some painkillers, and they barely touch it."

"I'm sorry about that. I can discuss your pain level with Irena. What would you say it is?"

"When I'm lying here? About a three. When I move at all? About a seven. All I know is that I'm thankful to be alive right now. Pain sucks, but at least I'm still kicking."

Kadon looked down and wrote a note on her tablet. "Okay, I'll discuss that with Irena and see what we can do. Other than that, how's your overall mood?"

Temkin adjusted the bed to a sitting position before he answered her question. "I feel kind of numb. I keep remembering things from the *Hercules*, but now it feels like that was years ago. I think about a couple of my mates over there and get nauseated."

Kadon frowned. "I'm so sorry for your loss. I know this is cliché, but it'll get easier."

The young man nodded as he rubbed his hand through his hair. "That's what they say, at least. I want to believe that's true. I've suffered a lot of loss in my life, Doc. It's never gotten any easier."

Kadon sunk deeper into the chair. "Time heals a lot, but it can't heal everything. Still, I hope you can give it some time. You'll feel better. No one will ask you to forget your friends, but I'm sure they would encourage you to look ahead rather than behind if they were here."

Temkin straightened his gown as he spoke. "I'll have to think about that."

Kadon's eyebrows lifted as she perked up. "Okay, time for a subject change. Sorry, this is the therapist in me. Can we talk a little about your childhood, like before your father left?"

Temkin swayed his head back and forth. "Sure. What would you like to know?"

"How was your home life?"

"To be honest with you, most of my memories are happy ones. I remember my mom making every occasion larger than life. She was funny, kind, and outgoing. I guess it was to balance out my dad. I found out later that my mom had two miscarriages before me. I think he'd have been just as happy for three."

Kadon looked down and quickly wrote some notes. "Ouch. What made you think that?"

"I've thought a lot about this, and I can't recall him telling me he loved me or was proud of me. He'd also complain to Mom that I was costing them too much money and that she was overprotective of me. I know those aren't great memories, but he greatly loved my mom when I was young. We never saw it coming when he left. It destroyed us."

"What makes you say he loved your mom?"

"I can remember him sitting on the couch, playing the guitar, both of them singing. After a few songs, he'd put down his guitar, and they would hug and kiss. It was the happiest memory I had as a kid. He also used to cook fancy meals and would make her laugh the whole time he cooked."

Kadon nodded. "That sounds nice."

"It was. It was just too short. After he left, my mom had to work all the time. Her parents died when she was a teenager, and she had no siblings. We were left with nothing. I had to grow up really fast."

The doctor wrote more notes on the tablet. "That must have been tough."

Temkin wielded an ornery smile. "Hey, Doc, are you writing a novel over there?"

Kadon looked up and cocked her head to one side. She smirked as she answered. "Notes help me to process. Sorry if it's disturbing you. If it makes you feel any better, I wrote a lot more with others."

He shook his head. "Not really. I feel like I'm being judged."

Kadon put down her tablet for a moment. "Well, in a manner

of speaking, you are. It's my responsibility to ensure your safety and the crew's. I need to determine when you're in a good enough place to reintegrate. If I give you a clean bill of health too soon, it could scar you for life. Sorry, but I don't want that on my head."

Temkin shook his head. "That's a lot of weight. I never thought of it like that."

She picked up her tablet again. "It's all part of the fun. My goal is to give everyone here the best care possible. Sometimes that's hard, but it's always rewarding."

Temkin closed his eyes and gripped the side of the bed. "I feel more comfortable knowing that. Thanks!"

Kadon noticed the move. "You are most welcome. I think that's enough for now. I'll talk to Irena about the painkillers and see you tomorrow when we can get you out of quarantine. I need to ask, are you in pain right now?"

"No more pain than usual... I'd say a three or a four. Thanks, Doc. See you tomorrow."

CHAPTER TEN

Adding It Up

Capalov knocked at the captain's door.

Eskar watched him casually walk in. "Come on in, Antoni. Have a seat."

"Good morning, sir." He said anxiously before sitting. "There is no Greg."

Eskar scratched his head while staring blankly. "Huh?"

The young man walked further into the room. "I checked the records you asked me to look at, and there was no Greg in that company. I also looked for Craigs, Treys, Grahams, and Greys. I don't know who he was talking to, but no one in his company had that name. Also, I watched the video again, and you can see the tattoo on his right wrist. It's definitely Temkin in the video."

Eskar tapped the table with his index finger. "So, maybe Greg was another nickname for Deke?"

"Yeah. That's gotta be it. I also thought that some people name their guns. It sounds crazy, but one of our neighbors named all his guns. Come to think of it, he was pretty crazy. By the way, nothing new in the latest data dump. I'll be expecting another dump in two hours. Do you want to watch the rest of that video?"

The captain took a sip of his coffee and sat back in his chair.

"Might as well. It's a good place to get started. I moved the console over so it's easier for both of us to see. Today is the day I need to determine if Temkin should be placed in the Brig or the VOQ, so we need to make some conclusions here."

Capalov studied the layout and gave an approving smile. He sat down and pulled up the video. "This is where we left off. I'm just going to continue it."

The feed showed Temkin running to another embankment and shooting two more men. After he checked their bodies for more clips, he returned to the warehouse. Temkin announced himself, then came in, shouting to his CO, "Hurry up! I've found us an exit. Just follow me."

The three squads followed Temkin out. In the distance, two IPF heavy assault vehicles were waiting to bring the men to safety. When the vehicle was in plain sight, Temkin collapsed, and voices around him called to pick him up. The last image on the feed was three men lifting Temkin to bring him to the assault vehicle.

Eskar turned to Capalov. "Well, that's definitely Navy Cross material. I don't think I've ever seen that kind of precision with rifles. All those men owe their lives to him."

Capalov sat quietly without a response.

The captain ignored the silence and continued. "I've Doctor Kadon coming here at 0830. Temkin is supposed to be out of quarantine at 1600. I figure that we can compare notes and determine the next best step."

Capalov's eyes drooped as he spoke. "I'm sorry we don't have all the data, sir. I feel like we have very little evidence to justify detaining him."

Eskar reached for his coffee and took a big sip. "Antoni, you've done a fine job so far. I think HQ intentionally holds up things like this to prove they're in charge."

A knock at the captain's door grabbed the attention of both men. "Enter!" Eskar said while lowering his coffee mug.

Doctor Kadon opened the door. "Hello, Captain. I'm sorry that I'm a few minutes early. I wanted to take care of something before our meeting officially started. Do you mind if I check your eyes here since you can't seem to figure out how to make it to the Med Bay?"

Eskar's face turned red. He tried to force a chuckle, but it sounded like a muffled cough. "I'm really sorry about that, Jill. Thank you for looking out for me."

Kadon's nose wrinkled, and an awkward smile came to her face. "What an ironic choice of words, and you're welcome. Is it okay for me to do this with Ensign Capalov present?"

Eskar looked at the young man. "Of course, as long as he doesn't mind."

Capalov uneasily responded, "Will there be any blood?"

The doctor snorted at the question, "Blood? Heavens no!"

The ensign gave an approving smile. "Then I'm fine."

"Great. Now, Captain, I need you to sit in the reading position for your console. Just sit where you would think was optimal for you to see the display clearly."

The captain turned the console to face him. He moved it back slightly, and the screen became blurry. "This is the position that I used to read everything at."

Kadon pulled a small tool out of her pocket and leaned over the captain. "Okay, I'm going to take some measurements. It won't hurt, but it's going to make some funny noises."

Eskar donned an ornery smile. "Do your worst, Doctor."

"I don't think you'd like to see that, Captain. For now, I need you to keep your eye open while the Presbyopiometer takes some measurements." She placed the small tool on his forehead and covered his left eye. The tiny device came to life, made a pleasant whirring sound, and would occasionally beep.

When it finished, she took it off and placed it over the right eye. "Okay, we're going to repeat this for the other eye."

Eskar nodded, and she continued with the same process.

When the device had completed its measurements, Kadon removed it carefully from the captain's head. "Okay, I'll have drops delivered to you by noon." She took out her tablet and studied the results. "Wow, your eyes are in poor shape. You really should have done this a while ago."

Eskar sighed as he spoke. "You say the sweetest things, Doctor. Thanks for doing this."

Capalov giggled, which caught Eskar's attention. The captain smiled, knowing he'd entertained a colleague.

Kadon finished studying the tablet and put it to her side. "So, Captain, you called this meeting. Are we all here?"

"Yep. I'd like to hear your thoughts concerning Temkin and to consider ours. We need to determine if allowing him free passage on our ship is safe. Since we won't be docking for over three months, I want us to ensure we're all good here."

Kadon frowned as he spoke. She then reached down and lifted her tablet. "After two interactions with him, I stand by my initial statements. He's highly intelligent, friendly, perceptive, and evasive. I was wondering how much we know about his childhood?"

Capalov spoke openly, "We're still awaiting more information about his childhood. For some reason, the records are sealed.

We're aware that his mother primarily raised him."

Kadon nodded. "When we took a CT scan to determine his injuries, I noted that he had spiral fractures on his radius and ulna, consistent with classic child abuse. He also had a broken collarbone. I'm convinced that he was abused as a child. This is also consistent with my interviews with him. He'd talk freely about his mother, but references about his dad were limited and vague. This is one of the mind's clever protection devices. It tries to help us blot out horrible things."

Eskar listened while he continued to inspect one of the reports on his desk. "Could that be why his records were sealed?"

Kadon pondered the question. "That's a possibility, for sure. One thing I'm getting in my conversations with Temkin is that he seems forthright and truthful, but there are a lot of barriers."

Eskar scratched his head. "Barriers?"

"Yeah. Temkin will freely talk up to a point. Then, deflection will occur. It happened multiple times while talking about his childhood. For instance, when I tried to talk about his father, he suddenly had a memory lapse, and his replies got vague. His father left them when he was younger, and I can sense some bitterness because of that."

Eskar cleared his throat. "I'd also point out that he's in Special Ops. He has been trained to lie. So, would you say we can trust his testimony?"

Kadon put her tablet down and stretched her neck. "It's hard to say, but overall, I'd say yes, he's being truthful. I watched your two interviews with him and compared them with mine. The heart rate monitor gives us some indication of his state as he discusses these traumatic experiences. All I can say is that his heart raised in rate when it should have.

"Let me explain this another way. When you are trained to lie, you can give all of the external appearances of being truthful, but there are indicators internally. Spies are taught techniques to fool the measuring devices, but the body will still give clues if you know how to spot them."

"Maybe it's just the old man in me, but my radar is up," Eskar spoke candidly, "He may be truthful, but something strange is going on with him. I can't put my finger on it, but I don't like the vibe I'm getting."

Eskar offered coffee to his two guests; Capalov refused, but Kadon willingly accepted. He poured two cups.

"I can understand that, but can we hold him on a bad vibe?" Capalov's head lowered as he asked the question. He looked closely at the captain to ensure he didn't overstep his boundary.

"That's a good question. Technically, I can hold anyone for any reason. This ship, as far as the crew is concerned, is a dictatorship. There are people I'll answer to back home if it's done inappropriately. The question is if that same logic applies to visiting officers as well. HQ would say it does, especially if there can be any threat to our mission."

Kadon took a sip of her coffee and nodded with approval. "Woah, this isn't the Navy coffee. It's the good stuff. Hey, Remy, I think I can buy you a couple of days."

"Oh yeah? How so?"

"When he comes out of quarantine, we can restrict him to the Med Bay for observation for a few days. His wounds are significant, and I'd like to do an MRI before I allow him to sleep on his own. I can take my time doing that."

Eskar couldn't contain his pleasure at this solution. "I like how you think, Jill."

"Hopefully, we'll get more information on him in the next data dump," Capalov said.

Eskar agreed as he spoke up. "In the meantime, while we're all here, let's look at what we got and make a plan of action."

Capalov cleared his throat before he spoke. "I know we have been focusing on Temkin, but what about his claim that this was a deliberate attack? I mean, we all kind of believe him, right?"

The three sat silently, contemplating. Finally, Eskar took the lead. "We need to consider that, but other than the black box, there's nothing we can investigate. Let's consider Temkin's testimony. Other than a glitch in the system, bad luck can explain everything else."

Capalov nodded in understanding. "Yeah, but what about the long-range communication?"

Eskar placed his hand on Capalov's arm. "You know, I thought a lot about that. If it were some sort of attack, why would they allow the short-range communication to work, knowing that it could be bumped to a long-range device?"

Kadon interjected. "Maybe whoever it was already got what they wanted. All they needed was enough time to procure something."

"Do you think it could have something to do with whatever was corroding in the forward Cargo Bay?" Capalov stared at his colleagues with wide eyes.

Eskar grinned with pride. "That's another good question. How close are we with the black box? Maybe it can shed some light on this. Plus, not to put too thin a veil on this, Temkin was Special Ops. If there were someone on the ship who could pull this off, it would be him. Also, he's all hush-hush about what he was doing out here in the first place."

Kadon sighed. "That's a distinct possibility. After watching your interviews, he showed every sign of mourning his friend's passing. Bigsby, I think he called him. He also implied other friendly attachments on that ship. It'd take a special kind of coldness to let all of them die like that."

"I agree, but that's something we need to consider," Eskar said. "We'll not have any evidence other than what we can conclude from the black box. I think our hands are tied at this point, but that doesn't mean we shouldn't be vigilant on this ship. We need to keep track of this guy because he'll be our guest for the next three months." Eskar sat back and took another sip of his coffee.

Kadon looked down at her tablet and nervously tapped her pen on the edge. "The good news is that he won't be going too far for a while. The damage to his leg will require a few more weeks to heal. So, at best, he'll be hobbled for the near future. I've also got to break that peachy information to him today."

Capalov looked at Kadon, and his eyebrows raised. "Captain, didn't he request a tablet?"

"He did. But he probably won't be carrying that thing around very much."

"True, but we could snoop to see what he's looking at on it, right?" Capalov spoke freely.

Eskar shook his head and scowled. "I don't know how I feel about that, Ensign. I'd like to believe we all have some level of privacy out here."

Capalov continued, "Captain, all traffic is monitored on the ship. It's just done by AI rather than by a human. The AI is programmed to evaluate words and actions and raise a red flag if something is egregious. We can elevate any account on the ship. It would still be the AI doing the heavy lifting, but it would warn us in time for us to do something. The other option is that we could keep denying his request for a device. He can't communicate with home because we're on a mission. He can read mail but can't reply."

Eskar considered Capalov's comments. *All options suck here*, he thought. "I see your point. I'm okay with giving him a tablet for now as long as we use the AI rather than us as the first line of observation. Hey, Jill, did you read my report on this name, Greg?"

"Yes. Did you find out if he was a soldier in the unit?"

Capalov boldly answered, "No, I did a check for all of that. We thought that maybe it was another nickname for Temkin. I also thought he might have named his gun Greg."

The doctor wrote something on her tablet, then spoke, "That's a possibility. I had a boyfriend who told me he named one of his guns after me: Ella Diablo."

Capalov's laugh cut the growing tension, but he had a curious grin on his face. "I didn't know you were named Ella."

Kadon carried a confused look on her face. "Nor was I named Diablo. It's just Spanish for she-devil... and it was kind of a joke. He had another gun named Vera, and I would ask if that was one of his ex-girlfriends, too. He denied ever dating a Vera, but I wouldn't put it past that sneaky liar."

Capalov looked embarrassed as he nodded in understanding.

"I might find a way to ask him about Greg in my next interview." As Kadon spoke, she reached back and fixed her hair.

Eskar stood to his feet. "I don't want to keep you both too long. Are we good to go for the time being?"

Everyone nodded, and Eskar added, "I'll let you know when our next meeting is. Until then, keep an eye out. Jill, I'll come down to visit him when you release him to the Med Bay."

Kadon smiled and then snorted. "Great. Are you sure you know where the Med Bay is?"

Eskar laughed. "I might have some recollection of where it is. Sorry, Jill. Thanks."

CHAPTER ELEVEN

Expanding Freedom

I have some good news, Mister Temkin." Irena glided into the Quarantine room.

"And what would that be, Irena?" Temkin sat comfortably in his bed.

"You are being moved to the Med Bay, Mister Temkin. Your quarantine time has expired."

Temkin couldn't contain his smile. "That's not good news - that's great news! Though you have treated me very well in here, Irena."

"Thank you, Mister Temkin. I will still be caring for you in the Med Bay, and you will require more attention for your recovery, but now you can interact with the rest of the crew. I also have the tablet that you requested. I apologize, but, because we are on a mission; you cannot respond to incoming messages, you can only read them." Irena's reaction conveyed little emotion, but in its inflections, it sounded happy.

Temkin tried to reach out to accept the tablet, but his hand shook so much that he lowered it to his side and allowed Irena to place the tablet on the table next to the bed. "I'll take anything right now. Thank you, again, for everything, Irena."

Irena continued cleaning items in the room as Doctor Kadon walked into the Quarantine and spoke, "Well, I guess Irena has already told you the news."

"As a matter of fact, Irena happily shared the great news with me. Irena also gave me this shiny tablet." Temkin pointed to the table next to the bed.

Kadon reached her hand out to shake Temkin's. "It's nice to actually meet you, as opposed to watching you through a window."

Temkin unsteadily reached up and shook hers. "It's nice to meet you too."

Kadon's smile eroded as she pulled up a chair. "Unfortunately, this isn't just a friendly visit."

"Am I already in trouble for something? I haven't even walked out of this room yet."

She shook her head as she said, "No, this is just our daily visit with a little extra debriefing."

"Ummm... okay."

Kadon rolled her eyes. "It's no big deal. I need to run some extra tests, including some MRIs."

Temkin sighed, "Oh, great!"

"Yeah, I need to do a contrasting MRI of your head and a couple of other sections of your body. You took a lot of damage over there, cowboy."

A coy smile took over Temkin. "Yeah, but I'm still tickin'."

Kadon snorted. "That's a lot better than the alternative."

"You ain't joking, sister."

Kadon sat in the chair next to Temkin's bed. "So... how are you feeling today?"

"Emotionally, physically, or what?"

Kadon's levity evaporated. "Don't be silly. You know what I mean."

"I feel my body is healing, but I don't feel any better." Temkin looked down and frowned, as if he was examining his own body as he spoke.

Kadon reached into her satchel and her tablet came out. "What do you think might make you feel better?"

Temkin paused and studied Kadon before answering. "Finding out what happened on the *Hercules*. My mind keeps going there. Something attacked us, and even when I say that, it sounds ridiculous to me. I can only imagine how it sounds to you and your captain."

Kadon leaned in a little closer to the patient and asked, "Do you think it could just be bad luck?"

Temkin took another long moment before responding. "I've been on the wrong side of bad luck many times. This was something more. I'm certain there was something intelligent behind this."

"Before saving you, the drones did a thorough sweep of the *Hercules* and came up with nothing."

"I know how unbelievable this sounds, but I'm telling you, we weren't alone up there." Temkin tried to adjust himself in the bed to aid his own comfort.

"Every time I tried to sleep, music would blare on the intercom. Someone or something was watching me, and it felt like it was thriving off my fear." Temkin's eyes darted left and right as he spoke, and his hand shook uncontrollably.

Kadon stood from her chair and placed her hand on his shoulder. "You're safe now. We're far from the *Hercules*."

Temkin calmed at Kadon's touch. He took a deep breath and

spoke. "If you believe me, then you don't know if we're safe or not. If you don't, then you think either I did all of this, I'm crazy, or I'm just one unlucky bastard."

The doctor considered Temkin's words before replying, "It doesn't even matter as much as you think. I believe you experienced something traumatic over there. All I know is that we saved you, you're here, and it's my job to help you get better."

Temkin's hands stopped shaking, and he became noticeably more relaxed. "Doc, I'm scared. I'm scared that what happened over there will happen here."

"I can see that. Let me ask you this: What do you think we can do about that at the moment?"

Temkin remained silent.

Kadon finally spoke. "Exactly! For now, let's fix what we can fix."

"You mean me, right?"

"In a manner of speaking, yes. Different subject: How did you get the name Deke?"

Temkin cocked his head. "Huh?"

"Your nickname. How did you go from Dillon to Deke?"

"Oh. When I was in high school, I played football. One of the coaches gave me that nickname because I'd repeat what he said in the huddles when I was captain. It started as 'The Deacon' and was shortened to 'Deke' somewhere along the line."

Kadon's stylus tapping on her tablet broke the silence in the room. "I see. Did you have any other nicknames?"

"In high school, I had the nickname Lupo."

"Lupo? Like Latin for wolf?"

"I think that's where it came from - I don't know."

"Any other ones, like maybe Greg?"

That grabbed Temkin's attention. "Where did you hear that name?"

Kadon backpedaled. "Oh, I think I read it in one of the reports."

"It's so weird. Three or four guys swore I went by that name when I enlisted and went to boot camp. All I could figure was that there was someone who looked a whole lot like me, and they got mixed up with me. Since then, it'll happen now and then. I don't get it, but that name seems to want to try to stick to me."

"So, it wasn't really a nickname or anything?"

"No, but once I told my mom about people calling me Greg, and she began to cry. It turns out that Greg was what she planned to name her first boy before she had the miscarriage."

Kadon frowned. "That's so sad. I'm sorry to dredge up that memory."

Temkin shrugged. "Yeah. But either way, not my nickname."

"Okay. That's enough stuff for right now. I hope you'll find your stay in Med Bay more pleasant than this room. If nothing else, we have a complete entertainment system at your bed. You can keep up with the latest soap operas or your favorite basketball team."

"It's the Nets, but basketball's out of season. Still, I get the gist. A room with some color will be nice."

Kadon looked around the room as she spoke. The shiny surfaces were all gray, and the only color in the room was the navy stitching on the white bedsheets. "Well, without basketball, maybe you can keep me apprised of what's happening in the soap operas. Med Bay is drab, but you're right. It isn't this drab."

He paused, then added, "Also, would it be possible to take a real shower? The electro-scrub can't replace a real one."

Kadon scrunched her nose. "Sorry, we're on a mission, and water must be conserved. We all get one water shower a month."

"Oh, yeah. I forgot. At least I'll have something else to look forward to."

Kadon nodded in satisfaction. "You and the rest of us! I think it's time for me to let you head to your new digs. Hopefully, you can get some rest."

As if on cue, Irena returned. "Mister Temkin, I have brought a wheelchair to take you to your new bed."

With noticeable exertion, Temkin made his way to the edge of the bed. "Thank you, Irena. I'm looking forward to seeing it."

He turned to address Kadon. "Goodbye, Doc."

CHAPTER TWELVE

Secured Secrecy

Eskar sat quietly in his quarters. The pleasing pulse of the core engines was the only distraction to a rare moment of complete solitude. Despite the tranquility, something troubled him.

He tried to suppress it with a small nap, but the past few days' events continued to nag at him. Frustrated, he rose and headed to his desk to study some more documents on Temkin.

A picture of his wife captured his attention and brought a momentary smile to his face. *Oh, my dear, this'd all be better if you were still here,* he mused as he turned on his monitor. The unexpected passing of his spouse five years ago turned Eskar's world into a somber prison. Because of that, he often volunteered for the most extended and dangerous missions.

The screen illuminated and informed Eskar that he had a message waiting. He opened the message:

Hello Captain,

I just wanted you to know that Temkin is in Med Bay.

I floated a question about the name Greg to him, and he became a little animated. Evidently, he's been called that before. His mother was going to name her first child Greg, but she had a miscarriage.

Maybe there's something to that, but his answers seemed reasonable.

I just thought you would like to be aware of my findings.

Sincerely,
Kadon

Jill is always on top of things. Eskar smiled as he closed the message. He thought for a moment, then reopened the message to send a one-line reply:

Thank you for the update. I'm grateful for your persistence.

-Eskar.

As he began to search for the Temkin reports, he noticed that he could see without squinting. "Wow! Those drops really did the trick," he told the empty room.

The loading was taking longer than expected. While waiting, he decided to make a call to Engineering. "Lieutenant Polson? How are things coming with the *Hercules* black box?"

The young woman on the other side spoke nervously, "Sir, we're still working on it. The damage to the drone was extensive, so we've been carefully taking the bird apart. I'd say we'll have it in the next few hours. Then it'll take a few days to analyze the data."

The answer was what Eskar expected, but he wanted to say something to encourage Polson. "Okay. Keep up the good work. I'm anxious to see what's in that box, so please help me stay informed."

"Yes, sir. I'll let you know when we free the box."

"Thank you, and carry on."

Eskar disconnected and looked down at his console. The Temkin files had loaded. *What the heck is the delay on the rest of those reports?* He thought while slapping his hand on the countertop.

As he sat stewing, a blip indicated a new message. He turned to look at the console again, and his shoulders slumped when he saw it was from Naval Command Headquarters, and it was titled 'Concerning Major Temkin.' *Nothing good starts with the word 'concerning,'* he thought while opening the message.

Captain Eskar,

Under no circumstances are you to engage Major Temkin in questions concerning his

mission on the Hercules. His role is of the utmost importance to interplanetary security, and the data stick you found and secured is a high-priority item.

We understand the need to find answers to what occurred on the ship, and we encourage you to investigate to the best of your ability without pursuing Temkin's role in his mission.

We considered aborting your current mission, but it, too, has the potential to save many lives. Please consider Major Temkin a crew member for the time being, and we will debrief him upon your return to Ice Rock Port.

Sincerely,
Admiral Lars Fergusson

Eskar gritted his teeth as he read the note. "Well, ain't that just lovely." He spoke into the silence of his room. Once again, the room refused to reply.

Taking a deep breath, he reached over to the intercom. "Capolov?"

The ensign quickly responded, "Sir?"

"I get a feeling that we won't be getting those sealed records any time soon. Let's focus on our real mission for now, but we still need to keep an eye on Temkin. Can I count on you to check in on him occasionally?"

"Yes, sir. I'll make a habit of it."
"Good... Good. Thank you, Ensign."

CHAPTER THIRTEEN

Making the Rounds

Doctor Kadon walked into Temkin's quarters in Med Bay. "You seem to be quite into that tablet."

Temkin jerked his head back to look at who was talking. He immediately grimaced, and his face showed he regretted the action. "Oh... Good morning, Doc. I've just been catching up on the news back home."

"Oooh. I'm sorry - I didn't mean to startle you," Kadon said. "That looks like it hurt."

Temkin nodded. "Yeah, but I promise it's getting better. The pain is only three or four, and I stopped taking painkillers yesterday."

"I noticed that... Good. I think we'll take the casts off your leg and arm tomorrow. Based on the last CT scan, you've healed pretty well. The regen stimulators seem to have done their job. You'll probably need a cane for a couple of weeks, but with therapy, you should be good."

Temkin patted the arm cast with his good hand. "All I know is I've got an itch that I'm looking forward to scratching when this baby comes off."

Kadon switched gears, "Anything new?"

"New? Oh... back home? They're putting up a new water treatment facility near my place. That's sure to change the value of the condo." Temkin laid back down in his bed and adjusted it to the sitting position.

"Where is home?"

"I own a place in Groton, Connecticut. To say I live there is a joke, but I've saved up enough that I'll be able to retire in five years with a decent pension and do something part-time to make ends meet."

"Sounds like you've thought about this a lot."

"Yeah, I have gotten a lot of job offers, and I already have a few things lined up that'll pay me double what I make now. I want to make good on my promise to my mom to stay in for twenty."

"So, you were seventeen years old when you entered?"

"Technically, I was sixteen, but I turned seventeen the same month my mother signed the consent papers. What about you, Doc? Do you plan on retiring?"

Kadon pressed her stylus on her upper lip as she stared into the air. A small smile crept into the corners of her mouth. "I rarely think about that, but I can't lie. I'd love to head back to Brazil and live in a place overlooking the water. Maybe someday, but no time in the near future."

"I've never been down there."

Kadon quickly pulled her tablet out of a large pocket in her coat. "It's beautiful. Like no other place on Earth, if you ask me." She handed her tablet over to Temkin. It showed scenic pictures of the Brazilian shorelines, breathtaking waterfalls, and sunrises.

"Those are amazing. Did you take these?"

"Yes, on my last visit. Two years ago."

"You have a good eye." Temkin handed her tablet back.

"Thanks. Most are pretty touristy, but I love 'em ."

Temkin's smile faded. "My bet is you didn't come down here to talk about retirement locations."

Kadon shook her head. "No... no... I've got a couple of things to talk to you about."

Temkin gave her a half-welcoming gaze. "Dig right in, Doc. My dance card is pretty open at the moment."

"Okay. I'd like to give you a few MRIs before releasing you. It'll be about four scans. I want to evaluate trauma on all your major organs and take one last look at any fractures."

"That's fine with me. I'm not claustrophobic or anything."

"Great. That's one less question that I have to ask. What about metal? Do you have any metal implants?"

"Some people said I have a tin head, but it isn't true. Other than that, no."

"Very funny, tough guy. Well, because I'm going to make contrasting MRIs, I need to break this into multiple sessions. I'm sorry, but the scans will take about an hour each. Any allergies?"

"Nope."

"We also have to wait forty-eight hours between sessions. I hope to do the first one right after we remove your casts tomorrow."

"Sounds good to me, Doc."

"Once all those are done, we will probably move you to the VOQ."

"I've never stayed in the VOQ."

"Me either, but I've heard they're much nicer than the standard officer's quarters. Visiting officers are VIPs on this ship."

Temkin puckered his lower lip as he nodded. "Something else

to look forward to, I guess."

Kadon began tapping her stylus on the tablet as she furrowed her brow. "So, next thing. I'm sorry, but I couldn't help but notice that you often end up on the floor in the corner as you sleep."

"I've noticed that too. I don't know how I ended up there."

"Are you sleeping okay?"

"Sometimes I am, but I'm still having a lot of nightmares."

The doctor took down some notes as she spoke. "Do you want to talk about them?"

"Not really, but I will."

"Okay. How about you give me the gist? Just an idea of what they were about."

"I think I can do that."

Temkin closed his eyes and took a deep breath. "The main one is that I'm still being chased by something that I can't see."

"That's not too surprising considering your circumstances."

"Yeah, but whatever it is knows me well, and I think it can't stand me."

"What would make you say that?"

"I don't know if I can explain the feeling exactly because I don't think I understand it myself. I get this impression in my gut that whatever is there wants to remove me but can't."

"Can't? What's stopping it — not that I want you dead or anything."

Temkin chuckled briefly. "I don't know, but it's like something is holding it back. So... I've got a question."

Kadon looked up from her tablet. "Ask away?"

"Have you ever been to a haunted house?"

"Yes, my parents used to make one in our backyard every year."

"So, for me, what makes haunted houses scary is that, from

the moment you walk in, something or someone is watching you, and you're helpless to prevent them from doing what they were planning on doing."

"I can see that." kadon said as she pondered the sentiment. "I've never thought about it in that way."

"That's how I feel in these dreams. Something that doesn't like me is watching me, and I can't do boo about it."

Kadon thought before she spoke. "This feels like a manifestation of what you just experienced."

"Maybe so, but I tell you, Doc, sometimes it doesn't feel like a dream. Especially since you have moved me to Med Bay. When it's completely quiet in here, I feel like something is still watching me. I worry that it has followed me from the *Hercules*."

The doctor put her stylus down and gave Temkin her full attention. "I don't think anything is here, but what do you think would make you feel safer?"

Temkin looked down and considered his response. "I've no idea. What I don't want is anyone else to be in danger."

"Would you like me to prescribe you something to help with your anxiety?"

"No. I'd rather avoid medication, if possible."

Kadon stood and patted Temkin on the shoulder. "Okay. I recommend working out again when we get these casts off you. Physical exertion is a better remedy. Let's get you fully healed, both physically and mentally."

Temkin pinched his lips together tightly. "I really hope so — because things are hard right now."

Kadon stood to leave. "Time will help, too. Get some rest, Deke."

Cast Away

M ister Temkin, it is time for us to remove your casts." Irena's passive voice was designed to calm patients. The med-bot pushed a small cart into the room. On the top was a collection of medical accessories.

Temkin looked over to see the table of tools. His eyebrows raised. "Irena? I must admit that this isn't the most comforting of moments in my stay here."

"I fully understand, Mister Temkin, but I am the most precise tool for this task. I have programmed your anatomy into my system and have determined the optimal path for removing the casts without any injury to your person. I believe that you will feel relief when the arm cast is removed. I have noticed it is rubbing your upper forearm, which I suspect has caused you some discomfort."

"As a matter of fact, it has caused quite a lot of discomfort, Irena. I'm looking forward to its removal." Temkin put his tablet to the side and sat up in the bed.

"With that in mind, Mister Temkin, if it is acceptable to you, I would like to start with your arm as soon as Doctor Kadon arrives." Irena's serene face conveyed no emotion, but Temkin's shoulders relaxed as the med-bot spoke.

"Am I late for the party?" Doctor Kadon walked in unannounced and at a brisk pace. She was already wearing gloves, a mask, and a paper-based apron.

Temkin looked over and smiled. "Not at all. Irena was explaining to me that the cast on my arm would come off first."

"Yes. Based on your last scan, I can see why you've been itching. It's a minor imperfection in the cast itself. No big deal, but definitely an aggravation."

Irena spoke, "Doctor Kadon, I am ready to perform the procedure if you are."

Kadon looked at Temkin. "Are you ready, Deke?"

"Where are we going to do this?" Temkin looked around the room as he asked.

Kadon smiled. "Right here. After this, we'll do the first set of MRIs. While you're in there, Irena will clean up."

"You're the MVP, Irena," Temkin said.

"Thank you, Mister Temkin. I am not sure what MVP means in this context. I am not on a sports team."

Temkin looked at Kadon and laughed. "Well, it means you're valuable and appreciated right now."

Irena paused for a moment as its neural network crafted the appropriate response. "Thank you. I am happy to be of service. If we are ready to proceed, Mister Temkin, I need you to lay flat on your bed."

Temkin immediately began to lower his bed from the upright position as Irena placed the table directly next to it. Kadon stepped out of the way to allow Irena maximum room.

Irena held out a mask for the major. "Mister Temkin, I would like you to put on these safety glasses and mask. The glasses are mandatory because of the laser, but the mask is optional. The fumes from cutting the cast can be quite pungent. They are not poisonous, but it will be more pleasant for you if you choose to wear this."

Temkin grabbed both offerings and placed them on his face. "Is this correct?"

Irena turned to face the patient and examined the mask. "Yes, Mister Temkin. Now, just lay back and try to relax. I would request that you keep movements to a minimum as I perform this procedure. Please let me know if you need to move so I can make it as safe as possible for you. Some patients would rather not look at me while I cut the cast off because I replace my right hand with these attachments. If it bothers you, you can look away or keep your eyes closed."

Kadon studied Temkin as he responded, "I'm fine, Irena. This isn't my first go-around with a med-bot."

Irena removed its right hand and replaced it with a small laser cutter. "This cutter is specifically designed for cast removal. Let us begin then, shall we?"

Temkin nodded. With extreme caution, Irena grabbed Temkin's casted arm with her left hand and began to cut through the casting material with the cutter. The laser made an understated humming sound. Small puffs of smoke and a flickering light occurred along the cutting surface. The burnt stench of residue filled the working area as Irena progressed further down Temkin's arm. Temkin never budged.

When Irena made the final cut, half of the cast fell onto the bed while the other half remained in her left hand. The falling portion made a pleasing thud as it fell.

Kadon stepped in. "Deke, may I take a look at your arm before we continue?"

The young man didn't flinch at the request. "Fine with me."

The doctor removed the cloth sheath that enveloped his arm and studied his upper forearm. "Just as I suspected. The cast was agitating you right here, wasn't it?"

Temkin reached over and scratched the spot that Kadon focused on. "Oh, that's so much better. Yes, Doctor, that's the spot."

Kadon smacked his hand away. "Hold on there, sport. Let me apply some calming cream to it."

Temkin frowned. "Sorry, Doc. I needed to scratch that for some time now."

"This cream will help. Try not to scratch it. Are you feeling any more pain?"

Temkin slowly moved the arm. "Actually, I feel a little dull pain near my wrist. I'd say it's a one or two."

Kadon examined the wrist. She pressed her finger into the fleshy part just below the thumb. Temkin didn't flinch. "I think you're fine. It's most likely some muscle soreness. Are you ready to do the leg?"

A wry look spread across Temkin. "I can't wait!"

Kadon rolled her eyes. "Okay, Irena. Do your magic."

Irena began to hold Temkin's injured leg. "Now, Mister Temkin, just lie back and try to relax. I would request that you keep movements to a minimum as I perform this procedure. Please let me know if you need to move so I can make it as safe as possible for you. Some patients would rather not look at me while I cut the cast off because I replace my right hand with these attachments. If it bothers you, you can look away or keep your eyes closed."

Temkin exchanged looks with Kadon and chuckled. "That sounds very familiar, Irena."

"Yes, Mister Temkin. It is my best response for procedures of this nature."

Temkin nodded in understanding. "Okay, Irena. It's a great response. Please carry on."

The med-bot made short work of the cast on Temkin's leg.

Kadon stepped in to examine the leg. "So, I told you that therapy will be necessary on the leg. I put a cane over in the corner for you to use for now."

Temkin replied, "Yes, you did tell me, Doc."

Irena interrupted, "Doctor Kadon, there is something wrong. My data stream from the server is intermittent. Safety emergency! Please stand back." The med-bot's head, which used optical projections to imitate human-like qualities, started to flicker.

As Kadon turned to face Irena, the med-bot's arm with the laser attachment began to glow vibrantly. The ground started to smoke where the laser was pointed. Irena's face went completely dark as the med-bot swung its arm wildly toward the doctor.

Kadon tried avoiding the beam, but the laser caught her upper left shoulder. Wincing at the discomfort, she could see the attachment swinging back and heading for her neck.

Kadon reached out her right hand to impede the med-bot's progress, but was going to be too late to stop the current trajectory. She snarled as the attachment moved at an unstoppable pace.

Temkin watched in horror as Irena lost control and, without hesitation, jumped off the bed to tackle the med-bot. Though he couldn't stop it, Temkin was able to grab the arm heading toward

Kadon. He gritted his teeth while wrestling to keep the arm away from the doctor.

The med-bot continued to struggle, then went limp.

Temkin got up from the floor and looked at Kadon. The doctor was holding her arm as blood trickled through her fingers. He turned and shouted out into the hall. "Help! We need some assistance in here."

He heard three sets of footsteps coming down the hall, in the distance, before he passed out on the floor.

CHAPTER FIFTEEN

Watchful Eyes

Captain, I think we have some eyes on us." Capalov stared at the screen without looking up.

Eskar heard his name and walked to Capalov's station to investigate what was discovered. "What do you have, son?"

"I keep seeing interference at the edge of our scanner's range, sir. At first, I just figured it was some type of asteroid RF interfering with the equipment. Then I captured this." The ensign stepped away from the console so the captain could clearly see what he found.

Eskar looked at a display showing an identified man-made RF signature. "That's Martian. I haven't seen that since the war. Have you run it against the database?"

Capalov looked down at the console and started typing. He quickly found the answer. "It's an MC Class-Six Frigate, sir."

Eskar looked at the screen as if to verify the data relayed by the ensign. "Class-Six? Are you sure it's not Class-Five? The belt is a long way from home for a Class-Six."

"Yes, sir. The signature is Class-Six, and a variant that came after the Martian Secession. Also, the scanner caught at least one other fainter Class-Five Frigate RF signature." Capalov looked up from the display. His face was filled with apprehension at delivering the bad news.

Eskar pondered the situation. *This can't be a coincidence*, he thought while moving to the command chair. "Lieutenant Walters, move us to REDCON-Two."

The lieutenant responded, "REDCON-Two, sir!"

Within seconds, the ship intercom systems announced that the ship was entering REDCON-Two. All crew members hurried to their assigned battle positions on the ship. Lighted signs in the halls and portals announced the Readiness Condition.

Eskar asked the ensign, "Do you think they've seen us?"

"Based on how they've stayed just beyond our scanning range, I'm going to have to say yes, they have, sir." Capalov looked squarely at Eskar.

"That ship is six times ours in mass, so let's find out for sure. Lieutenant Walters? Please announce we'll be making an aggressive course correction."

"Sir, yes, sir."

The intercom came alive again, warning of an imminent maneuver.

Eskar waited for the intercom to go quiet before he spoke. "Walters, go RF Quiet."

Walters pressed a few controls, and another announcement came over the intercom. "RF Quiet, sir!"

"Quinton? Bring the ship to a hard inertial stop. Immediately."

Navigator Quinton straightened in his chair. "Hard halt, sir!" He leaned over in his chair and spoke into the intercom. "All crew brace for hard maneuvers!"

The Gibraltar lurched to a stop as the crew held on to rails. There was audible creaking as the ship decelerated.

Eskar sat waiting. He took a sip of his coffee and quietly cursed how hot it was. *Let's see how good their navigator and captain really are.* "Keep an eye on the scanner, Capalov. This will be your one chance to see them."

An uncomfortable quiet overtook the Command Deck as the crew watched the ensign. Only the muffled sounds of the alarms broke the silence. Sweat poured from Capalov's forehead as he tried to stay focused on the scanner. Finally, the system rewarded him with a recognition blip—followed by the unnerving sound of two more blips.

Capalov shouted out, "Sir, one Class-Six and two Class-Five Frigates showed up and quickly disappeared."

Eskar grinned. "Well, I guess we have guests. What do you want to bet that three captains are giving three navigators tongue-lashings right now as we speak? Unfortunately, we're no match for that kind of firepower. Walters? Raise us to REDCON-One."

Walters replied, "Sir, yes, sir. REDCON-One!"

Eskar walked around the deck. It was as if he was using this as a teaching moment. "There's no sense in running. The Class-Five ships can easily catch us. Quinton? Let's get up to speed and back on course. If they wanted to kill us, they could have already done that... with ease."

"Yes, sir. Setting course and speed." Quinton's face remained stoic, but his shaking hands did not.

CHAPTER SIXTEEN

The Passphrase Is...

The intercom blared in the Med Bay halls. "Attention! We are in REDCON-One, REDCON-One. Please ensure all discretionary items are secure."

Temkin woke up with a deep breath. "What the hell's going on?"

A med-bot approached Temkin. Immediately, he recoiled at the sight. "Mister Temkin, I am Milla. I can see that my presence alarms you. I am another med-bot from the medical bay."

Temkin tried to relax, but his vitals stayed elevated. "Milla, did you say?"

Milla unemotionally responded, "Yes, Mister Temkin, Milla. I know you are concerned, but may I check you for concussions and other trauma?"

Temkin attempted to straighten himself in bed. His face betrayed the pain in his body. "Okay. Just don't change your hands to weapons."

"I do not understand, Mister Temkin. I am not permitted to use a weapon."

"Yeah? Don't tell that to Doctor Kadon."

"Tell me what?" Kadon walked in, grinning.

Temkin smiled as he inspected the attacked appendage. A lab coat covered her arm, but the flesh-colored bandage could be seen through the material. "Doctor Kadon, you're alive!"

"Yeah. Rumors of my demise were greatly exaggerated," Kadon said, then pointed to her arm. "I only needed a few stitches."

Temkin sighed. "So... you're okay? All I remember is that I was about to jump from my bed to stop Irena from slicing your neck when I blacked out. What happened to Irena?"

"I'm fine, and thanks for jumping into action. I'm a little concerned about you blacking out. We saw no evidence of concussion. The good news is that we have you scheduled for an MRI, and we'll check out everything. We're still looking into Irena. It looks like it got a series of bad data packs that confused its processing unit. I don't know if you heard, but it tried to warn me before it went crazy."

Temkin grimaced as he closed his eyes. "And that comforts me... how?"

Kadon stiffened at Temkin's reply. "Look, I'm just the messenger here. Besides, it was going for me, not you. Irena will be decommissioned after we ascertain what happened. Would you mind if Milla checks you out?"

Temkin shrugged. "That's fine."

Milla stepped forward. "Okay, Mister Temkin. I am going to check your vision. I will warn you that some people find the light I am going to shine in your eyes uncomfortable, but it will only be for a moment."

Temkin sat back in his bed and tried to relax. "Do what you have to, Milla." As he rested on his pillow, he asked Kadon, "Did I just hear that we're in REDCON-One?"

Kadon raised her eyebrows. "Yeah. I don't know what it's

about, but we just did a hard maneuver. I think the ship came to a halt. Then, a few minutes later, we started moving again and entered REDCON-One."

Milla continued to check the patient. "Mister Temkin, my examination shows your health is fine. There is no evidence of trauma. I have noticed that your heart rate has just increased dramatically. Would you like something to comfort you?"

Temkin shook his head as he turned to face Kadon. "Doc, I've got an idea of what's going on here."

Kadon cocked her head. "Yeah. A med-bot lost its marbles."

Temkin looked visibly irritated as he shouted, "No! About the REDCON-One. I think I know why we're in REDCON-One."

"Really? How would you know that?"

"I can't say, but is there any way you can get a message to Captain Eskar?"

Kadon's lower lip puckered. "You can't say? Okay, I'll assume that's what we're not allowed to ask you about."

Temkin looked apologetically. "Yes. I'm sorry. Can you get a message to Captain Eskar?"

"I can try."

"All you need to tell him is to remember what I've already told him."

"What you have already told him... That's it?"

Temkin nodded. "That's all you need to tell the captain. He'll understand. Let me tell you that this may be a matter of life or death for the ship. I don't think I can make this any clearer."

Kadon frowned. "Are you serious?"

"Serious as a heart attack," Temkin said while putting his hand on his heart.

Kadon listened to Temkin as a snarl formed on her face. "Well, crap! And that's a horrible simile to share with a doctor."

"Sorry, Doc. This is a huge deal."

The doctor turned to leave. "Okay, hang out here. I'll be back."

Temkin tried to add levity to the moment. "Is that a promise or a threat?"

Kadon waved as she exited. "Maybe a little of both."

Temkin smiled in approval.

CHAPTER SEVENTEEN

An Unwelcome Reunion

Capalov studied his tactical display. He manipulated the console repeatedly before informing Eskar, "Captain, our communications are being blocked."

Eskar sneered as he said "Dammit" under his breath. He looked at the map. "Quinton? See those asteroids over there?"

Quinton straightened in his chair. "Yes, sir."

"Can we get in close enough to drop a dormant drone on the surface of one of them?"

Quinton studied the chart. "Yes, sir. I believe we can, easily."

"Excellent. Set course, Quinton." Eskar called his second in command. "Mason? We need a dormant drone. Please set up a one-day dormant time, then have it send a coordinate distress signal to HQ. Ensure the message includes that we're being tracked by Martian ships and that our communications have been blocked."

Mason quickly replied, "I'm on it, Captain. Give me ten minutes."

Eskar spoke again. "Thanks, Mason. Get it done as fast as possible. Our window to do this will be small."

"Yes, sir. I'll do my best."

Eskar studied his crew. He could sense the combination of fear and tension in each of them. He saw Doctor Kadon slipping onto the deck from the corner of his eye. "Doctor Kadon. You shouldn't be up here."

Kadon's cheeks flushed. "Captain, may I have one moment of your time?"

In Eskar's head, a tidal wave of expletives flooded his imagination. Instead, he filtered all of them to, "Quickly, Jill. What is it?"

Kadon walked close enough that only Eskar could hear her comment. "I have a cryptic message from Temkin that he insisted I relay to you, sir."

Eskar looked confused. "I don't have time for this, Jill."

Kadon nodded rapidly. "I understand, but... hell, let me tell you what he said. He said to remember what he told you."

Eskar took off his cap and scratched his head. "What does that mean?"

"I don't know, but that's all he'd tell me. He said that this is an issue of life and death. I'm going to go now, sir."

Suddenly, Eskar's eyes brightened. "Oh. I understand now. Tell Temkin that I haven't forgotten."

Kadon looked thoroughly confused. "Okay, Captain. I'm going to go tend to my patient."

"Thank you again." Eskar approached the navigator and spoke. "Quinton, how close are we?"

Quinton smiled. "Sir, I think you could drop the drone right now."

"Excellent news." Eskar reopened a communication channel. "Mason, where are you with the drone?"

"Sir, it's ready to drop."

"Okay, Lieutenant Walters, make our RF as noisy as hell. Mason, launch in twenty seconds."

Walters engaged the RF generators, and the sound of multiple electric motors could be felt vibrating the ship. "Sir, we're in RF overload."

Mason chimed in on the intercom, "The drone has been successfully dropped on the surface, sir."

"Quinton? Set a course forward with very little shift in our present trajectory. When we're four thousand klicks from here, bring the ship to a gentle halt." Eskar filled his cup with coffee. He was about to take a sip but remembered to wait until it cooled. Saving his upper lip from the scalding-hot fluid made him smile.

"Sir, the course is set. We should be at a stopping point in approximately fifteen minutes."

Eskar moved over to study the ship's current track. "Good, good. Walters? Keep our ship noisy until we come to a full stop."

Walters nodded as he examined his console. "Yes, sir."

I need to say something here. Think, old man! Eskar cautiously took a sip of his coffee. He began to share with the crew through the intercom. "Everyone. We're soon going to be in contact with a Martian frigate. I want you to remember that we're Federation soldiers, and we need to handle this situation with the calmness that honors our leadership. Do not do anything out of sequence. I know some of you have ill feelings about the Martians. Right now, they're not our enemy. They're merely another country. Remember that as you man weapons. Are we clear?"

The crews on all decks responded in unison. "Sir, yes, sir."

That wasn't half bad off the top of your head. "That being said, it's an honor to serve with all of you. I look forward to completing our mission and returning safely to port."

The fifteen minutes felt like hours to Eskar. As the ship decelerated, Quinton said, "Sir, we're about to come to a full stop, as ordered."

"Walters, kill the RF generators."

"Sir, they're now turned off."

The whirring of the electric motors subsided. The only noise that could be audibly heard was the warning alerts of REDCON-One.

Eskar waited momentarily before speaking again, "Walters, drop us to REDCON-Two."

Walters looked confused. "REDCON-Two, sir." The warning tone in the halls changed as the Readiness Condition was lowered.

"Capalov, will you try to open a hailing message to our trackers?"

Capalov looked down at his console. "No need, sir. They've reached out to us."

"Okay, patch it to the mains."

The ensign pressed a few controls, and a video image appeared on the main displays of the control room. An older officer emerged on the screen. Her sturdy frame and piercing eyes made her look intimidating. She had a deep voice and a small but detectable smile. "Captain Remy Eskar? I'm Admiral Saarvi Shoapa of the *MCS Defiant*. I believe you know that you're outnumbered and outclassed here. I'd respectfully ask that you stand down."

Eskar gazed down at Capalov's display and could see Shoapa's Class-Six Frigate escorted by two more Class-Five Frigates. "Admiral Shoapa, we're complying with your request."

"Walters? Lower the shields and close the torpedo ports."

Walters looked at the captain as if he had been pushed under a bus. "Yes, sir. Lowering the shields and turning off the weapon systems."

Eskar wasted no time. "Admiral, as you can see, we've complied with your request. I'll remind you that we're not at war, and neither of our superiors would support any act of aggression."

Shoapa pursed her lips as she nodded. "An interesting choice of words. We were tracking a distress signal from one of your cargo ships and witnessed the ship's destruction by what looked like a weapon from your ship."

Eskar paused to consider his words at this minute. "Admiral, we, too, heard the distress call and arrived in time to find a single survivor from a crew of twenty-one. While attempting to rescue him, we discovered that the ship was about to self-destruct. Our team barely got out of the ship alive. If you're interested, I could send you our footage."

"That won't be necessary, Captain. I'd ask what two Federation ships are doing so far away from home?"

Okay, Remy, this is the time to slip in that phrase. I sure hope I remembered it correctly. Eskar shifted his cap, buying a few moments to gather his composure. "Ummm. We've been observing anomalies in some of the asteroids. The patterns concern us, and I suspect you're here for a similar reason. As it's said, 'High tide is coming.'"

The comment got an immediate reaction from the admiral. She leaned over and whispered something to one of her lieutenants. The lieutenant looked at Eskar and then whispered something back to Admiral Shoapa.

The silence was unnerving. Eskar tried his best to remain calm, but his hands nervously tapped on the table in front of him, out of the camera's view.

Finally, the admiral replied, "I understand, Captain. We should be prepared for that."

Eskar's eyes brightened as an audible sigh escaped from his mouth. "Where does this leave us, Admiral?"

Shoapa stared at the captain before answering. "Captain Eskar, I'd like you to send us your flight plan for the next two Kaladron sectors. I'd advise you to raise your shields because there's a significant amount of matter ahead. My ship will personally escort you through these two sectors. As long as you allow us to guide your ship, there will be no problem. However, if you choose to deviate in any way, I'll consider that an act of aggression and happily blow your ship and crew into oblivion. We've lowered our jamming devices, but we're monitoring your communications. Are we clear, sir?"

Eskar frowned, but was in no place to negotiate. "We're clear, Admiral. Thank you for your kind offer and understanding."

"Captain, before I go, I want to know if you saved anyone from the *Hercules*."

Eskar considered his reply. "Yes, but it was very precarious. We have one man currently in our medical staff's care."

It looked like Shoapa tried to conjure a smile, but it never fully developed. "Do you require any assistance with this man?"

Eskar shook his head, "No, I think he'll be fine. We may be a Corvette, but we have a very advanced Med Bay and one of the top doctors in the fleet. The survivor has not fully recovered yet, but we expect him to eventually."

The admiral accepted the answer. "That's good to hear. Please send us your flight plan, Captain, so we all can be on our way."

Eskar muted the conversation. He looked at Quinton. "Quinton, please send a fictitious flight plan to the admiral. I would suggest something essentially ahead of the current course that we're on."

Quinton considered Eskar's request and entered some numbers into his navigation pad. He then unmuted his coms. "Sir, the new flight plan has been sent."

Eskar kept his eye on the admiral. "Thank you, Quinton."

A beep could be heard coming from Shoapa's side. She turned to see what the message was. "Captain, we have the plan. Prepare to follow us, and we'll escort you beyond our frigates."

Eskar tried his best to be cordial. "Lead the way, Admiral."

"Good day, Captain."

"Good day to you as well, Admiral."

With that, the communication cut out.

"Quinton, keep an eye on that frigate. Please don't let us deviate one click off of our track."

Quinton nodded and took a deep breath before responding. "Yes, sir. We're tracking now."

CHAPTER EIGHTEEN

Meet the New Bot

Doctor Kadon walked into Med Bay. She stopped by her desk and surveyed her wound. After she had redressed the issue, she continued down the hall to check in on her patient.

Temkin sat quietly in his bed. When Kadon turned the corner, he smiled to welcome her. "Were you able to deliver my message to Captain Eskar?"

"Yes... And he told me to thank you for reminding him."

As Kadon spoke, the intercom announced that the REDCON had dropped from One to Three. Temkin stared into the air as he heard the announcement. "Hopefully, that helped."

Kadon scratched her chin. "What did you say to him?"

Temkin looked sheepishly at her. "I'm sorry, but I'm not permitted to share that."

Kadon rolled her eyes. "Some of that shh-shh-hush-hush stuff, huh?"

Temkin smiled like he enjoyed the aggravation. "Something like that, yeah."

"All I can say is I'm glad not to be in REDCON-One anymore. I don't care why right now. While we're here, I want to check you out." She grabbed her stethoscope and walked toward Temkin.

"I thought Irena already did that."

Kadon nodded. "Irena did before it wigged out. Milla checked you out a few minutes ago. Now it's time for a human to check."

"Milla... Milla. My bad. That's who I meant."

Kadon put the scope up to his chest. "I know. No worries. Milla won't be offended. Now, stay quiet for a moment." After taking some measurements, she asked him, "How does your wrist feel?"

Temkin lifted it in the air and moved it around. "It's a little sore, but all things considered, it feels pretty good."

Kadon smiled. "Cool beans. What would you say your pain level is?"

"One-point-five."

Kadon snorted. "Not one-point-three?"

"No, definitely a one-point-five."

Kadon smirked. "Okay, smart guy, how about the leg?"

Temkin gingerly stepped off of the bed. The first step caused him to grit his teeth. He tried to continue walking, but he grimaced with each step. "Okay, this is a lot more painful. I'd say a five-point-three in pain."

"Hobble on back here, gimpy. It'll take some more weeks to get that one back in shape. Still, it's a good sign that you can at least carry some load with it. That's why we got you a cane to use for a while and put you in physical therapy."

Temkin chose to hop back to the bed rather than walk. Almost effortlessly, he gently placed himself back in bed. The smile on his face indicated that he was pleased with his recovery.

Kadon typed some more notes into her tablet. "How are your dreams?"

"My dreams?" Temkin had a half smile as if he thought she was joking.

"Yeah. You know. Those things you have when you go to sleep? Are you still having nightmares?"

"Oh... Yeah, I've been dreading sleeping and still having those same nightmares."

Kadon tried to smile as her lower lip protruded. "I'm sorry, Deke."

Temkin shrugged. "It'll get better, right?"

Kadon patted him on the back. "Yes. It's just going to take some time. For now, let's reschedule your MRI for when we're back at REDCON-Four. In the meantime, here's an exercise band. I'd like to see you working that wrist out to ensure you recover full mobility."

"Will do, Doc." Temkin placed the band on the table next to his bed.

Kadon saw the band on the table, frowned, and pointed her finger. "I better see that has moved when I return."

Temkin burst out laughing. "Okay, okay, you got me!"

CHAPTER NINETEEN

Parting Without Sorrow

Captain, it's Admiral Shoapa hailing you," Capalov said, looking over from his station, his face showing little emotion.

Eskar nodded and raised his hand to point at the main display. "Put her on-screen."

"Captain Eskar, we've reached the end of our journey. We wish you Godspeed on yours."

"Thank you, Admiral. I wish you a safe return as well."

Shoapa spoke. "Before we part ways, I wanted to assure you that we had no intentions of harming you in any way. We were merely responding to the distress beacon, just as you were."

Eskar nodded. "Understood, Admiral. I appreciate your candor on this. Hopefully, we'll have more peaceful joint efforts in the future."

"I'd like that very much. I think we have all had enough war for our lifetime."

Eskar forced a smile. *Don't let your real thoughts show, old man,* he thought before he responded. "Yes. War is a terrible thing."

"Good day to you, sir. Shoapa out." With that, the screen went blank.

"Sir, the Martian ships have returned the helm to us. They're quickly moving away from our location."

"The best news I've heard all day. Quinton, let's drop to REDCON-Four. I want you to wait until the Martian fleet is out of scanning range, then change to our actual course."

Quinton stood to attention. "Sir, yes, sir. I'd estimate that will be in twenty minutes."

"Very good, Lieutenant. Carry on." Eskar hailed his second in command. "Mason, all communication jamming has been suspended. Send a self-destruct signal to the dormant drone."

Mason quickly replied, "Yes, sir. Consider it done."

Capalov waited until Eskar had given all deck orders before saying, "Captain, may I speak to you privately?"

"Of course. Let's walk into the planning room."

The two men headed away from their stations into a small room on the far end of the deck.

Eskar closed the door behind him. "What's on your mind, Ensign?"

Capalov stared nervously at the captain. "Sir, do you think the Martians could have jammed the *Hercules'* communication array? Depending on how it was jammed, all you would know is that no signals were being returned. When our array was jammed, it took me a few minutes to realize that something was intercepting our transmission. We figured it out quickly because we knew the Martians were following us."

Eskar studied the young man. *This kid is pretty sharp,* he thought before speaking. "That's a good thought, but why would short-range work?"

Capalov looked down and scoffed. "Oh yeah. Everything would have been jammed."

Eskar put his hand on the young man's back. "Antoni, I love how you're thinking. Asking questions and considering possibilities is rarely a bad call. I'm baffled by how the array could have been so selective as to only knock out long-range comms. That was a plausible reason that didn't check all the boxes."

Capalov smiled at the captain's compliment. "Do you believe the *Hercules* was attacked by something?"

Eskar fixed a button that had come open on his shirt. "You know, I don't know either way. I've been on ships that just seemed to be a magnet for bad luck. I've also been attacked by unrecognizable enemy weapons. Ultimately, the *Hercules* is gone, and we have to do our best to give it some sort of advocate. I'd love to find a smoking gun that points to someone just because bad luck is such a senseless way to die. Still, we're after the truth, and we need to be able to prove our truths, too. Keep thinking outside the box, and let's keep sleuthing it. We owe that to the *Hercules* and its crew, all right?"

"Thank you, sir. That brings a lot of things into focus."

Eskar heard his name on the deck. "Someone's looking for me. Are we done here?" He began walking toward the exit.

Capalov straightened. "We are, sir."

"Good. Let's see what's going on."

As Eskar reentered the Command Deck, Lieutenant Quinton spoke, "Sir, Lieutenant Polson is looking for you."

"Thank you, Quinton." He reached out to Engineering. "Polson, you were looking for me?"

Capolov poured a cup of coffee and handed it to Eskar as he spoke. Eskar gladly accepted it.

"Yes, sir. Can you come down to Engineering? We've finally retrieved the black box. I've got to show you what we've found."

"I'll be right down, Lieutenant."

As Eskar walked off the deck, he took a sip of the coffee and cursed when it scalded him.

CHAPTER TWENTY

Not What Was Expected

Because of the sloping of the ship's hull, the door to engineering required a single step down to allow it to be tall enough to accommodate entry. Eskar often chuckled at the oversight that required such an awkward design.

The door slid open as Eskar walked in.

"Captain on deck!" A young ensign declared as everyone stood at attention.

Eskar shied away from the pomp and circumstance of military etiquette. *No one is this important,* he thought to himself as he continued into the room. "At ease, everyone. I'm looking for Lieutenant Polson."

Polson stepped forward. "Sir. Thank you for coming down so promptly."

Eskar turned and walked toward her. "What have you got for me, Lieutenant?"

Polson bit her lower lip before speaking. "Sir. It's probably better that I show you."

Eskar raised an eyebrow. "Okay. Let's see what you found."

"Well, sir. It's not what I found, but rather, what I didn't find."

"I'm confused."

Polson walked over to a table containing hundreds of parts. "Sir, this is the remains of the drone that we recovered, and over here is the black box."

Eskar studied all the parts in amazement. "Lieutenant, that's a lot of work."

Polson pointed to two other shipmates. "Yes, sir. Zinto, Gibaldo, and I worked on this for days. A few hours ago, we finally got the black box out. We were pretty excited."

Eskar scratched his chin. "Were?"

"Um, yes, sir. The black box was entirely intact. Despite the massive damage to the drone, the box looked completely clean."

Eskar followed the conversation. "That's great news. So, have you attached the box to download its content?"

Polson bit her lip again. "We did, sir, and we discovered this." The young woman walked over and pressed a few buttons on the computer attached to the black box. The screen came alive with activity. Hundreds of small boxes showed up on the display. "As you can see, the date here shows the day the *Hercules* left port at New Coronado. Each box represents a video feed on the ship or a strip chart of a vital subsystem. For instance, if I click here, this is the reactor temperature at this date stamp."

Eskar examined the moving strip chart and nodded his head. "Okay, this is great stuff. Have you looked at later dates on the box?"

Polson's eyes darted left and right as she spoke. "Yes, sir. But something strange is going on. It's just much easier to show you." She manipulated a few controls, and the date stamp skipped to three weeks later. "This is when things first happened."

Eskar stared blankly at the screen. "What am I looking at?"

"Do you notice that only about two-thirds of the boxes are

available?"

"Oh yeah. I see that now." Eskar reached out and touched the screen. The box opened to the video feed on the Command Deck of the *Hercules*.

"Now, let me forward it another week." Polson incremented up the date. Only ten boxes remained.

Eskar shook his head and furrowed his brow. "Where are all the feeds?"

Polson began wringing her hands. "Gone. These ten boxes are all of the external cameras. Everything else stopped recording."

Eskar pressed, "How is that possible?"

"I don't know, sir. I checked to see if they were deleted. When feeds are cut, they retain artifacts on the media. There were no artifacts. The other two hundred and seventy-five feeds are completely blank. They're sending no signals to the black box. I have one instance that has me bothered. Let me just show you."

Polson reached down and clicked on one of the feeds. "So, this footage was taken in the last few seconds before this particular feed stopped." The video showed a small hall, and after a few seconds, the video feed went blank.

Eskar watched the video with a confused look on his face. "Okay... What am I looking at here?"

"Let me rewind it and play it at half speed." Polson allowed the video to play again slowly. She pointed to the screen and explained, "Two things, sir. Do you see that distortion that appears to be moving from left to right on the display? Also, can you see the shadow that tracks the distortion?"

Eskar studied the video feed and slowly shook his head. "What in the world?"

"I know, it's kind of crazy, right?"

"Could someone have stayed just out of the camera's sight as they killed the feed?"

Polson considered the question. "I suppose so. Maybe it could be video aliasing, but that's pretty unlikely, too. It seems highly irregular to me. Wouldn't you say, sir?"

"Irregular is an understatement. You got me. For now, let's just move on. You said that the external boxes were still working. Did they pick up anything?"

"Yes. At some point, someone did a spacewalk to manually open one of the Cargo Bay doors. We also noticed an explosion of some sort about a week before we rescued Major Temkin."

Eskar adjusted his cap. "Explosion?"

Polson started the stream to show what they discovered. "It looked like it might have been a small arms fight in the forward decks of the ship."

Eskar pointed to the screen and began to talk. "That's laser fire, for sure. See the color of the flashes?"

Polson continued, "After this event, all movement in the forward hall stopped, except for these three things I wanted to show you."

"What kind of things?"

Polson stared into the air as if trying to think of the best words to describe what she saw, then said, "Let me just show you."

A small light could be seen down the forward hull through one of the observation windows. Eskar got his nose inches from the screen. "What the hell is that?"

Polson quickly chimed in, "It looks like a flashlight to me."

Eskar carefully put his hand on the screen. "I can see that. You say this happened a couple of times?"

"Yes, sir. Three. I'm so sorry, sir, but that's all we found."

Eskar could sense the lieutenant's nervousness. He decided to address it directly. "Polson, you're fine. If the data isn't there, that's not your fault. Can you speculate why we lost all of the feeds?"

"I'd guess that it had to be deliberate."

"Why do you think that?"

"Each feed has at least three redundant paths. For the feed to stop sending, you could kill it at the source, but then the feeds would have died one at a time. From what I can see, there were four reductions in data. On the first one, ninety-two feeds stopped. On the second, another sixty-five stopped. Fifty were cut on the third and forty-six on the last. This rules out someone going and unplugging the feeds. Also, most of these feeds are monitored for other things, and someone would have noticed if the feeds were cut."

Eskar jumped in. "So they had to be cut in such a way as to not warn the crew."

"Yes, sir. My other thought was that the black box was faulty. I ran a full diagnostic on it and found it to be in complete working order."

"Hmm. Can you return and show me the feed that looks like flashlights?"

"Yes, sir." Polson manipulated the console, and the feed showed one of the events in question.

Eskar took a deep breath. "I wonder what they were looking for?"

Polson got close to look as well. "Maybe survivors?"

Eskar pointed at the lieutenant. "Maybe. Maybe Temkin wasn't the only one left alive on the ship. Polson, I know you've all been working hard to get this thing out. Would you mind studying it a little more and seeing if you can get any more information from it?”

Polson’s body stiffened as she spoke. “Not at all, Captain. I’ll get right on it.”

“Great, and great work, Lieutenant.”

“Thank you, sir.”

Eskar's mind spun with thoughts as he left Engineering, but one rose above the others: *It was time to pay a visit to Major Temkin.*

CHAPTER TWENTY-ONE

Evaluation

Eskar walked into the Med Bay to see Doctor Kadon with a puzzled look on her face. "Hey, Doctor, how are you?"

Kadon smiled as she turned her gaze away from her tablet. "Hello, Captain. I'm just looking at Temkin's fMRI results; they puzzle me."

Eskar walked over to see what was on her tablet. "fMRI? What's that?"

Kadon used her stylus to point to sections on the display. "It's called Functional Magnetic Resonance Image. Basically, it's a type of brain scan that evaluates function as much as structure. It lets us see how the patient's brain is processing information. See this area here? This spot is where memory and some language are evaluated, and Temkin's brain is the textbook-perfect result. But his activity is diminished over here, where emotions are processed."

Eskar studied the image, though he understood little of what he was looking at. "Could this be the result of his time on the *Hercules*?"

Kadon considered the question and slowly nodded. "Yes. That's a possibility. It could be a cognitive protection mechanism impeding his brain from attaching to the horror he had just witnessed. But that's not the only strange thing here. See these channels? They're like informational super-highways in your brain. Temkin's are off the charts."

"So he processes information quickly?"

Kadon adjusted her standing position and switched hands with the tablet. "Yeah, that's partly true. I looked at his last psych eval; his IQ was high. He was emotionally stable but showed signs of detachment. He also showed signs of acute sleep deprivation."

Eskar looked confused. "Okay…"

Kadon took a step back and put the tablet to her side. "If I were to give my psych eval of him right now, it'd be exactly the same."

"So he's behaving normally?"

Kadon frowned as she stowed her stylus. "Yes, more or less, but he's behaving in a manner that leads me to believe he understands what's being evaluated. I almost feel like he's telling me what I want to hear. I can't explain it, but he's kind and amicable, yet it feels like everything is calculated. I don't know if I'm making sense."

"It makes a lot of sense. Do you think Temkin is lying to us?"

"I truly don't think so, but I'm sure he's not telling you how he really feels about things. It's more like he wants to be liked and fit in rather than hiding some skeletons in his closet. I also think part of this is from childhood abuse. I don't know how it ties in, but I'm working on it. Do you get what I mean?"

"I do, Jill. I wish I could help you more. Is our patient visitable right now?"

Kadon turned and pointed down the hall. "Yeah, he's in room four. He's just getting out of his second MRI. That might make him a little crabby, but feel free to head on down. Having you listen as I process through this is a big help. Thank you."

"Glad I could help like that. I've no idea how all of this works, but I'm thankful you do."

Kadon blushed as she smiled. "Thank you, Captain."

Eskar made a flamboyant bowing gesture as he laughed, turned, and headed down to room four. Though only fifteen meters from where he had started, the walk felt cumbersome. The captain finally made it to the door and knocked.

A muffled voice from the room shouted, "Come in!" as the door slid open.

Eskar walked in. "Deke? How're you holding up?"

Temkin rolled over and began to adjust his bed to a sitting position. "I'm mostly good. I swear those MRI machines will drive you crazy if you let them."

"Tell me about it," Eskar said. "If I never have to be in one of those again, it'd be all right with me."

Temkin finally arrived at a comfortable position. "So, what brings you to my neck of the woods?"

Eskar scanned the room and noticed a chair. "Mind if I sit?"

"Not at all. Make yourself at home."

The chair was heavier than he expected, but Eskar managed to pull it over. "First off, I'm glad to see you recovering so quickly. How's the leg?"

Temkin looked down and frowned. "It's a hell of a lot better than when I first got here. Doctor Kadon gave me a cane, and I start physical therapy sometime later today. It hurts, but I'm amazed at tech that would let it heal so quickly."

"I know. I couldn't agree more. I broke my arm a few years back and could resume duty in less than two weeks. It's nothing short of miraculous. When I was a kid and broke my leg playing baseball, they didn't have tech like this back home. It took nearly three months for me to be back at it."

Temkin rotated his hand, "My wrist is in good shape too. The only real problem for me are the fractures in my ribs. They still hurt every time I take a deep breath. Too bad those machines can't help more with that." Temkin put both of his hands on his chest and rubbed. Though the action did little, it seemed to soothe him.

"You took a nasty jolt when the door opened. I'm glad you were able to survive it."

Temkin chuckled. "You and me both."

"So, I hate to bring up unpleasant things, but I was hoping you could assist me with a couple of questions that came up." Eskar looked Temkin straight in the eye as he spoke. The action seemed to surprise the young man.

Temkin regained his composure and shrugged. "Ummm, sure. How can I be of help?"

Eskar breathed a sigh of relief. "Great. When you made it from your quarters to the mess hall, I wondered how you got the command console?"

Temkin's eyes searched the ceiling as if trying to remember events. "Well, the one I used was from our makeshift station for boosting the short-range transmissions. It was in the quarters next to mine."

"Oh. What about the two life suits?"

Temkin cocked his head slightly. "The docking port was right next to the mess hall. They were easy to pick up."

Eskar laughed. "Of course. I guess I should have studied the ship layout better. So this is going to be the tough question, and

I'm sorry to have to ask it."

Temkin's momentary smile faded. "Okay... Ask away."

"You told me that when you hooked up the command console, nothing was living in the forward decks."

"That's right."

Eskar's tone became uncharacteristically soothing. "Are you sure of that?"

Temkin shook his head. "I checked multiple times. I still think something else was alive on that ship, but it wasn't human."

"Did you hear anything moving around?"

The young man's shoulders slumped as he tried to remember. "I'd hear things bump occasionally, but nothing that sounded like a person moving. One time, I heard a bulkhead depressurize. It scared the crap out of me. It took me a while to figure out what I was hearing. In fact, it wasn't even a thought that figured it out, but my ears popping at the change in pressure."

Eskar listened intently. "Why do you think part of the ship depressurized?"

"Got me, Captain. Maybe that corrosion finally caused a large-enough hole? Maybe whatever had caused all the other systems to fail on the ship was in control of a door?" Temkin tried to straighten up while talking, but the action only brought a painful sigh.

Eskar nodded as he stood and put his hand on Temkin's right leg. "That had to be pretty scary over there, son. I'm glad you made it out alive."

The action startled Temkin. "I'm having a lot of nightmares because of it."

Eskar's emotions were tugged by the comment. "I'm sorry about that, too. Time will help. Trust me, I know. I'll leave you be,

Kadon tells me you have another set of MRIs in two days. Then it's off to the VOQ for you."

"That's the rumor."

"Don't get too spoiled in that room. It's usually for dignitaries."

Temkin tried to force a smile. "I like the sound of that."

Eskar grinned. "Come to think of it, I probably would, too. See you soon, Deke."

CHAPTER TWENTY-TWO

Teflon

The knock at Eskar's door invaded his peaceful silence. He sighed deeply before responding. "Enter!"

Kadon slipped in. "Captain, is this a good time?"

Eskar straightened in his chair. "Sure. What brings you by?"

The doctor scanned the room until she found a chair to sit in. "Well... we just did the last MRI scans on Temkin. At this point, I've nothing else to hold him on. So I wanted to come by here and discuss what you'd like to do."

Eskar turned on his console and pulled up Temkin's record. "We still don't have access to those sealed records. HQ isn't helping us in any way here."

Kadon frowned as she sat down. "Remy, I don't think we have any reason to hold him."

"That's what gets me. This guy is squeaky-clean. Why do I have such reservations? I was down talking to him the other day. I gotta say, I really like him. He's nice, pretty funny, and doesn't play up the victim card. I feel like he's been dealt a bad hand, yet he keeps fighting, you know?"

"Yes. But why are you so hesitant?"

Eskar stood up and pointed to the coffee maker. Kadon

nodded and smiled. "Nothing is sticking, but there's a lot of circumstantial stuff that makes me uncomfortable. Have I told you about the black box on the *Hercules*?"

"No, what about it?"

"Hundreds of feeds on the log just went dead. We know nothing about what happened on the inside. I can verify that someone made a spacewalk. This kind of corroborates Temkin's account. But on the few feeds that remained, we also saw something that looked like a flashlight on the forward decks while Temkin claimed he was hunkered down in the mess hall."

"So what does that mean? Do you think he went up there? Maybe he was looking for survivors."

Eskar shook his head. "His account said he didn't go near the forward decks. So either he's lying, or maybe someone else was alive for a while up there, and possibly he had no idea. Either way, it's all unprovable."

"That's horrible. So, what do you think happened to the black box?"

Eskar stood at the coffee maker. He poured two cups and handed one to Kadon. "I don't have much experience with black boxes. I couldn't say. It seems pretty suspicious to me."

"Yeah... I'd have to agree. It seems like every time we near a conclusion, some more mud gets in the way. I can tell you that in my observations, I wouldn't assume he's the killer type. Did you hear what happened with the med-bot?"

"I heard that one of them went crazy and attacked you. I never liked those bots. They're too close to human for me."

"That's not precisely accurate, but close. They grow on you. They're programmed to be so pleasant. Sometimes, I like talking with them because their replies are uplifting. I know full well they're just algorithm-based responses. But they're so full of hope, you know?"

Eskar's eyebrows raised. "Sorry, Jill. I think they sound creepy, and they keep repeating your name. It drives me nuts."

"Yeah. I can see that, too. Anyway, here's more of the story. Irena warned me that it was losing control. When Irena lost it, its arm swung around wildly. The first pass cut my arm with the laser cutter, and it was heading for my neck next."

Eskar put down his coffee and leaned forward in his chair. "I didn't hear about all of this. What'd you do next?"

"It's not what I did. It's what Temkin did next. He leaped from his bed and tackled Irena." Kadon took a deep breath. "His action probably saved my life."

"Dang. I miss all the fun."

Kadon punched him in the arm. "So, here's the weird thing. After Temkin called for help, he passed out."

"What? Was he hurt jumping off the bed?"

Kadon took a sip of her coffee before answering. "Not that I could see. I'm guessing that the adrenaline of the moment got to him, but this guy has seen plenty of combat."

"Maybe he's in a lot more pain than he's admitting to? I know I passed out when I broke my arm in two places."

"That's a little different, but it's a possibility."

"So, back to the problem. I don't think I've got a choice here. I think we need to keep an eye on the guy and let him go to the VOQ." Eskar studied Kadon to see her reaction.

"Yeah. I don't see that any of the stuff we've discussed is concrete enough to justify holding him further."

"Let him go, Jill. We just need to keep investigating. We owe that to our crew and the crew of the *Hercules*." Eskar took Kadon's empty cup to the sink to accompany his. He stared in disgust at the collection of dirty coffee cups collecting in the bin. "In the meantime, I need to clean all these dishes. We'll talk later, Jill."

Kadon quickly rose and straightened her uniform. "Of course, Remy. Your coffee is the best on the ship."

"Thanks. I like it, too."

A knock at the door startled both of them. Eskar smiled at Kadon. "Man, I'm popular today." He turned to face the door. "Come in."

Capalov casually walked in. "Hello, Captain. I'm sorry to bother you."

"Not at all, Antoni. Please come in."

Kadon stood. "This is my cue to leave. Goodbye, Captain, and it was nice seeing you, Antoni."

"Okay, Jill, thanks." Eskar walked to the door with Kadon, then returned to the sink after she left. "I hope you don't mind if I do my dishes while we talk."

"No, sir. I came up here because I had another thought of something we can look at to get more information on the *Hercules*."

"Oh yeah? What would that be?"

"Our feeds from the drones. They were all streamed back to the ship. Maybe in their scouting, something else will show up." Capalov fidgeted with his hands as he spoke. It reminded Eskar of a child with something exciting to share.

"Of course. That's brilliant. Why didn't we think of that before?"

"It seems so obvious now. I was thinking that we could start with the drones that scanned Engineering. Maybe we could figure out the part they were trying to replicate."

"I like where this is going. Can you pull it up on my console over there while I finish up?"

Capalov brightened up at the request. "Yes, sir. Is it okay if I log you out?"

Eskar didn't notice the splattered water over his shirt until he felt the dampness. He noticed brown spots from coffee residue on his white button-down. "Of course. I need to go change my shirt. I'll be back in a jiff."

"Okay. It'll take me a few minutes to access the feeds anyway. The problem is that we don't know which drone went where, so it's a bit of guesswork to find what we're looking for. Do you have a notebook that I can use so I can keep track of the drones?"

Eskar spoke from his bedroom. "There should be one in the desk drawers just below the console."

Capalov pulled the drawer open and grabbed a small notebook. "Found it. Thank you." He began setting up the feeds. "I figure that we can look at four feeds at a time. We have twenty-four drone feeds to look at, so that'll make this about two hours of browsing, since we only care about their time on the ship."

Eskar offered Capalov water as he came to sit beside him. "I see you are already cueing things."

"Yeah. I quickly went through the first feed to determine when the ship engagement first occurred. Now, we can start all of the feeds at this location."

This kid is on it, Eskar thought as he sipped his water. "Great call, Antoni. I wish I could tell you what we're looking for, but I like your idea of looking at Engineering first. I see you have all twenty-four feeds up right now. I can barely make out any of them."

Capalov quickly pressed some controls. "Yeah, I'm looking for the ones that possibly went through Engineering. I can see Red-Three, Yellow-Two, and... maybe Yellow-Three... and Blue-Five. I say let's start with those four, and then we can pick more."

Eskar slowly nodded as Capalov placed some notes in the notebook. "Sounds like a plan. After we look at this, I'd like to see the drones around the Aft. I want to see how close that workstation was to the mess hall."

"Okay. What workstation?"

"Oh, I didn't tell you? Temkin said that he pulled the command station off a makeshift workstation that he used to modify the short-range communication array. I want to see if that holds water."

Capalov moved a lever, and the four desired feeds played simultaneously. "Okay, we can do that next. For now, get ready to put yourself to sleep on these feeds."

"If we only had popcorn... oh wait. I've got a box of it in the cupboard if would you like some?"

Capalov smiled. "I haven't had popcorn for a few years. That sounds great."

Eskar jumped off his chair. "Popcorn, coming up shortly."

The ensign continued to study the feeds. "Hey, Captain, I think I found a drone that went into Engineering."

"Great. The popcorn's almost ready."

Capalov paused the feeds. "Okay. I got a good picture of what they were working on. I'll wait for you."

Eskar quickly poured the popcorn into two bowls and hustled back. "I'm coming. We're already making good progress." He handed one bowl to Capalov while sitting with the other.

"Here's the workbench where it looks like they were putting the replacement part together." Capalov took a handful of popcorn and put some in his mouth. His eyes closed as he smiled at the snack.

Eskar chuckled at the ensign's response. "I'm glad you like it. Let me see what you are talking about here." Eskar studied the image. "Yeah, that looks like some sort of tailor-made part. Can you save that image and float it by Polson? I bet she'd know what they were trying to accomplish."

Capalov retrieved the image. "Yes, sir. I've saved the image and will head to Engineering after leaving."

Eskar couldn't take his eyes off the image. "Can you imagine being stuck over there, and this was your best hope of survival?"

Capalov didn't answer but slowly shook his head.

"So... Do you want to see about this makeshift workstation near the aft mess hall?"

"Of course, Captain. I think I saw the drone that searched that area earlier." Capalov pulled up a single feed and began to move through it at double speed.

Eskar pointed to the screen. "Stop there." Capalov couldn't respond quickly enough. "Can you move it back about five seconds?"

"Yes, sir." The young man quickly rewound the feed. "I think this looks like a workstation to me. How about you?"

Eskar ate some popcorn before speaking. "Well, I'll be. Temkin wasn't lying."

"No, sir. It seems plausible that there would be a command console here."

Eskar thought for a moment before continuing. "Antoni, I think we should look at any coverage of the forward bay with corrosion in it. Temkin said there was a container that essentially welded itself to the ground. I wonder if we would be able to see anything."

"I'm on it."

Eskar grabbed another handful of popcorn. "Good stuff. Let's see what else we can find."

Keys to Freedom

"H ello, may I enter?" Doctor Kadon asked from outside Temkin's Med Bay room.

"Come on in, Doc."

Kadon walked in to see Temkin sitting up in his bed with his legs draped over the side. "I see someone's ready to get out of here." She walked over to the corner and grabbed his cane.

As Kadon turned back around, Temkin grabbed the exercise band she had given him. "Just getting in my regular morning workout." The smile on his face let her know how 'regular' these workouts were.

She snorted and lifted the cane like she was going to hit him with it. "Oh, I bet. Just know, it's your body. I can't make you do any of this, but if you want full mobility, I'm telling you the best way to do that." She put the cane down and handed it to Temkin.

"I know, Doc. All joking aside, I've been using it. I've also been doing therapy with Milla. For being so pleasant-sounding, it has no problem inflicting pain. I've dated a few women like Milla." Temkin carefully slid out of bed and gingerly put weight on his newly repaired leg. His eyebrows raised, and he grinned as he stood. It wasn't until he tried to take a step that his dependence on the cane was evident.

Kadon studied his movements. "It's going to be a while, Deke, but you're already making significant progress. Are you ready to go to your new digs?"

"You bet. I hope it isn't a long walk."

"If you want, I can have Milla cart you over."

"No way. I need to get back on my feet… literally."

Kadon shrugged. "Suit yourself. It's about sixty meters."

Temkin nodded. "I'm good for that."

Kadon looked around. "Is there anything you need me to carry?"

"Yeah. The tablet and my sports band." Temkin's demeanor turned feisty.

"You better be using this damn thing, Deke. Oh, and we have standard-issue uniforms ready and waiting in your room."

"That's great."

"Also, I moved you up. Today, you can take a ten-minute water shower."

Temkin did a double-take. "You're kidding? This day's getting better with each passing moment."

"If I'm being honest, it's kind of my thank you for saving me from Irena."

"Well, that makes me even happier I did it. Are you planning on escorting me down?"

"If that's okay. If not, Milla can do it." The corners of her mouth subtly turned upward.

Temkin immediately put his hand up in a defensive pose. "No, no, no! I'm good with you doing it, Doc."

"I figured, and I've more good news. The VOQ is only fifteen meters from the mess hall."

At first, Temkin smiled, then he slowly frowned. "Food is good for sure. I'm not jazzed about being by a mess hall."

Kadon grimaced at her faux pas. "Oh, Deke. I didn't think when I said that. I didn't mean to upset you. I'm sorry." She delicately placed her hand on his right shoulder.

At Kadon's touch, Temkin's chest puffed up slightly as he took a deep breath and tried to muster a smile. "I know, and I get that this is a plus... especially with my leg like it is. I know you didn't mean it any other way."

"Well, do you want to head down?"

Temkin stood with the aid of the cane. "How far did you say?"

Kadon brimmed with positivity again. "About sixty meters. Are you ready?"

"I think so. Lead the way, Doc."

CHAPTER TWENTY-FOUR

At the VOQ

O kay, Deke. I'm heading back to Med Bay. Are you good for now?" Kadon asked with a smile.

"I'm great. This is one heck of a room." Temkin couldn't contain his excitement at the new residence for his next three months.

"It really is. I hope you enjoy the heck out of it. Get rest and shower because you stink a little."

"Aw, Doc, you say the nicest things."

Kadon shook her head and pouted. "Where do you want these items?"

Temkin looked around the room and pointed to the small table beside his bed. "Over there would be fine, and thanks for everything, Doc."

Kadon's smile returned as she walked over and placed his tablet and workout band on a table near his bed. "I'm glad things are working out. I'll be back in the morning to check on you." She headed for the door without waiting for a reply.

"See you tomorrow." He said to the empty doorway.

Temkin sat alone in his new room. The VOQ was quite a step up from his typical assigned room on a ship, and he didn't have to share it with another person. The room had a small kitchenette with a curly-maple wood veneer countertop. The refrigerator, sink, a small microwave oven, and two-burner stove occupied a single appliance space in the corner of the dining area.

Temkin looked at the bed. It was at least a double, possibly even queen-sized. As Kadon stated earlier, three newly pressed uniforms hung in his closet on a brass bar. Two pairs of shoes were at the base of the closet.

He walked over to the dresser and opened the top drawer to see underwear and socks were also stocked. He smiled as he slowly closed it.

A set of towels and a small collection of toiletries were nicely placed on the bathroom sink. As he entered the diminutive bathroom, a green light over the shower stated it was "usable." The light caused him to feel happiness for a brief moment.

The silence in the room troubled him, but the enticement of taking a hot shower was irresistible. Temkin quickly shed his gown and slippers. He limped into the bathroom, shaved, and cleaned his teeth. All were done with water-free devices.

Before continuing, he took a long look in the mirror. *Man, you're getting older.* He stared at the bathroom shower and was relieved to discover that there was a bar that he could hold while in the stall. He tried applying pressure to his leg, but the pain meant that most of the standing would be on his one good leg.

Temkin chose to hop into the shower. Studying the controls, he pressed the start button. An automated voice replied, "Mister Temkin. What temperature would you like to use for your shower?"

"Fifty degrees, please."

The system quickly replied, "Confirmed. You now have ten

minutes to complete your shower."

Small clicks were audible behind the shower wall, then water flowed. The initial cold water startled Temkin, but within a few seconds, the stream had a pleasant and invigorating temperature. He closed his eyes and allowed the hot water to spray on his face. Realizing he had little time to waste, Temkin grabbed the all-purpose stock wash and began cleaning.

The hot water pulsated on the back of his neck. Slowly, his eyes began to close. The water seemed further and further away as Temkin slid down and rested in the corner of the shower.

"**M**ister Temkin, you have twenty seconds left."

The automated voice awakened Temkin as he scrambled to regather his senses. With a deep sigh, he stood and pressed the stop button on the shower. *I wasted half that shower sleeping, h*e thought as he reached for a towel to dry.

When the shower door opened, he looked down to see a wet floor. *Water must have leaked out when I was sleeping. I'll have to clean this up after I dry myself.* He hobbled over to the bathroom sink to brush his hair.

The steam had fogged the small mirror, and at first, everything seemed normal. Temkin grabbed the comb off the countertop and ran it through his hair. Finally, he looked at the mirror and gasped. Handwritten into the condensation that enveloped the glass was a single word:

COWARD

Temkin brought both arms forward as he leaned on the countertop and gritted his teeth. He belted out a guttural scream as he clenched his fists. The shout seemed to calm him as he turned to find a washcloth. He reached over, wiped the word from the mirror, and stood motionless. With a newfound calmness, he continued combing his hair.

CHAPTER TWENTY-FIVE

Hard Work

Eskar didn't sleep well. His mind filled with ruminations of why there were three Martian frigates so far from Mars. The war crippled their fleet, though they fought valiantly. Allowing three or more capital ships to wander so far from home left butterflies in the captain's stomach.

"I don't have it in me for another war," he whispered as he prepared his uniform for duty.

A random thought caught his attention. Eskar chuckled when he realized they were even further from the Federation's domain. *I wonder what kind of conversations Admiral Shoapa is having with her team about our little rendezvous,* he mused as he decided to head to the Command Deck.

Heading down the hall, he spied Polson going to Engineering with a pace that indicated she was in no rush to get there. Her usually broad-shouldered posture slumped forward, and she stared at the ground before her. "Lieutenant Polson, how are you doing?"

Polson turned to see who had called her, then immediately stiffened. "Good morning, sir. I was heading to work on the black box. Late last night, I think we found something interesting."

"Interesting? I like the sound of that."

Polson smiled and looked down at the ground. "Yes, sir. I studied the feeds and decided to examine the windows where we saw the lights. On the second instance, I noticed something."

Eskar cocked his head. "Was it something or *someone*?"

"Someone, sir. It took me a few hours and grafting many frames together, but I got enough of an image to run facial recognition on it."

"Brilliant, Lieutenant! Did it find a match?" Eskar clapped his hands.

"Yes, sir. I just got the reply in the last data dump, but this is what was strange."

Here we go again: one step forward, two steps back, Eskar thought before he spoke. "Was it redacted?"

"No, that would have been par for the course. This is weirder. It came back with an officer named Major Ulysses Maric."

Eskar listened, but the line of thought confused him. "Okay..."

"Maric wasn't on the *Hercules*. He was allegedly stationed back on Earth and has never been reported as missing."

"What the heck? Is he Special Ops too?"

"It said nothing about that, but he was a Navy Seal. After I saw that, I looked at earlier feeds."

Eskar tracked perfectly. "What did you find?"

"Well, initially, nothing. But then I decided to check out crafts and drones that entered and exited the ship. After cross-checking all crafts, I've one unaccounted-for ship. An extra craft on the *Hercules* entered the ship after the major losses of feeds from the black box. I couldn't determine what kind of ship it was, but it was small and had extender cells."

"Whoa! Do you think that this is the reason we lost the feeds?"

Polson's head bobbled as she considered the question. "No sir, I don't know that for certain, but it might make sense. Maybe this was part of the special mission that we can't ask Major Temkin about."

"Also, wouldn't that extra craft have long-range communication?"

Polson smiled as she considered his question. "You know, I didn't think of that. That's an excellent point. I don't know what we can do with that, but I've gotta believe this ship could talk."

"Lieutenant Polson? Excellent work. Now, can you do me a favor?"

"Of course, Captain. What do you need?"

Eskar smiled. "It's not what I need, but what you need. Will you and your team take the day off? I appreciate all of your hard work, but I need you fresh. You look exhausted, and I suspect Zinto and Gibaldo need the same break." Eskar leaned over and spoke into his intercom. "Lebo? I'm ordering Polson, Zinto, and Gibaldo to take the day off. Can you make it without them for the day?"

Lieutenant Lebo replied, "Yes, sir. I appreciate your checking up on them. They've been double-shifting it for a while. We can hold things down as they rest."

Eskar looked up to see Polson's wide grin. "Thank you, Captain. Thank you so much."

"Of course. You three have done great work, but progress can wait twenty-four hours. Have a great day, Lieutenant."

"Yes, sir." Polson turned immediately and headed back to her quarters.

Eskar's mind was torn between processing Polson's information and being grateful that he was in a position to give her team rest. He decided to continue on to the Command Deck.

Capalov sat at his console, examining the information being presented. As he contemplated the results, he began rubbing his neck. "What the hell is going on?" He smacked the side of the console, then checked to see if anyone was watching. His eyebrows raised when he saw the captain take notice.

Eskar spotted him and walked over to investigate. "What's got you so perplexed?"

"I keep getting packet errors. At least that's what the console says."

Eskar scratched his chin. "Isn't that what I read about in the report for the med-bot that went wacko?"

Capalov nodded. "That's what happened. The tech team is looking into it, but it seems like it's affecting a lot of subsystems. This is the fourth or fifth time in the past couple of days that I've made simple requests only to have it respond with a packet error message ."

Eskar adjusted his hat. "Could the Martians have done this when they took over to guide us?"

"It's something to look into. We firewalled everything but the most basic navigation, but that doesn't mean their team might know a workaround. Let's just say I wouldn't put it past them. I'll head down to Electronic Security and let them investigate."

"Hey, Antoni? While you're down there, would you mind having them check our black box? I want to ensure we weren't losing feeds like the one on the *Hercules*."

Capalov considered the request. "Captain, that's a great thought. I will check that myself."

Eskar smiled. "That works for me too. Thank you, son. I ordered Polson's team to take the rest of the day off. I'd like you to finish these tasks and do the same. I appreciate all the extra time you put into this, but I need you at the top of your game when you're on this deck. Also, this is a gentle reminder: Right now, we're on deck. 'Sir' would be appropriate in our conversations here."

"Yes, sir. I'm sorry about that, and thank you." Capalov couldn't contain his excitement at Eskar's order for him to rest. He saluted, then turned abruptly to head for the exit.

CHAPTER TWENTY-SIX

Working Out

Temkin hobbled out of his room. Getting used to walking with a cane was more challenging than he expected. A young officer quickly passed, and Temkin called out to him. "Pardon me, can you point me to the gym on this deck?"

The officer stopped and turned to address Temkin. "Sure, it's just four doors down. See the gym sign hanging on the ceiling?" The young man pointed at the illuminated plaque.

Temkin felt embarrassed. "Oh wow. You'd think I'd have noticed that."

The comment brought some laugher. "My name is Howard, but my friends call me Hojo." He reached out to shake Temkin's hand.

"I'm Deke. It's a pleasure to meet you, Hojo. Thanks for helping me out."

"Well, good luck on getting the equipment in there. It's always busy. I'm sorry, but I'm running late. Hopefully, I'll see you around."

"No problem. Thanks."

Heck, the walk down there will be enough of a workout for today, Temkin mused as he began to head in that direction. Though the first few steps were difficult, the journey was easier than he expected. He reached the door and peered into the room.

As Hojo warned, the room was crowded. At first, Temkin was going to turn around and come back some other time, but determination got the best of him. He carefully entered the gym.

A few officers noticed him as he slowly limped in the room, but they quickly returned to their workout. Temkin scanned the row closest to his position. He spotted an open bench and smiled as he headed in that direction.

He was nearly at the device when a young man ran around him and sat on the empty unit. He looked at Temkin and said, "What, you wanted on this? I guess you should've got here faster. I see there's one available at the end there."

Temkin looked where the man was pointing, and his anger rose. The bench he referred to was at least twenty meters away. "Look, man. You knew I was heading here, and you jumped in front of me."

Unemotionally, the young man said, "Well, it's too damn bad you didn't get here a little earlier." He turned away and started setting up the bar's weight value.

Temkin steamed but realized there was little he could do in his current condition. He looked down the aisle and started heading to the other bench. "Have a great day, asshole."

The comment didn't go unnoticed. The young man immediately jumped up and got in Temkin's face. "Do you got a problem with me, pretty boy?"

Temkin only then realized this man was a half-head shorter. He stopped walking and looked him squarely in the eye. He gripped his cane tighter. "Nothing I can't fix, but that's an a-hole thing to do to a guy who's walking with a cane."

"Yeah? Is there something you want to do about it?"

Temkin's thoughts swirled. *Defuse this, Deke.* He considered his response. "Hey, man, I'm just here to work out. Peace."

"Peace? After you called me an asshole? It's a little late for that, pretty boy."

The young man tried to kick the cane out of his hand, but Temkin's reflexes were too quick. He effortlessly moved it, and the kick was ineffective. "I wouldn't recommend you screwing with me, little man. I'm wounded, but I'm not an invalid."

The crewman's eyes raged with anger. "What did you just call me?"

Temkin took a step back and put his one hand up. "Hey man, let's just go our separate ways—"

Before he could finish the comment, the crewman swung his fist and hit Temkin squarely on his jaw. Temkin's head snapped back, and he stood motionless for a few seconds. Then he closed his eyes as a maniacal smile overcame his face. He raised his free hand to rub his jaw as he chuckled and straightened his head. "Must I always be the one to solve the problems?" He angrily muttered as he stared at the aggressor. "Nice hit, tough guy. What are you going to do now?"

The crewman's eyes grew large as he reared back to strike Temkin again with an almost identical punch. This time, Temkin was ready. He reached out with his free hand and grabbed the crewman's fist, stopping it mid-swing. With the crewman's momentum broken, Temkin yanked him forward as his other hand dropped the cane and punched the helpless victim in the throat. "Wow, that looks like it hurt," Temkin said, grinning and never letting go of the crewman's other fist.

The young man gasped as he felt the impact. He raised his free hand to his neck as he fell to his knees, wincing and wheezing to allow air back into his lungs. His other arm was still held in the air by Temkin.

Temkin mercilessly twisted the arm, shooting pain through the attacker's body. By this time, others were approaching to stop any further violence. Temkin dropped the man's arm and leaned down to grab his cane. "I'm done here unless you want to continue, little man."

The crewman dropped to the ground, throwing both hands to his neck. Two young men kneeled to aid him, and two others moved in front of Temkin.

Temkin momentarily looked pale as the adrenaline left his body. "I need to sit down."

The two men helped him to the bench behind them. Temkin took a deep breath before he spoke while shaking his head. "How ironic; this is all he wanted."

Temkin sat down, slumped over, and rested his elbows on his thighs. His eyes closed as his head drooped.

One of the men looked more closely at Temkin. "I think he's out. That hit must have done more damage than it looked like it did." He reached down and lightly smacked his cheek. "Hey, buddy. You all right?"

Temkin's eyes abruptly opened as he took a deep breath. He looked down to see his adversary rolling on the ground, trying to catch his breath. The image horrified him. "What's going on?"

The man aiding Temkin turned to his helpers. "He's up again! Hey buddy, you okay? Everyone saw what happened to you. I'm sorry he attacked you like that. That was a fantastic move on his second punch. Here's a bottle of water. Drink up."

Temkin rubbed his chin before taking the water. As he sipped, he winced. "My jaw hurts."

"Yeah, I thought you were doomed after that first hit, but you lasted long enough to do that." The officer pointed down at the crewman gasping for breath on the ground.

Temkin looked down again in horror. "I did that?"

The officer cocked his head. "Are you being funny? I'm guessing it was a defensive reflex, but you put him down. Then you sat down here and briefly passed out."

Temkin nodded slowly. "I'm glad I sat. I'm sorry he's in so much pain."

"Shoot, he had it coming. You were right when you called him an asshole. The name's Nathan."

"I'm Deke."

"I know. I was on the team that pulled you off the *Hercules*. Don't mind Matthew." Nathan pointed to the man on the ground. "He's been a jerk for as long as I've known him." Nathan looked up and heard the rapid shuffling of soldiers. "Looks like the MPs are here. Sorry, Deke, but they're going to need your statement. Don't worry. Many of us will tell them what happened."

"Thanks... Nathan." Temkin pivoted in his seat to observe Matthew. By this point, Matthew had calmed and was breathing normally. Every time he looked at Temkin, his eyes quickly shifted away. Temkin couldn't recall the fight, as though the memory had elusively slipped through his grasp.

Facing the Music

W ell, you seem to make friends everywhere you go," Captain Eskar said to Temkin, glancing at the MP's report in his hand.

"Sorry, Captain. I tried to avoid it, but that guy had it out for me. I don't know what I did, but clearly, he was looking for a reason."

Eskar chuckled. "Matthew is a good kid, with very little going on up top. I watched the video. Did you really have to call him an asshole?"

"No, sir. I didn't. I shouldn't have let my temper get the best of me. I'm sorry about that."

"Deke, I wasn't looking for an apology. I'm looking for more maturity. I know you've had a crappy hand dealt you, but you knew the guy was no match for you, even in your crippled state. Am I right?"

Temkin's eyes turned to the floor, and his cheeks reddened slightly. "Yes, sir. I knew it. I gotta say I had no intentions of fighting him."

"But you called him an asshole, then backed it up with the

'little man' comment. Did you think he would let those just pass by?"

"No, sir."

"That's passive-aggressive, at best. I'd say that it's more active-aggressive. You stoked the fire, and Matthew Gircowski lit up like a Roman candle. As a major, you don't have this luxury. We ask the men under us to put their lives on the line. We can never forget our manners, even when they piss you off."

"Understood, sir."

"Deke, I watched the video. Matthew earned what he got and will have a lot of laundry to wash to remind him of that. You, on the other hand, what should I do about you?"

Temkin stiffened in attention. "I'll wash laundry, sir. I earned that too. And I'll try to do better in the future."

"Well, I appreciate your willingness to accept the consequences of your actions. I've got to discipline you, so here's what I'm going to do: You're confined to your quarters for the next three days. Only Doctor Kadon, the med-bots, and I will be able to speak to you. If you have to speak to someone else, you must request that from me via intra-mail. The med-bots will provide you with meals. And last, I want you to go down to the holding cell and apologize to Matthew after we're done here. Are we clear?"

"Yes, sir. We're clear."

"Okay. Hey, one more thing. Do you know a guy named Ulysses Maric?"

Temkin's eyes immediately shifted to Eskar. "Yes. We've worked on many missions together. I considered him a good friend. Is he on this ship? I haven't seen him in about six months."

Eskar studied Temkin. His answer was as perplexing as the question. "Ummm, no. His name showed up in one of our reports on you. I just wondered if you knew him."

"Ulysses was the best shot I've ever known. He saved our unit multiple times with his skills. He was also a great pilot. One time, we were being picked up by a YT-738 transport when the pilot noticed four drones approaching quickly. Ulysses used the 738's only drone to knock out those four. This guy was the perfect soldier."

Eskar's confusion continued to grow. "Would there be any reason he'd be out here?"

"Out here? In the asteroid belt? Hell no. He took a training position back on Earth to be with his wife and family. He trains elite SEALs. Unless the Navy needed a particular task accomplished, he's strictly a homebody. The last time I talked with him, he told me he loved his new work."

Eskar studied Temkin. *This doesn't feel like he's lying. I don't know what to make of this,* he thought as he once again looked at his report. "Well, that will be all for now, and Dckc?"

Temkin looked up. "Yes, sir?"

"Stay out of trouble, son. I've got enough crap going on without you stirring the pot."

"Understood, sir." Temkin saluted the captain.

"Get out of here. Now!" Eskar said with a smile on his face.

Unsealed

Capalov knocked on Eskar's door. When it opened, he burst into the room. "Sir, the report came in."

The sudden energy startled Eskar. "Come right in, son. Make yourself at home."

The ensign looked nervously at the captain. "Sorry, sir. I was just so excited."

Eskar furrowed his brow and smiled. "I understand, Antoni. Have you had a chance to look at the report?"

"No, sir. I came down here when I saw that it dropped."

Eskar reached over and tapped the MED icon on his communication module. "Hey, Jill, can you come down here? I'd like your eyes on something concerning Temkin."

Kadon responded quickly. "I'm on my way, Captain."

Eskar addressed Capalov. "I know you're excited, but I think we need to all look at this together."

"Understood and agreed."

"While we're waiting, could you take a look at my console? It's been a little glitchy lately."

Capalov immediately walked over to the console. "Glitchy?

How so?"

Eskar frowned as he played with the keyboard on the console. "It's driving me nuts. I make requests, and sometimes it responds, and other times it just hangs."

"Hmmm. Let me take a look." Capalov sat down and began typing. "Yeah, this is the same sort of packet error problem we've been having for a while now. I've already let Naval Tactical Data Systems know about it. Sorry. Hopefully, they'll solve it soon. For the time being, I increased the times it'll retry requests. It may be slower, but at least you're more likely to get what you're asking for."

"Hopefully NTDS will get back soon. Thanks for looking, Antoni." As Eskar spoke, a knock on the captain's door grabbed his attention. "Come in."

"Hello, Captain. You wanted to see me?" Kadon walked in.

"Yes, Jill. We finally got the sealed documents about Temkin. I was hoping you could look at them with us. You know, let's see if there is anything that might give us cause for concern."

Kadon clapped her hands and rubbed them together as she giggled. "This is exciting!"

Eskar grabbed another chair and offered it to Kadon. She graciously accepted. The three sat around the console as Capalov opened the portfolio. "I can see by the advisory that some of these pictures are graphic. Are you all ready for this?"

Eskar looked at Kadon, who was frowning as she listened to the ensign's words. "Jill, you don't have to do this. I can watch it and give you the CliffsNotes version."

Kadon straightened in her chair and put her chin up. "No, Captain. I'm fine. My only worry is that we may look at Temkin differently after viewing this, regardless of if he's innocent or guilty."

Kadon's words hit Eskar hard. He looked into the air as if evaluating their gravity. "I see your point, but I've got a crew counting on us to do our part to keep them safe. If this guy's a risk, I think it's our duty to see this through."

Kadon nodded. "I couldn't agree more. I think that's my hesitance here. I don't know what makes us qualified to do this."

"Absolutely nothing, but we've been called to step up. It's like getting called for jury duty. It sucks, but that's part of being an adult." Eskar tried to talk with such confidence that it would convince him also.

Capalov spoke up. "Captain, I couldn't say it better. I want to find the truth here, which might help us get a better picture."

Eskar looked at his partners in admiration. "Well, let's proceed, shall we?"

Capalov opened the first page and jumped back in his seat. "Holy moly!"

A picture of a young woman who was physically battered adorned the first page. Eskar flinched as he studied the picture. Her jaw was clearly broken, and her left hand had splints on three fingers. There was a healing scar over her blackened right eye. "What in the world happened to this poor lady? You think Temkin did this?" Eskar noticed a tiny hand holding her right hand.

Capalov spoke, "Not likely. This was Temkin's mother, Amelia Golding Temkin. According to this, she was severely beaten by her husband on the day of his disappearance."

Eskar did a double-take. "Did you say his disappearance?"

"Yes. According to this report, the officers found Dillon screaming for help over Amelia's body. It says here that his actions probably saved her life."

Eskar shook his head. "Well crap, this kid was born to be a protector."

Capalov put his finger on the monitor as he continued reading. "It says here that Deke was injured too." Capalov clicked the next page, and the picture of an equally battered young boy stared at them.

Eskar was getting sick to his stomach. "That's definitely Deke."

"Yep, it says that his collarbone and three ribs were broken. His left lung was punctured, he had a major concussion, and he was hospitalized for four weeks, where they had to induce a coma to help him heal. The only thing the police stated that he said was, 'He's gone.' They assumed he was referring to his dad. The report also said both victims showed signs of much more unreported abuse."

Kadon looked in horror. "What kind of man would do this to his family?"

Eskar shook his head. "A seriously sick one."

Capalov kept reading, then abruptly stopped. "Oh wow. Look here. It says that Deke fought back. His knuckles were bloodied, and they discovered a tooth that was found to be his dad's embedded in them."

Eskar frowned and squinted. "You're joking."

Capalov read on. "No. It says they ran DNA tests on the tooth and found it was unmistakably his dad's."

"How old is that kid? He can't be more than eight."

"Ten, actually."

"Ten? He's so small! Remind me when we get back to port to call my parents and thank them for how they raised me."

Kadon finally spoke. "Yeah, me too. Geez, this is horrible."

Capalov said, "That guy's a fighter. Man, he beat the crap out of Gircowski. Matt struck him, his head rocked back, and Temkin didn't flinch."

Kadon turned to stare at Eskar. "Well... this is news to me. Did you know about this, Captain?"

Eskar's face turned red as he tried to explain. "It was a minor scuffle. I dealt with both men. Temkin has been confined to his quarters for a few days, and Gircowski has laundry duty for the next month."

Kadon pressed on. "Did either of them need to be examined?"

Eskar replied quickly, "Winston was on gym detail. He made sure both men were okay."

"Winston? He's hardly the person to make that call." Kadon said, her jaw hardening and her eyes locking in on Eskar. "He probably has had CPR training and might know how to run the defibrillator. He's like a glorified lifeguard."

"Both men were offered more treatment, and they both refused. I can't force them to get help."

As Capalov looked away from the two of them at a nonexistent dust mote, Kadon studied Eskar for a few seconds before replying. "Yes, you can. You're the captain."

Eskar looked down. "That's true. I'm the captain. I guess I could've insisted, but I didn't think it was necessary, so that's on me. Sorry, Jill."

Kadon studied Eskar for a few seconds before replying. "Apology accepted. After we're done here, I'll go down and check on Gircowski and Temkin. For now, let's see what else we got."

Eskar took a deep breath. *Mental reminder: Don't cross Doctor Kadon.* His mind drifted to an argument he had with his wife, and the memory made him snicker.

Kadon's radar was up. She cocked her head as she asked, "What's so funny?"

Eskar thought of a few deflecting comments but chose to tell the simple truth. "Oh, I was just thinking about a funny story with my wife. We had a dog, and it was my time to walk her. I was about ten minutes late, and she explained why I needed to be on time when I walked her. As she was talking, the dog peed on the floor. I looked down and realized what had happened. We both felt so bad that we walked the dog together. It ended up being a two-hour walk, and we laughed about that night for years."

Eskar's smile faded as he remembered there were no more chances to walk with his wife.

Kadon intuitively placed her hand on his shoulder. "Chloe was an amazing person. I'm so sorry for your loss."

Eskar nodded. "Thanks." He paused a moment before continuing. "Hey, Antoni? What else do we have?"

Capalov scanned through the pages. "So, they found the dad three years later, dead in the cellar of an abandoned warehouse about a block from his residence. The body was too decayed for forensics to do much. There was a turned-over book cart and a rope around his neck... Whoa, geez!" Capalov jumped back in the seat as he turned the page. The pictures showed the gruesome corpse of Temkin's father. The drying and decaying body lacked certain parts taken by vermin over time.

Eskar frowned as he looked at the pictures. "Jill, didn't Deke say they thought it was a suicide?"

Kadon couldn't take her gaze off the pictures. "Yes. He said they'd concluded it was suicide."

Capalov regained his composure and continued. "It says that

in here too. His wallet, keys, and watch were still on his person, so it probably wasn't a robbery. Based on the fact that his driver's license had expired two years ago, they concluded that he died in the same year that he disappeared. With no evidence of malice, it was concluded that he committed suicide."

Eskar wanted to spit, but there was no place to do that with people present. Instead, he spoke plainly. "That's horrible."

Kadon quickly spoke up. "No, that's karma. That bastard got what he deserved. Before you feel too bad for that monster, look at page one. Those two people are the victims here. What kind of man brutalizes his own family?"

Eskar looked down. "Not a man at all. A coward, a bully, and a narcissist."

Capalov's eyes raised over the monitor. "Hey, Captain? Check this out."

Eskar's curiosity was piqued. He quickly spun in his chair. "What did you find?"

Capalov started paraphrasing again. "So, Deke's mom couldn't care for him during her recovery. She had no family or friends willing to take Deke in. Deke ended up in foster care for six months. During that time, he got moved to three different homes."

"That poor kid."

Capalov nodded as he continued to read. "Yeah, but according to the reports, he had a dark side."

Kadon leaned forward as if it would help her listen better. "What does that mean?"

The ensign put his finger on the monitor. "It says that one child was a notorious bully in the first home. Deke roomed with him and was picked on for about three weeks... Hold on. I'm just going to read this word for word... 'The bully struck Deke. Deke fell to the ground and was whimpering. As the bully came in to kick Deke, Deke suddenly jumped up and punched the bully so hard that he broke three of the bully's teeth.'"

Eskar watched slack-jawed. "Holy crap. You gotta wallop someone pretty hard to do that."

Kadon remained somber. "That bully didn't stand a chance. Deke was beaten up all of the time by a man. A boy his own age would be no match."

Capalov agreed. "Apparently not. Even though everyone agreed it wasn't Deke's fault, he got shipped to the second home. I swear, this kid got no breaks in life." He frowned as he shook his head in disbelief. "So, in the second home, the parents were arrested for drug use. It turned out that the dad was a dealer and the mom was a hopeless addict. No apparent abuse, but the mom insisted that she was afraid of Deke."

Eskar smirked. "Afraid of a kid? I'd be way more afraid of my husband if I were her."

Capalov interjected. "Hey, there's a clip here of the woman. Do you want to hear it?"

Both nodded, so Capalov began the stream.

After some initial setup, the feed showed Darea Ilson, the drug-addicted foster care worker. Her skin was rutted and her cheeks hollow. Her eyes looked sunken, and the whites were jaundiced.

Ilson spoke, "That boy was filled with an evil spirit that would only come out when someone

threatened him."

The agent replied, "Ma'am, can you explain that further?"

Ilson looked deeply into the camera. "That boy has an evil heart. He sat and carefully watched all of us. The first time I ever heard a peep from him was when I burned my hand on the stove. I saw him standing at the door... laughing." She shivered at the thought. "When I looked at him, he stopped and just stared at me. It was like he enjoyed watching me get hurt."

The agent asked, "Was there anything else about Dillon?"

Ilson's eyes grew large. "One time, when I was... ummm... indulging, I turned to get some candles to cover the smell, and he was quietly standing there. He handed me the candles. He must have been standing there for twenty minutes because I never heard no door open, and I locked the damn thing when I walked in. It felt like he was enjoying my pain. I could see it in his evil little eyes."

"This coming from a drug addict." Eskar was disgusted. Kadon began wringing her hands. "So far, I only have one question: How is Deke so normal?"

Capalov continued. "On to the third home. An older couple watched him for four months. They were Christian churchgoers. The wife said Deke was the best kid they had ever fostered. He was thoughtful, and they tried to adopt him. Deke's mom recovered to the point where she could reclaim her son. That's when they moved to New Jersey for a fresh start. Evidently, Deke was really attached to this third home. The adjustment back to his mother was hard. He ran away twice but quickly returned."

Eskar listened quietly to Capalov's narration. His stomach turned as he thought of the horror that Temkin had endured. "Is there more?"

Capalov nodded. "Hold on a sec... I'm reading on... Oh!"

Eskar's eyes looked up. "Something else?"

"Yeah. Deke's mom put him into therapy at the recommendation of the high school. In those sessions, he talked about recurring nightmares that he was having."

Kadon's head turned toward Capalov. "Nightmares?"

"Yeah. It says that Deke had nightmares, and in them, he killed his dad."

Eskar dismissed it. "That's just his imagination running wild. He was only ten when his dad passed away."

Capalov nodded. "Yeah, but he also mentioned that he dreamed about using a cart to carry his dad and hide his body."

Eskar stopped for a second. "So you're telling me that Deke, the undersized ten-year-old, was able to put a grown man two meters tall and that weighed over one hundred and thirty kilograms in a cart?"

Capalov objected. "I'm saying he had dreams about it."

Kadon jumped in. "Maybe he saw his dad commit suicide?

That's something you would blot out for sure. Maybe the dream was Deke's mind saying the dad committed suicide because of him. In essence, he killed his dad."

Eskar rubbed his chin as he pondered the idea. "That's deep, but I'd buy that."

Capalov raised his hand in the air. "Ding! Doctor Kadon for two hundred points. That's the exact conclusion that the therapist came to. They prescribed a light antidepressant and sent him on his way. A few years later, he was caught vandalizing a car, and the judge gave him a choice of serving time or joining the Navy. He chose the latter."

"I don't know about you two, but I need a break," Kadon said as she took a deep sigh. "This whole thing is depressing on so many levels."

Capalov replied quickly. "That's pretty much the end anyway."

Eskar stood up. "Well, Antoni, you've been reading so much that you didn't get to share your perspective. What are your thoughts here?"

The ensign pushed the keyboard back and stared down at the floor. "Reading this, I feel like I've had a really easy life. I had no idea how good I had it."

Kadon smiled. "Well said, Antoni."

Eskar continued, "I understand that, but what are your thoughts on Deke?"

"I don't think this helps us much. Deke had a bad childhood but overcame it, becoming a decorated war hero. Nothing here changes any of that."

Eskar patted Capalov on the back. "Son, your parents did a lot right with you. I'm glad to have your help with this."

"Thank you, sir."

Eskar recognized Kadon's hesitance. "Jill, it looks like you want to say more."

Kadon half-smiled as she scanned the room, trying to conjure what was bothering her into words. "Yeah, I do, but I struggle to explain it."

Eskar became concerned. "Is there something else that we're missing here? I need you to be comfortable to share what's on your heart."

Kadon nodded. "Yeah, that's part of the problem. Have we given any real consideration to the fact that the *Hercules* might have been actually attacked by something unknown?"

Eskar cocked his head as he spoke. "I haven't put much thought on this because I don't see enough evidence of it in what we've studied. Let me ask you this: Did you or your family ever own an unreliable car?"

A curious smile spread across Kadon's face. "Yes. My first car after college was a nightmare. It broke down perpetually and stranded me multiple times."

"Did you take it to the dealer to get it fixed?"

"Oh yeah, many times. They'd have it for a few days and inform me that they solved the problem. The car would work fine for a while. Then the exact same problem would re-emerge. My dad even went down there and gave them hell once, and it did nothing."

Eskar studied a loose thread on his shirt as he spoke. "Could you explain what was going on with your car?"

Kadon shook her head. "Not really. We called the car the voodoo-mobile."

Eskar chuckled as he pulled out his pocket knife and worked on the thread. "Exactly. We don't always know what's going on.

I'm sure you've worked on certain ships in our fleet that are considered *cursed*."

Kadon's eyes narrowed. "*Cursed*? You mean like the whole ship?"

"Exactly. Do you remember the IPFS *Raven*?"

"Do I? Heck, that poor ship broke down more than rookies on their first day at training camp."

Eskar gleamed. "Yeah. That ship had electrical problems all of the time. But we, in the Navy, considered that ship to be cursed, and we felt bad for anyone stationed on it."

Kadon paused before speaking. "Remy, I'm having a tough time drawing the lines here. Can you help me a little bit?"

Eskar continued, "Yeah... ummm... sorry. My point is that I'm not superstitious, but I believed that that ship was cursed, just like your voodoo-mobile. It's inexplainable why it was failing, but the data showed it time and time again."

"You think the *Hercules* was cursed?"

Eskar rubbed his sleeve where he had just cut a small thread. "Yeah, I kind of do. There are some unknowns over there that explain all that's happened, but we'll never be able to resolve that."

Kadon frowned. "Do you believe that Temkin was attacked by some unknown entity, then?"

Eskar considered the question. "You know, Jill, I don't really think he was, but that doesn't mean he didn't perceive that it was something beyond his experience. Personally, there's a fine line between the unknown and what we don't understand. In Temkin's case, it's far more likely that it leans towards the latter."

Capalov interjected, "So, no hocus-pocus-voodoo-stuff?"

Eskar shook his head. "I just can't see it. I've really considered this and think everything we see can somehow be explained."

Kadon nodded. "I can see that, Remy. Thanks for taking the time to explain it to me."

Eskar smiled. "Let's keep looking at the evidence. If something pops out, maybe it'll change my mind on this."

Kadon stood. "Of course! And on that note, I'm going to head over to check out Gircowski and Temkin."

Eskar smiled as he walked Kadon to the door. "Thank you, Jill. You're a huge help on this, and I'm sorry about not insisting that these men check in with you."

Kadon stopped walking and put her hand on Eskar's arm. "Remy, you already said sorry, and I accepted the apology. You don't need to bring it up again. I trust you, and I know there was nothing malicious here."

Her touch warmed his arm. "Okay, I just don't want you thinking less of me."

Kadon smirked and tilted her head. "I think your reputation is very safe with me. I'll talk to you later, Captain."

Capalov slipped by both of them to exit out the door. "Goodbye."

CHAPTER TWENTY-NINE

Checkup

Who is it?" Temkin asked from his chair. He sat, holding a bag of ice to his chin.

"Hey, Deke. It's Doctor Kadon. May I come in?"

Temkin slipped into some pants, put the ice bag in the sink, and sat back down. "Yes. Come in."

The door opened, and Kadon slipped into the room. "I came to check on you."

"I'm fine."

"I'm sure you think that, but I'd like to be the judge of your health."

Kadon walked closer. As she did, she noticed an ice bag in the sink. "What was that for?"

"I think you know, Doc." Temkin chuckled as he rubbed his jaw.

"I do. Do you mind if I take a look?"

"Would it matter if I did?"

Kadon shrugged. "Only a little."

"Well, then, look away, Doc."

Kadon held up her PortX camera. "Okay, look at me and smile for the camera." She took a few pictures. "Now let me get a side shot." Rather than having him turn, she walked to his side. "I want to take a few of your neck too."

Temkin sat motionless and calmly said, "Go right ahead."

Kadon took all the pictures she wanted, then pulled out her tablet. She opened the PortX application and began looking at the pictures. "Well, it looks like there's no cranial or neck damage."

"The pain I feel says something different."

"Yeah, I can see the contusion, but that'll heal. I want to check you for a concussion." She pulled her flashlight out and checked his eyes. "You look okay, Deke. You're doing the right thing with the ice bag." She reached over to the sink and handed it to him.

"Thank you." Temkin grabbed the bag and replaced it on his chin.

Kadon walked back in front of Temkin. She leaned down until she was at eye level. "So... how are you doing?"

Temkin looked confused. "You just said I was fine."

"No, I said your physical body was okay. How are you doing?"

"Oh... I'm okay, I guess. I didn't mean to start a fight. Sometimes, it's like I can't help myself."

Kadon found a chair and sat down. "Gircowski told me you came down to apologize to him."

"Yeah. It was Captain Eskar's recommendation, but it was the right thing to do. I didn't mean to hurt him like I did."

"He said that he didn't expect such a sincere apology from you."

Temkin nodded as he adjusted the ice bag slightly, trying to look away from Kadon. "I've had a lot of practice. I've done many stupid things in my life."

Kadon smiled. "Is that so?"

Temkin brimmed with pride. "Yes, ma'am."

"So, how are you sleeping lately?"

Temkin studied Kadon before he answered. "I think a little better."

Kadon pressed through the deflection. "Are you still having nightmares?"

"Sometimes. But now the dreams are mixing with some of my old haunts."

"Do you remember your dreams much?"

"Sometimes vividly, while other times, it's as if I've got a hazy first-person perspective. Right now, the dreams about the *Hercules* are very clear, but some of my older nightmares feel like I'm watching them through a dirty window. Does that make any sense?"

Kadon wrote some notes on her tablet. "Yeah, it does. Now, here's a tricky question. Which disturbs you more, the vivid dreams or hazy ones?"

Temkin sunk in his chair as he considered the question. "The hazy ones, for sure."

"Why do you say that? Especially with such certainty."

"With vivid dreams, I can see everything going on, so I can at least prepare for what's ahead, even if it's terrible. When it's hazy, I don't know what will happen. I feel like I'm always caught off guard when things occur."

Kadon nodded as she kept writing. "I can see that. I think we all feel like we want some control. Not knowing weakens us, but sometimes, not knowing lets us relax in ignorance. Still, I'm with you on vivid dreams... Now, switching gears for sec... How did you feel when you struck Gircowski?"

"How did I feel? Ummm... honestly, I can't say that I

remember… it's all kind of hazy."

"You can't remember how you felt?"

"No. I can't remember striking him. I remembered him hitting me and then it all became a blur. I do remember looking over at him rolling on the ground, and feeling terrible for him."

"Hey, I don't want to lose sight of this. Are you saying you can't remember striking Gircowski?"

"Not really. It is all kind of hazy, you know?"

Kadon thought before answering. Then she wrote some notes. The silence made the atmosphere uncomfortable until she spoke again. "I'm guessing the adrenaline kicked in and training took over. Sometimes we do things out of response rather than premeditation."

"Yeah, maybe. I still felt so bad for the guy."

Kadon stopped writing and leaned back to study Temkin. "Why did you feel terrible for him?"

"Well, I know his type."

Kadon looked confused. "His type?"

"Yeah, when I was in high school playing football, we always had guys who wanted to prove they were the best on the team. The best players rarely needed to prove they were great. But these young men would pick fights, insult, and try to show how great they were. In the end, they just looked like idiots. If their blunders were too big or one of the top dogs called their bluff, they would just disappear, never to be heard of again on the team. Gircowski was like those imposters. But I didn't need to expose him. Yet looking at him while sitting on that bench, I realized that's exactly what I did. I felt terrible."

"Kadon paused again. "That's empathy. It's generally a good and virtuous thing to have. The imposter of empathy is sympathy. Empathy is putting yourself in someone else's shoes, while sympathy is feeling bad from a position of power. They seem very similar, but one will cause your heart to change, and the other will make you believe that the person is somehow lesser because of their situation."

"I've never heard it explained like that. That really gives me something to think about, Doc."

Kadon smiled. "Well, that's a good start." She began to write something down on her tablet when she frowned. "These dang packet errors are driving me mad."

Temkin's head snapped around, and his eyes widened. "I'm sorry. What did you just say?"

"I said that I keep getting packet errors on my tablet. It's really annoying. Captain said he was having the same problem. Are you all right, Deke? All of a sudden, you look pale."

Temkin stood up and limped over to Kadon. "Doc, would you mind if I looked at your tablet? You can close out whatever app you're running to take notes."

Kadon studied her patient for a moment. She exited some applications on the tablet and handed it to Temkin. "It's all yours, especially if you can help it stop doing this."

Temkin took the tablet from her. "Is it okay if I use your stylus?"

She handed him the stylus. "Of course, help yourself."

Quickly, he began looking at some settings on her tablet. Kadon could hear him mumbling things under his breath. Temkin's stance became restless, and his actions became more deliberate on the tablet. He finally looked at Kadon. "How long have you been getting these errors?"

Kadon had to think momentarily. "I'd say it has been about a week. Maybe a little more."

Temkin eyes were darting wildly. "Crap! Crap! Crap! I need to talk to the captain as soon as possible."

Kadon's face transformed from curious to worried. "Deke? What's going on? What's gotten you so rattled?"

"This is what happened on the *Hercules*. I don't know how or why, but I'm telling you something has followed me over here."

"I don't think I fully understand what you mean here, Deke."

"I told you, or the captain — I can't remember now — that we started having random strange behavior on the ship. These sorts of faults were the same kind of stuff we saw there. And it only grew worse. I think we're being attacked. And I've no clue what to do about it." He handed the stylus and tablet back to Kadon.

Kadon moved quickly to stand from her chair. "I'll go find Remy and have him come here immediately." She turned and headed out of the room.

CHAPTER THIRTY

Infestation

Kadon walked through the halls with purpose. She stopped by Eskar's quarters only to find nobody around. Next, she walked over to Command Deck, and he wasn't there either. She noticed Capalov on duty and decided to speak to him. "Ensign, have you seen the captain?"

The ensign stopped what he was doing to give Kadon his full attention. "No. But he should be here any minute."

Kadon looked around as she bit her lower lip.

Capalov stepped away from his station. "Doctor, is something wrong?" The doctor seemed too distracted to respond, so the ensign reached out and touched her arm. "Doctor?"

Kadon refocused on him. "Oh. Well... I don't know, but I need to find the captain."

Capalov heard the captain walking in. "Doctor, he's right here."

Kadon turned to see the captain with a welcoming smile. "Oh. Captain, I'm so glad you're here. I've got an urgent request from Major Temkin. He asked for you to see him as soon as possible."

Eskar cocked his head as he adjusted his cap. "I don't work for him. Why the hell does he need to see me? What could possibly be so urgent?"

Kadon trod lightly. "Sir, Major Temkin believes we're experiencing a similar attack to the one on the *Hercules*."

Eskar's attention was fully engaged. "You've got to be kidding me."

"I wish I were, but I mentioned to Temkin that we were getting packet errors on our server requests, and he freaked out. It was like he saw the ghost of an ex-lover's father."

Eskar turned to the second in command. "Mason? You've got the helm."

Mason stood to attention. "Yes, sir."

Eskar then turned to the ensign. "Capalov? I need you to recheck our black box and ensure we still have all our feeds."

Capalov saluted as he headed to the door. "I'm on my way, Captain."

Eskar followed Capalov out with Kadon in tow. "Doctor, I don't like where this day is heading."

"Me either."

The short trip to Temkin's quarters was only interrupted by the brief elevator ride down two levels. Neither Kadon nor Eskar said a word.

When they arrived, Temkin was standing at the door. "I'm so glad you came down, Captain."

Eskar nodded. "Kadon gave me a quick synopsis. Can you explain to me why you think this is an attack?"

Temkin studied the captain as he cleared his throat to speak. "On the *Hercules*, we started getting packet errors on all interactions with the host. I've watched host computers die in the past, but two planetary-class military units with the same errors? I don't think this is a coincidence."

Eskar understood the reaction. "It's unusual, I'll give you that. I'm sure Captain Haynes tried something."

Temkin shook his head. "No, sir, we didn't realize what was happening until much later."

Eskar stared at Temkin, trying to determine the next logical step. "Do you have any suggestions?"

Temkin turned away as he thought about the question. "Maybe it's like some kind of virus that has infected the mainframe. No matter what, I'd alert NTDS immediately to see if they can combat it. Captain, I hope I'm just plain wrong on this, but it's got me on edge."

Eskar tried to console the young man. "Deke, you did the right thing by alerting me. I promise to look into everything and hopefully get some answers."

Temkin nodded. "Thanks, Captain. I know it isn't much to go on, but thanks for taking it seriously."

Eskar was about to finish when his communicator lit up. He pressed a switch to reply. "This is Eskar. Go ahead."

"Captain, Mason here. We're being hailed by the Martian frigate that guided us earlier."

The captain replied, "I'm on my way." Eskar looked at Temkin and Kadon. "Pardon me, but I must go tend to some business. Deke, I'll get back to you soon."

CHAPTER THIRTY-ONE

And It Gets Worse

Eskar quickly returned to the Bridge. As he walked in, Mason met him at the door. "Sir, Admiral Shoapa has hailed us three times. It must be urgent."

Eskar nodded. "Put it on the mains."

The screen came to life, but the picture was distorted. Admiral Shoapa was visible, and her lips were pursed as she waited for a reply.

Eskar responded. "Admiral Shoapa, this is Captain Eskar."

"Captain Eskar, we have an emergency, and you're the closest ship to us."

What the heck is going on? Eskar thought before replying. He noticed Capalov return to the Bridge, and motioned for him to come over and listen to the conversation. "How can we be of assistance, Admiral?"

Shoapa didn't waste time with pleasantries. "A few hours ago, the two escort frigates collided. We don't know what happened, but it was fatal to both ships. We're taking on survivors but have lost at least forty."

I swear that this universe has gone mad, Eskar thought. "Send us your coordinates, and we'll make haste to your position."

"I'm sending you the coordinates now. I've also handwritten them because our mainframe is acting erratically. Here they are." Shoapa held up the note. In the background, the remains of the two collided frigates took up most of the monitor.

Eskar studied the wreckage in horror. "Shoapa, we're on our way. Keep us informed."

Mason spoke up, "Sir, it looks like we can reach their position in two hours and twenty minutes."

Eskar addressed the monitor, "Admiral, I don't know if you heard that, but we're over two hours away. We'll make every attempt to get there as soon as possible. In the meantime, I'll try to relay messages about the situation to our headquarters and Martian Command. Is it okay for me to request more help from the Federation?"

"Yes, any help would be appreciated. Thank you, Captain."

The monitor went black, and Eskar wasted no time. "Walters, I need you to reach out to HQ and then hail Martian Command. Let them know of the situation." Eskar reached down and tapped the MED icon on his communication module. "Jill, I need you to begin preparing for wounded incoming. We have a massive collision between two Martian frigates."

Doctor Kadon replied quickly, "Yes, sir. I'm on my way to Med Bay."

Lieutenant Walters interjected. "Sir, it appears that our long-range communications are down."

Eskar didn't bat an eye. "Raise us to REDCON-One-point-Five. We're also under attack."

"REDCON-One-point-Five, sir."

"Walters, get Admiral Shoapa back on the line."

"Yes, sir. I've hailed her."

In a few moments, the admiral returned to the screen. "Captain Eskar, I didn't expect to hear back from you so quickly."

"It appears that our long-range com is down too. I believe we're all under some kind of attack. We're on our way to you. Hopefully, we can figure this out together."

Shoapa's jaw tightened at the news. "We agree with your assessment and await your help, Captain. I apologize, but we have many wounded that we're attending to. I must get back."

"Understood, Admiral. We're still on target to reach you in just over two hours."

Once again, the screen went black. As it did, Eskar's eyebrows raised. He turned to his XO. "Mason, can we rig another dormant drone to launch and send messages for HQ and Martain Command?"

Mason replied, "I don't see why not, sir. What do you want them to say?"

"Can you send the last ten minutes of the conversation I had with Admiral Shoapa, then send our current coordinate, our destination, and the coordinates of the wounded Martian fleet?"

"Yes, sir. I'm on it. How long should it be dormant?"

Eskar thought for a moment. "Three hours. Long enough that any signal coming from our ship will be weak."

"Three hours, sir. I'll take care of it."

Capalov spoke up, "Captain, how do you know the long-range communications will work on the drone?"

Eskar took his hat off and wiped his forehead. "I don't, but it's a hunch. The dormant drones are intentionally unattached from our ship electronically. We load them with commands through a data card. If this thing is attacking our subsystems, the drones may have a chance of working long enough to get the message out."

"That's a great idea, sir. I hope it works."

"Me too. Capalov, something is attacking our mainframe, and we need to discover what it is and how to stop it. I need you to get with NTDS and coordinate that effort. We need as many eyes on this as possible." Eskar sipped his coffee, only to curse how scalding hot it was.

CHAPTER THIRTY-TWO

Rescue Preparation

Doctor Kadon hurried down the main corridor as the REDCON-One-point-Five alarm sounded. Shortly after, the sound of the four main engines resonated in the halls around Med Bay. Milla met her at the portal. "Doctor Kadon, I have begun preparations for the incoming patients. Nina and Seja are doing the same."

Kadon could see the progress that was already being made. Makeshift cots, pillows, and blankets were on one side of the bay. In another section, medications specifically dealing with radiation exposure were stockpiled. "That's good news, Milla. I've ten more crew members coming down to assist. I have something to ask you because I need an unbiased answer."

Milla paused for a moment before answering. "I would be happy to answer any questions you have, Doctor Kadon. I have advanced logic circuits and algorithms designed for problem-solving and resolution."

Kadon nodded. "Exactly! That's why I need to ask you this question."

"What is the question, Doctor Kadon?"

Kadon looked up, trying to phrase this question in the best way possible. "I've been thinking we should bring Irena back online for this emergency. Do you think that's too risky?"

Milla quickly replied. "That is a good question, Doctor Kadon. According to NTDS's report, what happened to Irena could happen to any medical robot on this level. They have increased our redundancy checking on faults and added an extra failsafe in case of a significant crash, as Irena experienced. The risk has been mitigated significantly. Irena is also the med-bot with the highest proficiency rating for trauma treatment."

"So you're saying you think it would be okay for this emergency?"

"Another medical robot would be invaluable at this time, Doctor Kadon. I calculate the risk to be minimal. But this would be a breach of Navy protocol. You must file a report explaining the justification for such an action. When we returned to port, you would also possibly have to face an inquiry."

"I think it can help save lives. That's what I care about. I don't care about facing a board."

"Doctor Kadon, I suspect your mind was already made up before you asked the question."

Kadon snorted at Milla's revelation. "Maybe so, but I'd have stopped if you cited a major objection."

"Understood, Doctor Kadon. Irena is still down in NTDS. Would you like me to go down and recommission it?"

"No, I'll do it. I'll need to sign the paperwork anyway."

"Understood, Doctor Kadon. I need to return to preparation."

Kadon's head shook as she closed her eyes. "Oh... of course, Milla. I apologize for monopolizing your time."

"Not at all, Doctor Kadon. I will welcome you and the extra help we will get with Irena."

Kadon turned and jogged down the halls to NTDS. The trip left her winded, but the moment's excitement kept her motivated. As she took the last step down to enter Engineering, she heard Temkin call to her, "Jill, what's the rush?"

Kadon turned to see Temkin hopping down the hall rather than using his cane. "Hey, Deke, a major collision occurred between two Martian frigates. We're doing everything we can to prepare for incoming survivors."

"Why are you down at Engineering?"

Kadon realized who she was talking to. "Well, I'm trying to get Irena back online to help."

The comment startled Temkin. "The killer med-bot?"

"Oh, don't be so dramatic."

Temkin crossed his arms and cocked his head. "No, seriously. That thing almost killed you."

"It was an understandable issue that has been addressed. But Irena's help would be huge with all the incoming wounded. I'm temporarily giving it a stay of execution."

"Well, that all sounds okay, but let's hope Doctor Slaughterhouse doesn't come for a visit."

Kadon pouted. "Really, Deke? More drama?"

"Hey, I'm just calling it as I see it."

"Sorry, I don't have time for this right now. I'll come to talk with you later."

Temkin turned to leave but quickly spun back to make one last statement. "Hey, Doc. It's the right call. Without a doubt."

"Thanks, Deke. See you soon."

Kadon walked into the NTDS station. The entire crew was busy preparing for the emergency. She noticed a young man stowing electronic devices in a large metal cabinet. Quickly, she ran over and tapped him on the shoulder. "Pardon me."

The young man turned to look at her. "Doctor Kadon, can I help you?"

"I sure hope so. I was looking for the med-bot brought down here a couple of weeks ago."

"Irena?"

"Yes, that's the one. I need to reclaim it for this emergency."

The young man scratched his head. "I don't know if that's allowed."

"In an emergency, I can commandeer a piece of equipment. I'll fill out any paperwork I need to make that happen."

"Of course, sir. Let me see where it was stowed." The young man went to a terminal and started typing. "Hmmm." His brow furrowed as he investigated further "Where the hell did you go?" He looked up to see Kadon staring at him. "Sorry, sir."

"No apology needed. By the way, what's your name?"

"Alan Wittle, sir." He straightened even further.

Kadon regretted putting more pressure on Wittle, but she needed to press further. "At ease, Alan. Any luck finding Irena?"

"No, sir. I believe we stowed it at the previous REDCON-One event. I'm going to have to search the cabinets for it. Don't worry about the paperwork. I'll find it and send it your way."

"Really? You don't mind?"

Wittle shook his head. "No, sir. It'll be in Med Bay within the hour."

"Thank you, Alan. I appreciate your help on this. Oh... One more thing. Can you ensure Irena has the same safeguards you put on the other med-bots?"

"Yes, sir. I'm happy to help. It'll be updated with our patches as well."

Kadon quickly exited and returned to Med Bay to aid in the preparations. When she arrived, the bay was filled with crew members working to prepare for the rescue effort. For a brief moment, she was overwhelmed with emotion at the outpouring of helpers. She regained her composure and headed to work. As she was setting up different types of aid stations, she noticed Ensign Capalov working.

"Hey, Antoni. Doesn't Eskar have you doing enough?"

Capalov turned and saw it was Kadon. "Doctor, I volunteered for this. It's my honor to help. When I signed up for the Navy, I really signed up for this. I wanted to help people and make a difference."

"Well, you're doing both. I'm glad to see you down here."

A familiar voice resonated behind Kadon. "Doctor Kadon, I am ready for instructions."

Kadon turned to see Irena standing and ready for action. "Irena, it's good to have you back. I believe we're going to need many more radiation kits. Can you oversee that?"

"Of course, Doctor Kadon. I will begin immediately." Irena turned and headed to the far corner of Med Bay. Milla walked by Irena, and the two med-bots conversed momentarily.

Kadon smiled. In her heart, it was like having an old friend back. After working with the med-bots for as long as Kadon had, she recognized each one had a slightly different personality. Irena was her favorite of the group.

Kadon was still captured with watching Irena when another familiar voice startled her. "Where can I help?"

She turned to see Major Temkin standing behind her. "I know you're supposed to be in your quarters, but we can use all the help we can get. There's a stool over there. Would you mind folding these towels and placing them in bags?"

"Not at all. I'd be happy to get to do anything to help."

Kadon snorted. "Well, quit your talking and get to work, Mister."

Temkin stiffened up pompously and saluted Kadon as he smiled. "Yes, sir!"

CHAPTER THIRTY-THREE

Helping Out

C aptain, we're ten minutes out."

Eskar studied the status display. "Walters, can you raise Admiral Shoapa?"

"Yes, sir. It's coming on mains now." Walters linked the communication, and the main display came to life.

"Admiral Shoapa, we're near your position. How can we be of the most help? Our ship and crew are at your disposal."

The admiral continued to look away, and the Martian Bridge was brimming with activity. "Captain, you've arrived just in time. We're able to track you. The good news is we were able to re-seal the *Cuda*. It can't move, but life support is fully functional. The *Wraith*, on the other hand, is unsalvageable. Our electric protective field has about ninety minutes of life left. Once that's gone, no life is sustainable on that frigate. We're taking in survivors as quickly as we can. We could use your help in rescuing the crew."

Lieutenant Walters showed Eskar scans of the three ships. "Admiral, I'm looking at scans of the ships. We're heading to the *Wraith* now. We'll go to the opposite side of your frigate and launch every rescue craft we have."

"Understood, Captain. Thank you for any assistance you can provide. We're very grateful."

Eskar stared out the forward port windows. "We're happy to help. I'm looking now, and your frigate is within our visual range. I don't see the other two yet, but I suspect it won't be long."

Shoapa frowned. "We can see you. Just follow the trail of smoke."

Eskar looked closer and noticed the dense smoke cloud to the right of Shoapa's ship. Slowly, as it came into view, the moment's horror captured the captain. *Lord in heaven, help those people,* Eskar thought as he began to catch his first glimpse of the *Cuda* and *Wraith*. Both ships were still attached to each other, and smoke billowed from the connected area between the two. The dull-blue electrical shielding covered the large cavity created by the collision.

As Class-Five Frigates, the *Cuda* and *Wraith* were massive and intimidating. The design was quite contrary to that of their federation counterparts. The Federation frigates had smooth exteriors with the occasional protrusion, while Martian exteriors had many appendages with an occasional run of smoothness. On Federation ships, engines and cannons were integrated into the hull, yet those looked like they were attached as afterthoughts to their Martian counterparts. The *Gibraltar* looked to be a quarter the size of these ships.

The forward sections of the *Cuda*'s hull were still impaling its sister ship. The *Wraith* clearly took the brunt of the damage, with *Cuda*'s nose entirely through the *Wraith*'s body. As Eskar looked down the crash lines, multiple lifeless bodies floated around the wreckage.

Eskar studied the collision from the safety of his Command

Deck on his diminutive Corvette-Class ship. His mind was having a difficult time wrapping around this surreal moment. "Admiral, we have visual. We'll do everything in our power to help."

"Affirmative, Captain. Godspeed to you and your crew. I'm leaving this channel open so we can continue communicating through this operation."

Eskar nodded. "Understood, Admiral." He turned away from the mains and tapped an icon on his comm module. "Mason, are we ready to launch?"

Mason quickly replied, "Yes, sir. We have thirteen rescue crafts and about thirty drones ready to launch at your command."

"Thanks, Mason. I'll let you know soon." Eskar quickly addressed the navigator, "Quinton, bring us in as tight as you can on the other side of those wounded frigates. Watch out for those smoke plumes. That stuff is dense and sticks to everything."

Lieutenant Quinton manually steered the Corvette into position. "Yes, sir. Less than thirty seconds until we're in position."

The *Gibraltar* adeptly navigated into position and came to a complete stop. Eskar spoke to the admiral, "Sir, we're in position. We can launch at your command."

Shoapa nodded. "Launch at your discretion, Captain."

"Yes, sir. Help is on the way." Eskar contacted his second in command, "It's time to launch, Mason."

"Affirmative, Captain. We're launching."

The Corvette shuddered as dozens of smaller craft began their rescue mission. Eskar stood on the deck with great pride as the rocket plumes from the Mantis ships caused their viewing port to vibrate.

The Martian contingent had already set up loading areas for stranded crew members. The Mantis ships lined up and quickly accepted survivors to the *Gibraltar*. It only took ten minutes for eight of the thirteen Mantis ships to return with a full cargo of refugees.

The Mantis ships quickly unloaded to waiting teams and prepared to return to the rescue effort. The pilots kept up a relentless pace in their race against the collapse of the electronic shield. Some of the slower-loading ships, full of injured crewmen, used auxiliary entry points. The better pilots gave these ships extra leeway as they entered the bay.

Eskar watched as his entire crew behaved as a single unit, with near-flawless execution. He found it challenging to keep his emotions in check in the face of such bravery and valor.

Within an hour, over two hundred Martians were loaded onto the *Gibraltar*. Mason hailed Captain Eskar. "Sir, we have secured all the remaining crew of the *Wraith*."

Eskar smiled and couldn't help himself as he gave a jubilant cheer. "Well done, well done!" He turned to the monitor to address Admiral Shoapa. "Sir, our rescue effort was a success. We have secured the remaining crew members. Our medical teams are working on helping the wounded while tending to those who are merely displaced."

Shoapa beamed. "Captain, I'm very impressed. Your crew behaved courageously out there and are a great credit to the Federation."

"Thank you, Admiral. Our business isn't concluded yet. Just as you've surmised, we think we're being attacked. Our survivor has also confirmed that this is what stranded the *Hercules*. I want to come over and discuss how we can work together to fight this battle. I'm of the opinion that one of our ships needs to run for Martian territory while the other waits with the *Cuda*. I think it makes more sense for your ship to head back."

"I'm in complete agreement. Please come over so we can plan this as soon as possible."

"I'm on my way, sir." He hailed the commander and the ensign. "Mason, Capalov, I need you to attend a meeting with me on the Martian frigate."

Capalov responded immediately. "I'll meet you in the Launch Bay, sir. On our way over to the *Defiant*, I'll share with you what we have already found."

Mason answered next. "I'll be in Launch Bay Four-L with Honner as our pilot."

"Excellent. See you both in five minutes."

CHAPTER THIRTY-FOUR

Triage

Doctor Kadon moved adeptly from cot to cot as she addressed the most critical patients. Her efforts benefited from the presence of Milla and Irena. They remained vigilant and invaluable in the execution of their duties. Three cargo bays served as the holding facilities for most of the survivors. The two larger bays housed the healthier refugees, while the smaller bay acted as a triage for the wounded and injured.

It was the crew's duty to collect those who hadn't survived the collision. Drones vigorously searched through the wreckage to find lost souls. The grim task netted the bodies of forty-six additional fallen Martian crew members. The drones carefully brought the remains over to the *Gibraltar*.

Eskar directed the team to place a shipping container in one of the launch bays currently under repair. Martian Naval officers reverently walked the fallen soldiers to a container which was equipped with a climate control unit. The duties of the officers included preparing the bodies for storage. Every attempt was made not to lose sight of the cost of precious life.

Eskar deemed it most appropriate to allow the Martians to tend to their own, and he asked Captain Ari Tregevek of the *Wraith* to select the team for this onerous task. Tregevek volunteered himself and somberly selected his team. He took a moment to salute Eskar. As one who had experienced the tragic deaths of those under his command, Eskar lowered his head to stop the tears from falling, then hugged Tregevek rather than following protocol. Tregevek returned the gesture.

Med Bay was reserved for the most critical cases. The team placed forty patients in the Bay, and Kadon was doing her best to help every one of them. The surgical mask and protective goggles helped hide her look of fatigue, but those close to her, like Eskar, could see the signs.

Eskar stopped in to check on the medical team. He quickly scanned the room and found the doctor tending to a young man. When she paused, the captain spoke. "I was just checking in to see how things are going."

Kadon didn't notice Eskar initially, but she spun to look at him when he spoke. "I assume you're asking as the captain?" Kadon took a defensive stance, resting most of her weight on her left leg, further from the captain.

Eskar's smile faded. "No, Jill. I'm asking as your concerned friend. You look exhausted."

The comment moved Kadon. "Oh... I am, but sleep can wait. Many of my patients can't."

"I understand, but just make sure you're getting some rest."

Kadon thought for a moment before replying. "Right now, we need a bigger facility and more medics."

"You're on your own for that, kiddo."

Kadon shook her head and rolled her eyes. "I know, but thanks for checking in on me."

"You bet. I'll let you get back to it."

Eskar moved on to check other areas, leaving his friend to do what she did best.

Kadon watched Eskar depart as she walked to the next patient in the ward. She called to Milla, "Milla, can you scan this young man's leg? I think there's something more going on here than just this superficial wound."

Milla quickly reacted. "Of course, Doctor Kadon." Milla leaned down and examined the leg. "You are right, Doctor. There is a metallic sliver that is embedded in the bone. I would recommend immediate surgery to remove this."

Kadon was ready. "Let's do it, Milla. Seja? Prep for surgery." The good doctor looked down at her patient. "What's your name, sir?"

The young man couldn't open his eyes. He turned his head slightly and whispered, "Molique."

"Okay, Molique. We'll need to operate on this leg, but you should be fine."

The young man nodded, then grabbed Kadon's arm and whispered, "Thank you for saving my life."

Kadon didn't know what to say. "Hang in there, Molique. It'll get better soon."

Seja gracefully walked over and began speaking. "Mister Molique, please do not be alarmed. I need to place a mask on your face to anesthetize you for your surgery. I assure you that it will only take a few seconds." Before the patient could object, Seja placed the mask over his face. As stated, Molique was asleep in less than ten seconds.

Milla operated as Kadon watched. Milla patched the young man's leg up with the sliver dislodged, and the damage it had done was repaired. It looked over at Kadon, "We are finished here. The operation was a complete success."

Kadon smiled. "Excellent work, Milla." As she spoke, she noticed Irena watching the operation. Before the unfortunate accident, Irena would have been the robot to perform such delicate operations, but the doctor couldn't risk that. Kadon felt deep empathy for the med-bot and the circumstances that forced her to pick Milla.

Rather than watching the operation constantly, Kadon felt like Irena focused on her a large part of the time. Kadon found the attention unnerving. At one point, she called out to Irena, "Irena, can you see how we are on radiation kits?"

Irena responded, "Yes, Doctor Kadon. I will do that immediately." She headed to the port side of Med Bay and began an inventory check.

The ten minutes Irena walked away gave Kadon time to gather her composure. Milla needed her full attention, and Molique was counting on it.

After the surgery, Kadon decided to listen to Eskar's gentle reminder and take a small rest. She walked to her office and took off her goggles and mask. When she sat in her chair, she saw a message from NTDS. *Shoot, I bet I need to sign something for Irena. You know how the Navy loves its paperwork,* she mused as she listened to the message.

"Ummm... Doctor Kadon. Sorry to leave you a message. This is Alan Wittle from NTDS. I've looked all around our office and can't find the med-bot. I suspect it was stowed tightly away during the last REDCON-One incident. I promise I'll keep looking for it and keep you informed. Goodbye."

Kadon's head cocked as she slowly turned to watch Irena, still vigilantly doing inventory.

CHAPTER THIRTY-FIVE

Gathering of Minds

Eskar walked into Launch Bay Four-L and saw Mason and Capalov waiting for him. "Gentlemen, are you ready to head over?"

Mason quickly replied, "Yes, sir. I have Lieutenant Honner prepping the ship. I think this will be the first time I've been cordially invited to land on an active Martian frigate."

Eskar grinned. "These past few weeks have seen a lot of firsts, Major. Be on good behavior, and don't make them regret inviting us."

The men made their way into the waiting Mantis craft. After they were all secured, Capalov started speaking. "Sir, we think we have discovered what's happening in the mainframes."

"Well, that is good news."

Capalov nervously smiled. "Yes, but it's not all good news."

"Oh? How so?"

"Well, it looks like it's actually some sort of AI codex."

Eskar was confused. "Codex? Like some ancient book of rules?"

Capalov paused and took a deep breath. "Kind of, yes. This algorithm looks like it was based on some twenty-first century code outlawed about the same time we colonized Mars."

Eskar was doing his best to follow. "So it's like a virus?"

"Yes and no. It's malicious like a virus but more like an intelligent cancer."

Eskar shook his head. "You've really got me lost here, son. Can you help me out?"

Capalov relaxed in his chair and spoke carefully. "Sorry, sir. So... in virtual worlds, a virus is a foreign program that *infects* the host with something designed to compromise its subsystems. Part of the design of the virus is its ability to catch rides to other subsystems. In doing so, it infects the new unit with the same sort of code. Does that make sense?"

"Affirmative. I'm following. Please carry on."

"Now, we found something that behaves more like cancer than a virus. It's also code, but the code lays in wait, watching traffic and patterns of the host. It then intelligently inserts itself so the computer thinks it's part of the normal operations. In other words, it's entirely stealthy to the computer's security systems. Unlike a virus, it doesn't attach the same code to other subsystems. Instead, it creates viable communication that allows it to morph its core code to maximize its damage while keeping itself undetectable..."

Eskar remained engrossed in the information, but some questions nagged at him. He finally stopped Capalov to ask for some clarity. "So, I've two questions right now. If it's undetectable, how did your team... ummm... detect it? Secondly, is the cancer contagious?"

Capalov smiled. "You're on it, Captain. Let me answer the second question first. Cancer in living things isn't contagious. But in a computer, it's like an ecosystem, allowing the 'cancer' to travel from subsystem to subsystem, even onto different machines. The answer to the first is a little more convoluted. We wiped a device clean and then introduced it to the mainframe. At first, there was no effect whatsoever. After about thirty minutes, we noticed that the memory usage of the subsystem had nearly doubled, yet when any diagnostic was run, it would report everything was good. We also noticed that all functionality on the device was slowly being corrupted. We then tried this with two unrelated devices, and the same thing happened."

"Holy crap. So all of this came from the *Hercules*?"

Capalov's face filled with an uneasy smile. "It's hard to say. We did tap into their communication system, but now we don't see how an audio comm link could act as a carrier. In the case of the frigates, it most likely happened when they took over our guidance control. That type of connection is the ship's processor talking to the other ship's processor."

Eskar frowned. "So, we're somehow at fault for this tragic accident."

Capalov mirrored his captain's expression. "In a manner of speaking, but there's a reason this code is considered highly illegal in both the Federation and with the Martian separatists. Somehow, this was planted on the *Hercules*, and the ship and its crew paid the ultimate price for it."

"We can add hundreds more to that list with these frigates."

"Yes, sir." The ensign looked down and away from Eskar.

"Do you think any of this ties back to Temkin?"

Capalov contemplated the question for a longer time than Eskar expected. "Temkin could have brought the Codex, but he had no real access to the ship for weeks. We saw *activity* within a week of rescuing him. Temkin was still in Quarantine when we gave him the tablet. After finding this cancer, Temkin was my first inclination, too. I checked his activity, and other than an exuberant love of sports and current events, he didn't go anywhere unusual. About once a day, Temkin passively checked his emails and looked at the stock market. In Med Bay, he seemed to listen to a lot of music through the entertainment system. I'd say he used the tablet for input and interacted pretty blandly with it."

Eskar was pleased with Capalov's insight. "Temkin was part of electronic warfare, and he's no idiot. He probably knew we would monitor his activity. Could he have hidden his activity from us in some sort of way?"

"I thought of that, too. I've considered what else could have been done. I'm gonna say it's certainly possible, but I don't see any evidence of that right now. Sorry to switch gears a little, but we'll land shortly. I'm very concerned about these frigates. Based on their interaction, this cancer has proven deadly in a few days, but maybe our electronic security is better. It bothers me how easily this has spread."

Eskar took in what the ensign was saying. "Temkin still bothers me. We need to keep an eye on him. I hate that he's on my ship and I can't ask about his orders. As far as the frigates, what about stopping this... cancer? Do we have a way to exterminate it?"

Capalov shook his head. "We're working on isolating it based on heuristic properties that we've found, but in many of these subsystems, the best we can hope to do is to stop it from spreading and growing."

"So we're stuck with a bunch of nonfunctional equipment. And a threat that, at best, we can hold at bay."

Capalov sighed. "Yes, sir. I could be wrong, but that was my takeaway."

"We need to share this with the Martians. Hopefully, between our team and theirs, we can come up with a more acceptable solution."

Lieutenant Honner spoke over the intercom. "We're two minutes away. We've been cleared for entry. Secure yourselves for landing."

Eskar put his hand on Capalov's shoulder. "Thanks for the debrief, son. I'm going to ask you to share with Admiral Shoapa, but there's to be no mention of Temkin. Let's keep this to a status of 'we've all been attacked, and its origin can be traced back to the *Hercules.*' Am I clear?"

Capalov nodded. If there was any disappointment in his countenance, he hid it well from Eskar. "Yes, sir. I understand completely." He looked out the starboard window at the Martian ship. "Man, their ships are even uglier the closer we get to them."

The comment drew chuckles from Mason and Eskar.

The Mantis ship gracefully landed on the frigate and shut down its thrusters. Eskar was the first to exit and could see Admiral Shoapa waiting for him at the entry gate. Eskar smiled and walked directly to the admiral. He saluted her, and she returned the salute. "Admiral, it's good to meet you in person."

In the background of the bay, Eskar could see crowded rooms of extra passengers. Many looked lost and still in shock at the day's events. The admiral noticed his gaze. "It's a pleasure to meet you as well. As you can see, we're pretty full right now. I'd like us to go somewhere quiet. Unfortunately, most rooms on our ship are occupied right now. I've decided to take you to my quarters If that's acceptable. It'll be big enough for our team and the three of your team members."

Eskar looked at Capalov and Mason. "These two will attend. Lead the way, Admiral."

Shoapa nodded as she turned and headed to an exit on the bay's far side. As Eskar and his team walked down the halls, he couldn't shake the awkwardness of willingly being on a foreign warship. He studied the halls. The craft was much more spartan in design than Federation vessels, and the atmospheric pressure was significantly lower. Eskar kept adjusting his jaw, trying to allow his ears to pop.

The halls were narrow and lined with occupied cots. Eskar was familiar with the shocked look on the faces of the officers he encountered. Walking the halls of ships after brutal battles was not unfamiliar to him. He could feel the ironic twist that those battles were often with the separatist fleet. He studied the crew, and their loyalty to their cause was as evident as any crew on a Federation craft.

The groups finally arrived at Shoapa's quarters. As she opened the door, Eskar also noticed how much smaller the quarters were. Two guards stood inside the door, and one was stationed outside. Shoapa had four aides walking in with her. Eskar and his team followed.

Shoapa spoke, "I'm sorry. I know these chambers aren't as large as your Federation ships. We have brought in extra chairs so we can all sit tightly, if not comfortably."

Eskar did his best to be a diplomat. "This is an amazing ship. There's nothing to apologize for. It's designed for war, and the space is optimized for that purpose."

Shoapa smiled. "Captain Eskar. You may not know this, but I was a captain in the Federation long ago. I'm aware of how cramped Martain warships are. I appreciate your understanding."

Crap, I wish I'd known that. She's a traitor, too. At least she didn't insult me. Mental Note: Never become a diplomat. I'm not too fond of all this idle chatter. Eskar smiled internally but chose to nod rather than give a full reply.

Shoapa continued as everyone sat around a planning table. The table was active, and every touch was registered in the interface. "So, I know none of us have much free time, but we need to make a plan here for a path forward. I want to introduce you to my team. It's probably easiest if I just go around the table."

Shoapa pointed to the first individual. The man was easily 2.1 meters tall and one hundred and fifty kilos. The chair he sat in looked like a toy compared to his massive physique. "This is Captain Shendai Boorikan. He's the head of our security detail and troop deployment." Boorikan grunted at the introduction.

"Next, we have Lieutenant Gina Centor. She's our electronic intelligence officer." The mousy young woman avoided eye contact.

Shoapa turned and nodded to the older man to her left. "I believe you've met Captain Ari Tregevek of the *Wraith*, and this is Captain Ursula Beaumont of the *Cuda*." The two captains smiled and dipped their heads.

"Thank you, Captain Eskar, for your aid today." Tregevek spoke, "You have an excellent team, and I'm honored to serve with you in these difficult times."

Eskar bowed at the compliment. "The honor is mine, Captain. Perhaps I should introduce the two officers with me. To my left is Ensign Antoni Capalov. He has been the lead on the discovery of this electronic threat. To my right is Commander Jacob Mason.

He's in charge of all military and logistical operations." The two men nodded at their introduction.

Shoapa wasted no time. "Well, with introductions done, let's get down to business. Have you had any luck in determining what has attacked our ships?"

"We've found something that appears to have infiltrated all of our ships from the *Hercules*. Rather than letting me butcher the explanation, I think it would be best if Ensign Capalov explained."

Capalov's eyes opened widely, and he took a deep breath. "Thank you, Captain and Admiral. Our team isolated a Codex that we believe is causing all of this. Our assumption is that it attached to our subsystems when we communicated with the *Hercules*. It latched on to your fleet when you escorted our ship through your controlled sectors."

Centor listened intently, leaning slightly forward. "So it's like some sort of software virus?"

Capalov nodded, and his shoulders loosened at the question. "Yes, but it's an intelligent virus. It's using an AI algorithm to hide itself in our subsystems."

Centor added, "So it's using some kind of rogue AI at its core?"

Capalov responded, "We think so. This type of Codex has been outlawed by both the Federation and Martians. Whatever it is, it's complex and tough to contain."

Centor's lips curled as she subtly sneered. "So you infected us with some reprobate Codex, and now you don't know how to stop it? And you expect us to believe you had no knowledge of this?"

Shoapa quickly stepped in. "Lieutenant Centor, that will be all. This crew didn't need to help us, and they put themselves at risk to come to our aid. I expect you to remember that when you address them."

Centor looked down and fidgeted with her hands. "Yes, sir."

"I apologize for my lieutenant's zeal, Ensign. Would you please continue?"

Capalov looked at the young woman across from him as he spoke. "I think we've discovered a possible way to contain it, but whatever damage it's done is basically permanent."

It was time for Captain Eskar to step in. "I'd like Ensign Capalov to stay here and work with your team. He'll act as the liaison between our group and yours–if that's acceptable to you, Admiral."

Shoapa looked at her officer, then at Capalov. "As long as they can behave. We don't have time for finger-pointing right now. We can let people with more pedigrees than us figure this out later." The two officers looked down.

Capalov spoke first, "That won't be a problem, Admiral. If I were in Lieutenant Centor's shoes, I'd think the same damn thing. Excuse my language." The comment made Centor look up as Eskar winced.

Shoapa nodded with pleasure. "I like this one, Captain Eskar. He's a good egg."

Eskar smiled, but he firmly put his hand on Capalov's shoulder. "Yes, he shows great promise. And youth covers a lot of sins."

Shoapa went right back to business. "Okay, that's settled. Now, Ensign Capalov? As far as your team can tell, you said that any systems down are down for the count. Am I right?"

"Yes, sir. It seems to put a priority on long-range communication." Capalov leaned his elbows on the table and spoke passionately on the subject. "Our ship suffered the same problem as yours. We have also checked all our fighters and maintenance ships. All of them have the same problem."

Shoapa leaned back in her chair. "So what can we do?"

"Well... Captain Eskar did something that I think was pretty brilliant. He ordered us to launch some dormant drones and set their timer so that we were out of reach of its short-range radios before they activated. Hopefully, they could get distress signals out before the Codex could shut them down."

"I'm impressed. That is indeed brilliant."

Eskar spoke up. "We put messages hailing both your and our headquarters. With any luck, they're heading this way now."

Shoapa turned to Eskar. "So, how will we know if they worked?"

Eskar tilted his head and sighed. "Hopefully, someone will show up and help, but I don't think we can wait for that."

Shoapa leaned forward and placed her hand on the table. "I agree. I believe we need to return to the closest base to bring back help."

Eskar nodded. "I know you've thought about this, too. I talked with your chief medical officer, who confirmed that seven patients need more care than we can give them on the *Gibraltar*. I want to transport them here to give them the best chance of survival. Before that, I hope our teams can develop something to stop this virus from spreading. I'm just thinking about the problem when we contact any other vessel. If we can't quarantine this thing, it'll infect everything it touches."

"Agreed, Captain. At this moment, the priority is stopping this virus... or whatever they call it. Lieutenant Centor, you need to work with Ensign Capalov to this end. Is that going to be a problem?"

Centor stiffened. "Not at all, Admiral. We'll get right on it."

"Very well. You and Ensign Capalov are dismissed."

The two officers stood and saluted, then turned and left the room.

Shoapa turned back to Eskar. "Captain, I believe we have a plan for the short term."

"I'll have these injured soldiers moved to your ship as soon as possible, so when you're ready to leave, it'll minimize the delay," Eskar said. "If you'd like, we have more room on our ship for more passengers."

"I think it would be wise to allow for more room on your ship in case more problems arise with the *Cuda*."

Eskar's brow furrowed. "Wow. Good point, Admiral. Speaking of the *Cuda*, our drones keep examining the collision. We don't see an easy way to detach those two ships."

Shoapa shook her head. "Agreed. They're lodged together very tightly."

"I'm concerned about the stability of the *Wraith*'s reactor. The drones are reporting a breakdown of the core. Has your team assessed this, too?"

Shoapa took a sip of tea before replying. "Yes. We've seen the same thing. I don't understand, but our drones couldn't disengage the core. We think we have about three to four weeks before it's critical."

Eskar pondered the comment. "Would you mind if I put some engineers on the task of separating the ships? I'm concerned about the *Cuda*'s safety."

"That would be a great use of time. Captain Tregevek and his engineers will be there to aid you with any insight into solving this problem."

Eskar respectfully corrected Shoapa, "It's not a problem yet. Let's hope it never gets there."

"Of course, Captain. Also, when we have left this terrible situation, we plan to destroy the two frigates. I wanted to share that with you so it won't come as a surprise when it occurs."

"Admiral, we would do the same. No surprise here."

Shoapa looked pleased. "Good! It looks like we all have our work cut out for us. Unless you have anything else, I think we've covered enough to keep us all busy for the next few days."

There was some small talk as Eskar stood to exit. He reached out to shake Shoapa's hand. "Thank you, Admiral. I believe this has been very productive."

Shoapa met the captain's hand. "I think so too. We'll be expecting and preparing for the wounded to arrive. With any luck, we can begin our return to Martian territory within twenty-four hours."

CHAPTER THIRTY-SIX

Go Over Old Notes

D octor Kadon stared down at her tablet. The last twenty hours had passed like a whirlwind, and she could feel the fatigue in her neck and lower back. *I need to get some better shoes,* she thought as she massaged her neck and lamented the plight of getting older.

From the vantage point of her desk, she watched Irena and Milla continuing to tend to patients. Occasionally, Irena would look over at her, stare momentarily, then return to the task it was doing. Every time Irena looked over at her, her discomfort grew.

She decided to study more of the report on Temkin. She recalled Capalov saying something about his mother placing him in therapy at the recommendation of the high school. Kadon decided that was a worthy place to start.

Kadon opened the report on her tablet and was forced to look at the pictures on the first page. She sadly studied the young boy. Many of the wounds in this picture remained on his recent CT scan. Her heart broke for him. "Aw, Deke, what the hell did that horrible man do to you?" she whispered as she continued to the next page of the report.

Finally, she arrived at the section concerning his therapy.

Capalov's paraphrase was primarily accurate, but there were specific details that he either missed or didn't feel were important. Scanning the report, certain aspects caught Kadon's eye.

The mother brought her son in for a polygraph. She believed he may have been involved in the death of her husband. The mother was fearful, as Dillon would often become temperamental and have fits of rage. One incident resulted in the mother's boyfriend being badly beaten by Dillon. The boyfriend refused to press charges, but it ended his relationship with Dillon's mother.

Based on her choice of a husband, my money is this guy had it coming to him, Kadon thought as she read on.

In agreement with the mother, the high school counselors recommended that Dillon seek professional help. The mother insisted that her son be given a polygraph.

I can't even imagine what kind of life this mom has had. Kadon leaned in closer to read on.

After months of counseling, it was determined that Dillon had some vivid dreams about his

father's death. This raised some concern, so the counselors agreed to perform the polygraph. The test concluded that Dillon hadn't killed his father but knew more details than were released to the public concerning his father's death. The counselors concluded that Dillon may have personally witnessed his father's suicide.

Wow! That makes sense, but he was cleared. We came to the same conclusion, but it would have been a lot easier to come to it if Capalov had read us all of this. Kadon sat up momentarily and pondered how they got to the same assumption. She nodded and continued examining the report.

Because of her fears, the mother didn't want Dillon to return home after he was cleared of suspicion for the murder of her husband. With a history of minor criminal activity, it was determined that the best place for Dillon was to enlist in the Navy. Part of the agreement was to seal his records to give him every opportunity to succeed in the Navy....

"Are you reading anything juicy?" Temkin popped into Kadon's office.

His voice startled her so badly that she dropped her tablet. She quickly reached down and grabbed it, closing the report she was reading. "Deke, you scared the crap out of me. I was... um...

checking our inventory on some products. Weren't you supposed to be confined to your quarters?"

"Three days ended one hour ago. Besides, this place is so crazy, who's going to notice anyway?"

Kadon tried to calm herself, but her hands shook. "I would, for starters. I also noticed you came down to help while you were supposed to be in your room. What can I do for you?"

Temkin comfortably leaned on the doorframe. "Actually, I came down here to ask you the same question. Is there anything I can do to help? My room is driving me crazy."

Kadon looked around and saw the med-bot moving past the hall. "Irena was doing inventory. I'm sure it could use some help."

Temkin smiled. "I thought you were doing inventory."

Kadon's eyes grew large. "Umm... yes I was doing an inventory of the antibiotics, not physical materials."

"Oh. You sure looked pretty into it while reading those exciting spreadsheets," Temkin said as he crossed his arms.

Kadon could feel sweat trickling down the small of her back. "I've been working twenty hours straight. I doubt I'm into anything right now." She tried to look up at Temkin but could only briefly glance at his face. Instead, she turned back down as if examining the tablet for damage. *Dear God, I could never make it as a spy,* she chuckled to herself.

Temkin took a step closer. "You should go get some rest, Doc. If you would like, I can escort you to your room. Sure, I'm walking with a cane, but I've got some saucy gusto." He held out his free arm as if he were an escort.

Kadon tried to laugh, but it came out as a high-pitched wheezing sound. "No, I need to finish up this work. Go talk to Irena. I'm sure she can find something for you. There's so much to do here, it feels like there will never be enough time to get everything done."

Temkin cocked his head as he spoke, "Okay, Doc. I hope you get some rest." He waited an uncomfortable moment before turning around and hobbling over to Irena. Irena stopped what she was doing to converse with the major.

Kadon took a deep breath as her heart rate lowered. She waited until she could hear Irena interacting with Temkin, then reopened her tablet. She closed her eyes for a moment before continuing. *Deke's timing is uncanny and totally creepy,* she thought before opening up his case file again.

Looking at the case file, she noticed a link to an interview with Deke's mother. She pulled her earbuds out of her pocket and scanned the perimeter to ensure it was Temkin-free. When that was verified, she pressed "play" on the clip.

A middle-aged man began to speak. "Miss Temkin—"

Amelia Golding Temkin held up her hand to correct the counselor. She had aged considerably since the picture in the portfolio. Her hair was short and colored dark brown. A small scar stretched from her left temple to her widow's peak, which looked rather gray. She also had excessive makeup on her left cheek. "It's Miss Golding. I go by my maiden name."

The counselor's right eyebrow raised. "Oh, I'm

sorry. Miss Golding, can you describe your concern for your son?"

"First off, I love Dillon very much. He's a great young man, but certain things concern me."

"That's understandable. I can see that he has many great qualities. Right now, I'm more interested in what would bring you here today to visit."

Amelia's head drooped to focus on the table in front of her. Her finger traced the pattern of the tabletop. "Dillon is so loving. He never wants anything bad to happen to me. One time, I came home from work late. I had a terrible week, and Dillon knew it. You know, that boy cleaned the entire house and made me dinner. I felt like a queen."

The counselor agreed. "That's very nice, Miss Golding. Did he do stuff like that often?"

"Oh, yes. He was always looking out for me. But I guess that's part of the problem."

The man cocked his head slightly. "I'm not sure I'm following, Miss Golding."

She nodded. "I was afraid to bring any

boyfriends home to meet him."

"Did he treat them poorly?"

Amelia started retracing the tabletop. "Not initially. He was very inclusive. But... well... take Rubin for example."

"Was Rubin one of your boyfriends?"

"Yes. Rubin was an accountant and liked to take me to nice restaurants. He never let me pay and even opened doors for me." Amelia initially smiled, but it quickly faded as she described her boyfriend, and a million-mile stare overtook her.

"How did he get along with Dillon?"

"Dillon, good... mostly. Things were great until I burnt the chicken one night. Rubin yelled at me and threw the chicken in the trash."

"Did he hit you?"

"Rubin? Well, I did burn the dinner."

"Miss Golding, did he hurt you?"

"Ummm... he did grab me, pushed me back into

the kitchen, and demanded I cook something edible. I deserved it. As I said, the chicken was really burnt."

"Okay, I understand, Miss Golding. I want to talk to you later about this. This type of behavior is unhealthy, but we're here to talk about Dillon. I assume Dillon did something next."

Amelia scowled. "Dillon jumped over the kitchen table and threw Rubin to the ground."

"Did Rubin get up?"

"He tried, but Dillon kicked him in the face. He told Rubin that no one treats his mother like that. He then picked Rubin up by the hair and demanded he apologize to me." Amelia's eyes grew large as tears started falling.

The counselor wrote a few notes on his tablet. "Did Rubin apologize?"

"Did he have a choice? Of course he did. When my son let him go, he grabbed a knife off the table and threatened to use it on my son if he ever did that again."

"What did Dillon do next?"

"Dillon got between me and Rubin. Rubin lunged at him, and Dillon kicked the knife out of his hand. Rubin tried to punch him, but Dillon was too fast. His punch just flew around in the air. Dillon punched him two or three times in the ribs. Rubin ran for the door while shouting some terrible things at me."

"Miss Golding, in the law's eyes, Dillon did something wrong, but this man was abusing you. I have to say something that I probably shouldn't say. Ma'am, it sounds to me like that man got what he deserved. I see the bruise on your left cheek that you're trying to cover with makeup. Did Dillon do that, or did your boyfriend?"

Amelia slowly rubbed her fingers on her cheek. "Don't you see? I burnt the chicken." She shook her head as more tears fell. "Dillon has never laid a hand on me."

"So, you're saying that Rubin did this then? Don't worry, Miss Golding. You're safe to speak here. We're just trying to get the full truth. Rubin won't know, nor will Dillon."

"Well... Rubin did hit me. But that doesn't matter. He's never coming back again. This eventually happens with all of my boyfriends."

The counselor looked like he had much more to say but chose to table it for now. "Okay, Miss Golding. Why exactly did you come to me then?"

"When Dillon gets like this, it isn't Dillon anymore."

"I don't understand."

"I'm telling you, it's like someone who looks like Dillon has taken over. This version of him is aggressive, angry, and capable of doing bad things."

"So he has a nasty temper?"

"Yes... I mean, no... He becomes a different person. Listen! I know my son, and this is not my son when this clicks in. It's someone different."

"And you fear for your life?"

Amelia looked at the counselor like he was crazy. "Are you listening to me? No... I fear for whoever attacks me."

"This is a real tricky question, Miss Golding. Did you fear for your ex-husband's life?"

Amelia stared blankly. "Adam?"

"Yes, ma'am. Did you fear for Adam's life?"

Her attention returned to the pattern on the table. "I was beaten so badly at the time that I don't remember much. It took me three months before I could eat anything other than smoothies. I honestly didn't fear for Adam. But I remember seeing the rage in Dillon's eyes. I'll never forget that."

The counselor continued writing. "So, Dillon was furious?"

Amelia was taking deep breaths, and her eyes expanded. "He turned to me."

"I'm sorry. You said that he turned to you?"

"Yes. When I told Dillon to stop hitting Rubin, he turned to me and asked me why. Then he said the craziest thing."

"What did he say, ma'am?"

"He said... umm." Amelia looked up as if trying

to recollect Dillon's exact phrase. "It's not like I haven't stopped bad men before, Mom." Amelia's face filled with fear as her hands trembled uncontrollably.

The counselor tried to remain calm. "What did that mean to you, Miss Golding?"

Amelia sharply turned to face the counselor. "To me? I can only guess he means he got into it with other boyfriends I brought home and maybe my ex-husband. I fear he might have hurt or even killed my ex-husband, and I want to know... no... I NEED to know."

The counselor stood. "I think this is a good place to stop, Miss Golding. I really want to talk to you further about your ex-boyfriend, Rubin..."

The video stream ended, and Kadon sat slack-jawed in her chair. She looked up to see Temkin working with Irena on inventory. A subtle frown grew as she decided to add more to her personal notes. "Out of the frying pan, into the fire," she whispered as she rapidly tried to capture her thoughts with trembling fingers on her notepad.

CHAPTER THIRTY-SEVEN

Possible Solutions

When Eskar returned to the *Gibraltar*, he headed to the Bridge. "Sir, Admiral Shoapa is hailing you."

"Put her on the mains." Eskar took a sip of his coffee before responding and regretted it. "Ouch!"

The screen lit up to a smiling admiral. *A rare sighting indeed!* Eskar chuckled to himself. He straightened his posture and placed the coffee to the side. "Admiral Shoapa, you look pleased to see me."

Shoapa snickered. "Well, I am, sort of. Our teams found a workaround to inoculate the virus. We successfully tested it and have implemented it in our frigate. Capalov and a team are heading over to do the same on your ship."

"That's great news."

"We also believe we have a possible origin for the virus," Shoapa said as her smile diminished.

Eskar cocked his head. "You have my full attention, Admiral."

"Yes... well... one of our tech teams spotted the signature. It was small and hard to notice, but this code originated back on Earth when China had its own space program."

Eskar nodded. "Really? What is that, like seventy years ago?"

"Yes. It was one of the many code bases that were outlawed when pirates used it to cripple the Moon base back in 2074."

"Still, we're talking over thirty years that virus has been around."

Shoapa continued, "We've encountered it out here with mercenaries. Not nearly this aggressive or complex, but from the same family tree... if you know what I mean."

Eskar removed his cap and scratched his forehead. "I do, Admiral. How'd they get ahold of it?"

"My guess is that it never went away. Words like 'outlawed' only affect those who follow laws. The lawless ignore them anyway. This little gremlin has had thirty-plus years to mature. Our team would place this under the class of CHAI-type viruses."

"I'm not familiar with that type."

"CHAI stands for Combat Hardened Artificial Intelligence. It means it had its origins somewhere in the military. In this case, the now defunct China National Space Agency."

Eskar agreed with the assessment and wanted to dig deeper. "My question is: How did it get to the *Hercules*?"

"If I were a gambler, I'd bet there were rogue elements on that cargo ship, smuggling contraband under the noses of the Federation. I seriously doubt anyone would intentionally infect their ship with this virus, so maybe it accidentally got loose."

Eskar considered Shoapa's theory as he bravely took another sip of his coffee. "All I know is that virus is responsible for hundreds of deaths right now, and it kills me that it might be possible that whoever did this can get away with it."

"I understand, Captain, but right now, we need to deal with the dilemma at hand. Our solution can only contain the virus. Whatever has been broken is still broken. We have no long-range communication, and neither do you. I'm preparing our ship to head back toward our closest base, hoping to get aid."

Eskar looked at his crew and the ship. "Sir, we're prepared to watch over all three ships."

"Captain, I've been looking at the reports you provided us on the *Wraith*, and I believe your assessment is correct. We need to focus on detaching the *Cuda* from the *Wraith*. Unfortunately, I must leave this responsibility in your hands, hoping I can get help and bring it back."

"Understood, Admiral. We've continued getting data. The reactor is the biggest issue. The radiation is already beyond EP-suit levels. We will continue our efforts to separate the two ships."

Shoapa looked down at a paper handed to her as Eskar was talking. "With any luck, we have time to bring enough help to merely deboard the *Cuda* and destroy the two ships in place."

"With that in mind, Admiral, would it be prudent to attempt to unload as much crew off the *Cuda* as possible? We could easily hold another hundred or even more if we opencd up a few bays."

Shoapa's head cocked. "Captain Eskar, there are over four hundred on that ship. I think our best efforts should be focused on our vessel getting help and yours trying to detach the two ships."

Eskar didn't like the choices, but in his heart, he knew she was right. "Okay, Admiral, we'll focus our attention on that." He turned to see Capalov and the tech-team enter the Bridge. "Admiral, I see the team has come to inoculate our ship. When they have finished, I'll return your crew to you immediately."

"That's good news, Captain. I appreciate your understanding."

"Of course, Admiral. Eskar out."

The screen blanked, and Eskar turned to the matter at hand. "Capalov, it's good to see you again."

Capalov smiled. "It's good to see you too, Captain."

"Rumor has it that you've some good news for me."

"I do, sir. The inoculation device is in here." Capalov held up a small box. "We're going to need the Bridge for about thirty minutes."

Eskar grinned as he took another sip of his coffee. "The Bridge is yours. Do your magic. These Martian team members have a flight to catch."

"Yes, sir. Okay, folks, you heard the captain. Let's get on it."

Eskar held up his hand. "Ensign, can you explain to me what you're preparing to do?"

"Oh... of course, Captain." Capalov held up the small box. "This contains a computer that looks like a virtual ship when we connect it to our network."

Eskar was slightly confused by the explanation. "What does that do for us?"

"Let me explain, sir. So, how this virus seems to work is by sending satellites to subsystems. These satellites must get frequent messages from the mother virus to behave as they do. If these messages are somehow interrupted, the satellites immediately go from gremlins in their subsystems to all-out attackers of the subsystem. While they attack, they begin to make a new version of the mother virus in their subsystem."

Eskar followed but still failed to make the connection. "So, the mother virus has some sort of DNA embedded in the satellite subsystems?"

"Yes, Captain. It's kind of perfect. If the mother virus is compromised, the satellites build another mother virus.

Essentially, they make a new queen for them to follow."

"So, how does the virtual ship help?"

"I'm glad you asked, Captain. So, this virus was explicitly designed to cripple capital ships. It goes after three central systems: the communication, the navigation, and shielding."

"What about weapon systems?"

"We believe it tries, but the security systems on them are too complex for it to figure out, sir."

"So it does have limitations."

"Oh, yes, sir! We're taking advantage of one of them."

"I'm all ears, son."

"Okay… so… One of the other features of the virus is that it understands if it's being attacked."

"How does it do that?"

"The virus has many layers, and when one is permeated, it immediately tries to migrate the core to some other system."

"So when it's attacked, it flees."

Capalov thought for a moment, then answered. "Yes, Captain. It tries to find a suitable home for it to continue business."

"Does it inform its satellites?"

Capalov shook his head. "I wish it would. Then we would know exactly where they resided."

"Ah. That makes sense. Also, you said they start making a new mom if they don't hear from the current mom."

Capalov couldn't contain his grin. "You've got it, Captain."

"Okay. What do I have? I don't see how any of this helps us."

"We'll attack the mother virus with a protocol clone that'll take over talking to the satellites. The mother virus will find a gaping hole in our virtual ship that it can migrate to. When this occurs, we detach it from our network while still feeding the satellites the 'all is good' message with the protocol clone."

"That's why we still can't get our systems up. The satellites are still doing their job of crippling the subsystems," Eskar said as he straightened his cap.

"Exactly. The original intent of this virus was to render ships helpless so that marauders could easily take what they wanted from them without a fight. We're still working on a way to get rid of the satellite viruses, but that'll take a good bit of time."

Eskar patted Capalov on the back. "This is amazing how you all figured this out. Well done, son. Now, don't let me stand in your way. Let's trap this mother virus."

"We're almost done, sir."

Eskar's eyebrows raised. "Really? Wow, that doesn't seem so bad."

"All things considered, that's true, sir. But this doesn't stop the virus. It only stops it from spreading more."

Eskar smiled. "Well, Ensign, it looks like your work is cut out for you then."

Capalov heaved a deep sigh and nodded.

CHAPTER THIRTY-EIGHT

Sleuthing

"Hello, Doctor Kadon." Alan Wittle stood to attention as she entered the NTDS bay.

Kadon smiled and cocked her head. "Alan, isn't it?"

"Yes, sir. I read your reply, and I don't think I understand. I promise you that we didn't release Irena to you. I can't explain why it showed up in Med Bay."

"I understand, Alan. Were you able to complete my second request?" Kadon asked as she leaned on the counter that separated her from the young man.

Wittle nodded and frowned. "Yes, sir. And, as you suspected, we found the feed where Irena walked out of here. It was a few days before your request."

"Did you see who went in and out before that time?"

"We did, but the person seemed to know where our cameras were. Still, we got images of him walking in. But no facial shots; the bill of his cap strategically covered his face."

Kadon was unfazed in her questioning. "Did the man limp?"

Wittle looked confused. "Limp, sir?"

"Yes. Did the man walk with a limp or carry a cane?" Kadon's eyes narrowed on Wittle.

Wittle slowly shook his head. "No, sir. I don't think he did. Would you like to look at the clip with me? I can pull it up. It'll only be a couple of seconds."

"I would, Alan. Thank you."

"Of course." Wittle turned his monitor to give Kadon a better view. "So here's the clip of him coming through the front entry. He had an access card, so he had to have some level of upper clearance."

The video showed a person dressed in black with a Marine baseball cap on. The clothes were baggy, but any movement revealed a large-framed male as the suspect.

Wittle continued, "It also looks like whoever this was knew his way around the room. Look how he effortlessly walked to the storage bins, and it only took them two tries to find what he was looking for."

Kadon closely studied the stream. "Have you shown this to anyone else? Maybe they could recognize the person."

"Yes, sir. The entire team has reviewed this, and no one recognizes the perpetrator. We also reacquired Irena, and before we scrubbed its memory, we queried to see if it remembered its kidnapper. There was no running memory of the incident. All Irena remembered was arriving at Med Bay. You were the first identifiable human that it interacted with."

Kadon continued to watch the stream. "This guy sure knew how to cover his tracks. Is there any chance you could trace Irena's whereabouts off of the ID tags?"

"We thought of that too. But they were intentionally damaged. We gave Irena a new ID tag, erased its memory, and applied the latest patch to its processing system. If you would like, you can officially walk it down to Med Bay right now."

Kadon smiled. "You got that taken care of quickly, thank you. I could really use Irena's help right now. Also, could you send me those feeds? I'd like to study them more myself."

Wittle tapped a few keys and then looked up at the doctor. "Yes, sir. The feeds have been sent to you."

A familiar voice distracted Kadon from talking to Wittle. "Doctor Kadon, it is good to see you again." Irena gracefully glided into the room.

As Kadon turned to her, she noticed Wittle took the time to clean Irena's exterior. He even repaired the scratch that occurred across her nameplate. "Irena, you look amazing. It seems like they took good care of you down here."

Irena replied quickly, "Yes, Doctor Kadon. They were able to fix my programming, and they replaced my nameplate with a new one. I apologize for the confusion earlier. I did not know, or I would have turned myself in."

Kadon listened, and in her mind, Irena's answer was as close to an emotional response as a med-bot could get. In Kadon's heart, she was happy to have her friend back. "I understand completely, Irena. All I can say is that we could use your help in the Bay with all these extra passengers." She turned back to Wittle. "Alan, thank you for all of your help. If you come up with any more ideas, please let me know."

"Yes, sir. I'm so sorry for the confusion. We'll continue to investigate. This theft is a severe offense. I'm glad you followed up with us so we could be aware of the situation."

"I think I'm going to take Irena down to Med Bay. Have a good rest of your day."

"Thank you, sir. You too." Wittle saluted as Irena and Kadon walked out of his office.

CHAPTER THIRTY-NINE

Babysitting

"Captain Eskar, we're prepared to depart. I've put you in charge, and both the *Wraith* and *Cuda* captains answer to you." Admiral Shoapa smiled as she delivered the news.

"Thank you for trusting us, Admiral. We won't disappoint you. Please hurry back so this entire fiasco can come to a conclusion."

Shoapa chuckled. "Understood, Captain. We'll do our best to comply with that order."

"Safe travels, Admiral, and we look forward to hearing from you soon."

The screen went blank as Ensign Capalov commented, "Sir, the *Defiant* has fired up her thrusters and is heading away from our position."

"Thank you, Ensign. Put the *Defiant* up on the screen."

"Yes, sir." The main display lit up with a picture of the large frigate heading home.

Exhaustion suddenly overwhelmed the captain. Eskar turned to the second in command. "Mason? You've got the helm."

Mason stood to attention. "Sir, yes, sir."

Eskar headed to his quarters and found Lieutenant Polson standing outside, waiting for him to arrive.

"Captain? Might I have a moment of your time?"

Eskar looked at the young woman and nodded. "Of course, Lieutenant. How can I help you?"

"Sir, I've found two things I feel I need to bring to your attention immediately."

Eskar took off his cap and rubbed his forehead. "Would you like to come in for a moment so we can talk about what you've found?"

Polson looked at the door that slid open. "Yes, sir." She quickly walked into his quarters.

Eskar walked in and headed to his kitchen counter. "Please take a seat. Can I offer you some coffee?"

"Um... Yes, sir. That sounds nice."

Eskar prepared the maker for some of his premium blends. He spoke freely. "So, you said you had some things to tell me?"

"Yes, sir. Ensign Capalov brought a picture to me of something being created on the *Hercules*."

"Yes. I told him to visit you. I figured you'd be the best person to determine what that contraption was trying to replace."

"Thank you, sir. I think I figured out what they were trying to replicate."

Eskar smiled. "Finally, some good news. What was it?"

"It looks like they were trying to replicate a diverter for the cold-fusion reactor, sir."

A small bell went off on Eskar's coffee maker, and he poured two cups of his homemade brew. "Now, I'm no engineer, but aren't diverters a common part of the reactor?"

"Yes, sir. I checked our inventory, and we have two on hand." Polson took the offered drink and nodded politely.

"That makes sense. So, I have to ask, what do you think

happened to the ones on the *Hercules*?"

"About that, sir. I think I've got an answer, but you aren't going to like it."

Eskar stopped drinking his coffee. "I don't know if I like the sound of that."

"Sir, I think that the spare diverter was the source of the corrosion in their Cargo Bay."

The information shocked Eskar. "What?"

"Yes, sir. The diverter is a combination of materials designed to allow the helium products to exit the reactor safely. The spare parts must be stored in a stabilizing gel to ensure they don't become reactive with metallic materials."

Eskar put down his coffee to give Polson his full attention. "So, when you say 'reactive,' I'm guessing you mean corrosive?"

"Yes, sir. In this case, it would be hyper-corrosive. I'm guessing here, but I'd say whoever did this placed the spare part in one of those containers in the Cargo Bay. Maybe the bag containing the part got damaged and started leaking the gel... If that happened, it would only be a matter of time as to when the corrosion process would begin."

Eskar nodded. "But the corrosion happened so quickly."

Polson took another sip of her coffee before answering. "Yes, sir. The oxygen-rich environment is perfect for allowing this to occur."

"So, somebody on this ship made this happen."

"It appears so, sir... Yes. I'd also say that the part they were making wouldn't work either. If they had installed it, it would have lasted an hour before shattering."

"Well, that's terrible. Maybe the engineers figured that out before they installed it."

"Possibly, but I don't understand why anyone would do this on the ship where you reside. It doesn't make much sense to me, sir."

Eskar raised his eyebrows. "That makes two of us... Wait a minute. What about this extra man on the ship? Could he have done this?"

"Anyone could have done it, sir. But how can we prove it?"

Eskar tilted his head as he nodded. "That's a great question. Maybe see if there's a way we could correlate when the part was taken. Now we know what to look for. Is there a chance the part was stolen before the black box cameras started freaking out? I know we have a camera in the spares room. Maybe it caught someone taking the part from the bin?"

Polson considered the question. "Sir, I can look into that for sure."

Eskar rubbed his eyes and yawned deeply. He then stood, letting Polson know that this meeting had come to an end. "Great, then I think we have a plan forward."

CHAPTER FORTY

Chance Encounter

Capalov headed to the mess hall to refill his depleted tanks. The thought of forgoing the eating of food crossed his mind, but his weariness could wait. As the door slid open, he saw the *Wraith* and *Cuda* wreckage through the observation windows. It would have been a spectacular view if deaths weren't involved. Instead, it made him slightly ill to his stomach.

He managed to turn and see what was on tap at the grill. The teriyaki chicken was not high on his list, so he settled for a cheesesteak hoagie, fries, and a small brownie.

Capalov sat in an open space by himself and began eating his meal. The brown material that was supposed to be beef tasted more like chicken. And the fries were limp and greasy. Still, it was good enough to fill his stomach.

"Are you gonna eat that?" Temkin giggled as he sat down next to the ensign with a gleaming smile. Leaning his cane on the side of the table, he carried a tray with a grilled chicken salad and Jell-O. "Is it okay if I sit here?"

Capalov smiled and nodded, but the smile turned into a frown as he surveyed Temkin's tray. "Sure, have a seat. Yeah, the food here isn't great, but I've had worse."

"Really? Where?" Temkin smiled.

"Boot camp. I swear the Great Lakes Training Center cook was trying to kill us."

"Selco?"

Capalov raised one eyebrow. "Yeah, how did you know that?"

"That old man was trying to kill us fifteen years earlier." Temkin let out a hearty laugh that Capalov matched.

"You had that old coot too?"

"Yep, and the three henchmen."

Capalov looked confused. "The three henchmen?"

"Yeah, Bostick, Kramer, and Hildago."

"I know Kramer and Hildago. Bostick must have moved on."

Temkin shrugged. "Well, it was over a decade ago. Maybe Bostick is the head of another hall where he's trying to poison other recruits."

"How'd you make the switch?"

Temkin leaned back momentarily. "The switch to what?"

Capalov finished off his fries. "You know, to Special Ops? How'd you make that switch?"

Temkin nodded. "Oh, that. My CO thought I'd be a shoo-in for electronic warfare. When I took the test, three men approached me and offered me a position in Special Ops. I initially turned it down but thought about it that night and decided to make the change."

Capalov's grin grew. "Is it exciting?"

"Sometimes it is, but mostly it's a lot of detail work and observation. You spend most of your time preparing for your task. You have to consider contingencies and countermoves and evaluate all outcomes. It's much more tedious than I was led to believe."

"If it's so bad, why have you stayed in it?"

Temkin took a bite of his salad and studied Capalov's face. "I didn't say it was all bad. It's a lot of work, but I feel I'm doing good and helping. That's why I stay in it."

"I want to be Special Ops someday."

Temkin shrugged and kept eating. "You never know. Maybe they'll come up and tap you on the shoulder."

"That would be awesome."

"Just make sure you research and know what you're getting into. That's my warning to you. If you can handle it, it'll be good. If it shocks you, I'd run as far from it as possible."

Capalov leaned back in his chair. "We've been doing Special Ops kind of stuff the past few days."

Temkin stopped eating for a moment. "Oh yeah? What have you been up to?"

"Just keeping busy with one emergency after another."

"This ship seems to keep you hopping, doesn't it?"

"We all gotta do our part, you know?"

Temkin chuckled. "I don't feel like I'm doing much of any part right now. I feel like the third person on a date."

"This virus has wreaked havoc on our ships," Capalov said as he ate his brownie.

"I know. I'm thinking about all the lives that damn thing cost. It makes me sick to my stomach." Temkin shook his head as he picked up the plastic cup of Jell-O.

"Yeah. Doctor Kadon said we lost another one today. It's deplorable."

"Hey, Antoni, if there's anything I can do to help, feel free to ask. It's not like I've much else to do right now." Temkin quickly finished off the Jell-O and wearily stood to his feet. When he straightened, he grabbed the cane and began to walk away.

"Okay, Deke, I'll keep that in mind. For now, could you put in a good word for me at Special Ops when we return to port?"

Temkin raised his hand in the air. "We'll see, Antoni. I might not be the one you'd want to put in a good word for you."

Was he joking? Capalov thought. "It's a start. See you later, Deke."

CHaPTer FOrTY-one

Do What?

Eskar returned to the Bridge from a restless night of sleep. He was thankful for the darker room; walking through the brightened halls irritated his eyes. He immediately headed to the coffee maker for a fresh fill.

Capalov greeted him with "Good morning, sir. I'm glad you arrived early. Captain Tregevek has already inquired for you."

"What's got him so excited?" Eskar blew on the coffee before sipping.

Capalov shrugged. "I think something is going on with the *Wraith*."

"Thanks, Antoni. Can you get me a private line to speak with him?"

"Of course, Captain. I'll do it at once."

Eskar used the opportunity to walk around and greet the crew on deck.

The ensign delivered, as promised. Eskar's headset lit up, and he answered, "Captain, I'm going to walk into a private room so we can talk." Eskar followed Capalov into the briefing room and shut the door. "What can I do for you, Captain?"

Tregevek spoke with a heavy Slavic accent. "Captain, thank

you for taking my call."

"Of course. Is there a problem?"

Tregevek wasted no time. "Yes. I believe we have a severe problem with the *Wraith*."

"Is it what we discussed two days ago? We've been monitoring the rise of the radiation levels too."

"That's the exact problem. The engineers believe the radiation is now leaking into the *Cuda*."

Eskar's eyebrows raised. "Wow! That takes this problem to a whole 'nother level."

"Yes. We estimate we have a few hours before it's dire, but we might have a solution."

Eskar could hear the tenseness in Tregevek's voice. "Captain, I'm all ears. Short of firing on that ship, I don't think we have enough time to separate them..."

"Captain, before you speak any further, let me say that's exactly what we believe you need to do."

Eskar was confused. "I don't understand. Do you mean you want us to open fire on the *Wraith*?"

Tregevek took a deep breath. "Yes, Captain. We want you to fire three strategic shots to break the *Cuda* free of the *Wraith*. I understand that this sounds a little crazy..."

"A *little* crazy? No, sir. This sounds a lot crazy. First off, you're asking me to fire on a Martian ship. I understand why, but this would be considered an act of war. Secondly, we're putting the lives of the *Cuda* at risk. Don't we have time to put charges on the ship to do the same thing?"

"Remy, I understand everything you've said... and I completely agree. The truth is, we only have a few hours and can't place charges quickly enough. I've had my team assess the two hulls, and we've found the optimal three points to attack with your thirty-centimeter cannons."

Eskar shook his head. "Captain, the concussion of those shots will jar the entire crew of the *Cuda*. My ship will have to be moving forward to fire those cannons. It'll add some uncertainty to the shots. Also, the *Cuda* is without thrust. Even if we dislodge the ship, it's still in close proximity to the *Wraith*."

Tregevek took a deep breath. "Captain, we've considered the concussion and believe it's entirely survivable. The fact that your target is standing still makes the shots much easier. This should compensate for the added complexity of needing to move to fire your cannons. Our team believes they can fire up the *Cuda*'s engines. Once they start, though, they'll continue forward until they're out of fuel. We estimate that it'll be approximately twenty-two minutes and four hundred kilometers from the *Wraith*."

"What about reserves?"

"The two nonfunctioning engines will provide enough power to keep the batteries charged. Captain, we believe this is the best solution and have little time to waste here."

Eskar's head was spinning. He knew Tregevek was right in his heart, but the operation would tax everyone involved. "Captain, I don't see another option at this time. I know this sounds odd, but I request you to come to our Bridge and be the one to fire on your own Martain ship. This whole thing is already a mess. I don't want to be the one who started another interplanetary incident."

Tregevek chuckled. "Captain, I understand the difficulty of this. I'm sure we're both breaking laws that could have us removed from our positions or even court-martialed. I understand the sentiment, and I'll be up when you're ready for me to fire on my ship. I've just sent you a message with the locations you need to target. I'll also inform the captain of the *Cuda* of our intentions and that she should prepare her ship for immediate action."

Eskar shook his head. "This is wild, Captain. I hope you know what you're doing. I'll contact Captain Beaumont in ten minutes, after you've had a chance to brief her."

"It sucks, Captain, but it sounds like we have a plan."

Eskar could hear the drop in Tregevek's voice. The weight of difficult decisions is something all captains understood and respected. "I know you're right, Ari. This is our best bet. Let's hope it keeps the crew of the *Cuda* safe."

"Our prayers are with them now, I appreciate your understanding. Tregevek out."

Flirting

"Sir, are you supposed to be down here?" Lieutenant Polson noticed an unfamiliar face in Engineering.

Temkin turned around to address her. "I'm Major Temkin. My clearance allows me down here. Here's my badge." He handed her his credentials.

Polson studied the ID, studied his person, then walked over to the door and allowed the badge to scan. The light turned green. "So... you're the famous Major Temkin. How can I be of assistance?"

"If you could direct me to where the circuit board station is, it would be much appreciated. I need to repair this board, and I didn't want to bother anyone." He held up a small board that looked like a medical-grade circuit board and handed it to Polson.

Polson examined the board. "I can do that for you if you'd like."

Temkin shook his head. "No. Actually, I've so little to do right now, it would be great to have something to physically work on. Plus, I find working with boards like this kind of cathartic... You know what I mean?"

Polson gleamed. "I know exactly what you mean. Come over

here, and I can set you up. All the basics will be there. If you need anything else, I can probably find it for you."

"Thank you so much. You wouldn't, by chance, have a Tre-X programmer, would you? I figured I could rig one up using a standard programmer, but it would be so much easier if you happened to have one." Temkin smiled and leaned on the wall by his cane.

Polson giggled as she shuffled in slightly closer. "Well, you're in luck. I happened to have the Tre-X-II programmer. It's twice as fast and supports the new nano-Tre protocols."

"Nice! Would you mind if I borrowed it for a day or two? I'm in the VOQ if you need it for something."

"Sure. We're so busy with other stuff, I won't need it for months. Here you go." Polson reached into a drawer by Temkin and handed him the device. As he grabbed it, their hands touched, and Polson's face grew flush. "Umm... let me take you to the circuit station. There's a chair there, too, so you won't have to stand the whole time." One lock from her hair bun escaped and drooped across her left eye. She shrugged her shoulders and quickly moved it behind her ear with her left hand while staring at the ground.

"It's too bad you must keep your hair all bound up in the bun. I bet it yearns to be free."

The comment brought a smile to Polson's face as she turned to walk to the station. "You have no idea how true that is."

Temkin followed her through two rooms to a darker corner of one of the primary tech areas. As they walked, he noticed a familiar part lying on a table near the station. "Isn't that a diverter?"

"Yeah, I was looking into the project that your crew on the

Hercules was working on."

"Were they working on a diverter?"

"Yeah, but they weren't doing a very good job of it."

Temkin looked confused. "How do you know how good a job they were doing?"

"We have video of it from the drones when we rescued you... Well, when they rescued you."

Temkin chose to sit. "Oh, that was one horrible day."

"You lived. That's gotta be worth something."

"Yep. Thanks to you. Well... I mean, the crew of the *Gibraltar*." Temkin donned a knowing smile.

Polson smiled. "Touché, Major."

Temkin changed back to the subject at hand. "So, they sucked at what they were doing?"

Polson regathered herself. "Oh... yeah. This design looks very unlikely to work."

"I knew the engineers over there. They were pretty smart."

Polson was in her element. "Maybe so, but it looks like the device was made in extreme haste. First, the welds were terrible and overkilled. If you know how a diverter works, you'll know that a smooth surface along the transfer chamber is necessary. This design would have allowed pockets and eddies to form, eventually destroying the reactor and probably all of the crew."

Temkin looked impressed. "It sounds like you know your stuff, Lieutenant."

Polson crossed her arms and smiled. "Reactor science was my specialty in the academy."

"Well, I guess for me it's a good thing they didn't put that part in. I wasn't on that team. For what it's worth, my part actually worked."

"I'm sorry about the rest of the crew. I know that must be really hard."

Temkin's half-smile turned south as he nodded. "I had some exceptional friends on that crew."

Polson started to take a few steps backward. "Yeah. I'll leave you to do what you came down here to do."

"Thank you. And I promise to get the programmer back to you soon."

Polson turned and walked back to the front offices of Engineering as Temkin watched the young woman exit. When she left the room, he momentarily glanced at the diverter and snorted. Finally, he began working on the PC board he was holding.

After a few minutes, Polson returned to the room. "Major Temkin, you left this in the front office." A look of surprise overcame him as she handed him his cane.

"Oh, thanks. I'll need that."

Polson held out the cane for Temkin to clutch. "By the way, can I call you Dillon?"

Temkin smiled and leaned back in his chair. "No, you can call me Greg."

CHAPTER FORTY-THREE

Friendly Fire

Captain Tregevek stepped onto the *Gibraltar* Bridge, guarded by two Federation officers. Eskar quickly moved to greet him. "Captain Tregevek, welcome onto our Bridge."

Tregevek looked around, and all eyes were on him. "Thank you for inviting me here, Captain. I must admit that in all my life, I never would have expected to be on the Command Bridge of a Federation ship."

Eskar smiled and ceremoniously ushered Tregevek forward. "I imagine not. In all of mine, I could never have envisioned a scenario where I'd have willingly invited a Martian captain onto my Bridge. It's good to see you, Ari." The two men shook hands.

"Likewise, Remy. Do you think we're ready to do this?"

Eskar nodded as he looked at his crew. "I think we are. I have Captain Beaumont on the mains so we can coordinate this with the *Cuda*."

The main screen came to life. "Good evening, captains. The *Cuda* is as ready as possible with such short notice."

Tregevek looked at Eskar and stood quietly. The courtesy didn't go unnoticed. Eskar nodded and began to speak. "Captain Tregevek and I are ready to proceed. Captain, did you have anything else to add?"

"Ursula, we have ships prepared to begin emergency evacuations should the need arise. Captain Eskar and I concluded that, by using the Mantis ships and three cargo boats, we could rescue one hundred and twenty-five to one hundred and fifty more people. I know that isn't comforting, but it's better than zero."

Beaumont frowned as she looked down. "Let's hope that's unnecessary. Thank you all for your efforts. We discussed this at length with our crew, and we've already drawn up a contingency plan. We understand the sacrifices and risks and are prepared should that emergency arise."

Eskar spoke up. "We'll do everything in our power to ensure it doesn't." Without waiting for a reply, he looked around the Bridge and began to speak. "Ladies and gentlemen, we're going to do something unprecedented today. We're going to fire upon a Martian vessel. I know we've all been briefed on our duties, but I wanted to remind you that we don't take this action lightly. This is a last resort, and many lives are at stake. The gentleman to my left is Captain Tregevek. It's his ship that we'll be firing upon."

Eskar took the moment to face Tregevek and smile. "For this reason, I've asked him to command us to fire upon the *Wraith*. We all have a duty to perform for this to succeed, and this is his. Are we clear?"

The crew stood to attention and replied with a resounding, "Yes, sir."

Eskar nodded and turned to his navigator. "Walters, are we ready to make our attack run?"

"Yes, sir. The course is plotted, the target points have been entered, and we're ready to begin."

Eskar spoke with more bravado. "Excellent. Mason, are you on tap?"

Mason replied through the intercom, "Yes, sir. All Mantis ships are prepared for the emergency. We're in position on the far side of the *Cuda*."

Eskar turned to the Martian captain. "Captain Tregevek, we're prepared to respond to your orders. I'm temporarily giving you the command to give the attack order. Everyone who has heard me relinquish this responsibility, respond with a simple acknowledgment of 'aye.'"

The Bridge crew shouted, "Aye."

Eskar smiled. "Very well. Captain Tregevek, the Bridge is temporarily yours."

Tregevek stepped forward. "Before I give the order, I wanted to acknowledge how well this crew has represented the Federation. From the crews of the three ships you came to help, we sincerely thank you... Now, without any further ado, Lieutenant Walters, raise us to REDCON-One."

"REDCON-One. Yes, sir." Within seconds, alerts furiously chirped through all decks.

"Okay, Walters, energize the cannons and begin our run."

"Yes, sir. Starting our attack run."

As the doors covering thirty-centimeter cannons began opening, the Bridge shuddered. The rumble wasn't surprising to the crew, but it caught Tregevek off guard. He looked at the floor and smiled. "That's what I call power." The comment got a chuckle out of Eskar.

From the main screen, Captain Beaumont spoke, "Captain Tregevek, when you opened the cannon doors, we saw one of the defense grids come to life on the *Wraith*."

"Are you sure, Ursula? That ship is dead," Tregevek frowned as he questioned the other captain.

"I'm certain, Ari."

Capalov interjected, "Captain, I'm also picking up activity readings from the *Wraith*."

Tregevek put his hands behind his back and widened his stance. "What do you see, Ensign?"

"Sir, it looks like some automated defense systems came to life when we energized the cannons and launch tubes. Only one set of the six on the ship is functional."

Tregevek continued, "What's our range?"

"Four-point-seven kilometers, sir."

Lieutenant Walters spoke, "Sir, we're almost to attack speed."

Tregevek at once turned to the navigator. "Lieutenant Walters, correct? I need you to perform evasive maneuvers immediately."

"Yes, sir. Evasive maneuvers. I'm changing course now."

The *Gibraltar* lurched to the left as the vessel's mass worked against the requested goal. Both captains grabbed the handrail as the ship changed direction.

Capalov shouted, "Sir, we have incoming missiles!"

Tregevek punched the guardrail. "Fire countermeasures. We need to bank hard again. A second volley will be coming shortly. Walters, stow the cannons and prepare for a second maneuver on my mark." He looked over at Eskar to explain his actions. "The range of those missiles is five kilometers. We need to get past that mark."

Eskar nodded. "Understood, Ari. You know your ship. You should direct us out of this."

A rattling of countermeasure volleys shook the Bridge.

"All missiles missed, sir." Capalov didn't stop to look up as he spoke.

Tregevek continued to command. "Walters, adjust the course to 310-42 at max speed. Engage now. Prepare to fire the EMP tunnel at the incoming missiles."

"Yes, sir. Adjusting course. The EMP system is active."

Capalov spoke up again. "Second wave coming in."

"Evasive maneuvers, Walters."

Walters focused on the tracking system. "Evading now, sir."

The EMP tunnel cannon fired multiple times.

Capalov took a deep breath before speaking again. "All incoming missiles accounted for and neutralized, sir. No new threats found."

"Are we beyond five kilometers, Ensign?"

"Yes, sir. We're at five-point-four kilometers and growing."

"Well done. Bring us to idle."

Walters adjusted some controls. "Setting to idle, sir."

Tregevek looked at Eskar and breathed a large sigh of relief. "Captain, I didn't expect this, but some of the automated defenses on my ship are still operational. I believe we must take these out before we can complete our mission. It's only one of the six stations, but that unit can tear this ship in half. I'm returning the Bridge to your command, sir."

Eskar walked over to Capalov's station. He studied the active defense pod. "Ari, I believe we can take care of this problem, but because this will require us to divulge military tactics, I must ask you to step off the Bridge while we handle it. I'm sorry if this makes you uncomfortable."

Tregevek smiled and patted Eskar on the back. "No, I understand this completely. And for the record, you have my blessing to take out that defense station in any way necessary.

As an observation, I noticed that the defense station could not see the Mantis ships sitting on the other side of the *Cuda*. It's possible that you could manipulate this to aid our position."

Eskar nodded as he realized what Tregevek observed was accurate. "That's a great observation, Ari. I think we'll try to take advantage of that." He turned to the display. "Captain Beaumont, forgive me, but I must also disconnect with you briefly."

"I understand, Captain. Ari's correct. You could use the *Cuda* to mask a Mantis attack run."

Eskar took his cap off and rubbed his forehead. "Be prepared for our Mantis ships to do exactly that, Captain."

Beaumont nodded as the screen went blank.

"I'm glad I could help with killing my own ship. I'm trying to pretend this doesn't bother me, but I assure you it does. I'll be just down the hall when you feel it's acceptable for me to return."

Eskar looked at the two escorts. They understood his orders without him saying a word and followed Tregevek as he exited the Bridge.

As Tregevek left, Capalov spoke, "Sir, Commander Mason is hailing us."

"Mason," Eskar said, "I take it you saw what just happened."

"Yes, sir. We noticed that the defense systems didn't even acknowledge us. I think we could take it out if you want us to."

"That's been the conversation here on the Bridge. Captain Beaumont suggested we could sneak up on the defense system using the *Cuda* as cover. I think that sounds plausible."

With Mason's microphone active, Eskar could hear the chatter coming from the pilots. "We agree with this assessment, Captain. We recommend making two attack runs. The first would be to take out the sensor arrays, and the second would attempt to disable the weapon systems and launchers. Both runs will start by hugging the *Cuda*."

Eskar closed his eyes and considered the actions that needed to be taken. "How many ships are we talking about, Mason?"

"I'd say four on the first run and three on the second."

Eskar pursed his lips. "Beyond the fact that you're attacking a defense system, is there any risk to the *Cuda* or any other personnel?"

Chatter could be heard on the line as Mason consulted with his pilots. "Umm... no, sir. We'll be on the far side of the *Wraith*. Far away from the *Cuda*. The Tyber missiles we'll use are very targeted in their impact, so I don't expect much concussion to get back to the *Cuda*."

"Okay, Mason. Time is of the essence. We need to make those runs immediately."

"Understood, Captain. We're on it now."

Capalov interjected, "Captain, we're seeing four Mantis ships moving into formation. They're coming in tight on the *Cuda*."

Eskar turned. "Put them up on the main screen, Ensign."

"Yes, sir."

The four monitors that comprised the main screen changed to tactical displays. Two monitors showed virtual images of the ships with positional and rate information superimposed on each vehicle. Another monitor focused on the defense system of the *Wraith*. The final monitor showed the vitals of each of the attacking vessels.

With incredible precision, the four craft flew near the surface of the *Cuda*. As they broke over the 'horizon' of the frigate, they made a sharp turn and sequentially fired missiles at the *Wraith*'s defense systems. The eight missile trails lit up the hull of the dying ship as they passed at a high velocity, approaching their target.

One by one, the Mantis ships turned off and rapidly ran to the safety of hiding behind the *Cuda*. Eskar watched in anticipation of what would happen next. The screens showed the eight missiles closing in on the defense system.

Capalov studied his monitor and declared, "Sir, I can see their defense system reactivated."

The comment made the back of Eskar's neck tense up. He rubbed it with his left hand to try to alleviate the stiffness. All eyes on the Bridge watched as the missiles hit the defense array successively. With each small explosion, the mood in the room brightened.

"Sir, their defenses couldn't respond fast enough. We got eight positive hits."

The Bridge personnel cheered.

Eskar quickly went to his intercom. "Mason, all eight missiles connected. It's time for the second run."

The commander replied, "Affirmative, Captain. We're beginning it now."

Three more Mantis ships began a similar run, using the *Cuda* as coverage. The display on the Bridge changed for the next sortie, showing the three ships in formation. On the ship's vitals screen, the status of one of the craft changed from green to yellow.

"Captain Eskar. One of our ships' navigation systems is faulting. We'll be continuing with only two ships."

Eskar could feel the sweat forming on his forehead. He removed his cap while pulling a handkerchief out of his pocket and blotting his brow. "Understood, Mason. Carry on."

One of the three Mantis ships slowed and turned away from the formation as the two remaining crafts continued to deliver their payloads. Following a nearly identical path to the first run, the two ships covered the ground quickly and fired their weapons.

This time, there was no activity from the defense system. The missiles hit both the silos and the turrets without resistance. Three of the four fired missiles succeeded in neutralizing their threat.

Capalov analyzed the damage. "Sir, I believe we need another run. The defense system is still about fifteen percent active."

Eskar nodded and quickly spoke to Mason. "Mason, I think you need a third run at the system. There's still some activity on the unit."

"Understood, Captain. We have identified the functioning components and are now setting up for a third run."

"Thank you, Commander."

"Yes, sir. We're ready and running."

Two more Mantis ships made the now-familiar run at the defense system. The four launched missiles destroyed the remaining targets.

"The defense unit's neutralized, sir. I've scanned the *Cuda*, and they're reporting no casualties," Capalov declared.

Eskar clapped his hands. "Well done, Mason. Now clear those ships so we can make our attack run."

He turned to a security guard. "Claven? Will you go retrieve Captain Tregevek?"

"Yes, sir."

Eskar next asked Capalov, "Antoni, please get Captain Beaumont back on the line."

The display changed to show Captain Beaumont smiling just as Captain Tregevek reentered the Bridge. "Captain Eskar. We can see you were successful in neutralizing the defense grid. Like Captain Tregevek, it feels awkward for me to congratulate you on this."

Eskar chuckled. "No need for congratulations yet, Captain. I'm about to return my Bridge to Captain Tregevek for our attack run. I need you to confirm that you're ready for us to do this."

Without hesitation, Beaumont responded, "Yes, Captain. We're in position and are ready to engage our engines."

"Excellent! Stand by as we prepare to make this run again." Eskar turned to Tregevek. "Captain Tregevek, once again, I'm giving you temporary control of my ship."

Tregevek stepped forward and saluted Eskar, who returned the gesture. "Okay, Walters, are we lined up and ready to try this again?"

"Affirmative, sir. On your command."

Tregevek spoke to the main screen. "Captain Beaumont, we're beginning our run."

"We're ready, Captain."

"Very good. Walters, reenergize the cannons and begin our run."

Walter sat up in his chair. "Yes, sir. Beginning the run." Once again, the rumble of the cannon doors physically shook the Bridge.

Capalov gave a status update. "Sir, we're approaching attack speed and closing in on the *Wraith*."

"Grazinski? Fire the first shot on my mark."

"Yes, sir. Ready to fire."

Tregevek pointed at the lieutenant. "Fire now."

"Firing the round, sir."

The cannon shot caused the ship to decelerate and shudder rapidly. Tregevek grabbed the handrail to steady himself. The ship recovered and began accelerating at the target.

Tregevek spoke again. "Prepare the second shot."

"Ready to fire, sir."

"Fire now."

Capalov analyzed the first impact. "The first shell was a perfect hit." The reverberation of the cannon caused his cap to fall off. He leaned over and picked it up off of the deck.

Tregevek looked at Eskar and smiled. "Excellent news. Grazinski, ready the third round."

"Yes, sir. The round is ready to fire."

"Fire now."

"The second shot was acceptable, sir." Capalov held his breath, waiting for the final round. "The last shot was another bull's-eye, Captain."

Tregevek wasted no time. "Ursula, what's your status?"

Beaumont leaned over. "The shots were jarring, but we have confirmed that the last shot broke us free."

Tregevek shouted, "All right! It's time for you to engage your engines."

Captain Beaumont pointed to someone off-camera and said, "Engage the engines!"

The *Cuda*'s engines sputtered but began generating thrust. The ship had little maneuverability, so the initial asymmetry of the first engine created an unexpected yaw. The misguidance caused the ship to scrape its side along the hull of the *Wraith*.

Warning alarms blared in the *Cuda* as crew members attempted to assess the damage. The video feed sputtered a few times as power fluctuated on the frigate.

Finally, the ship broke free and started heading into open space. Meanwhile, the *Wraith* spun uncontrollably. Debris from the *Gibraltar*'s attacks along with the nose of the dead frigate collided with the exiting ship. Each hit caused the *Cuda* to shudder.

The spinning ship came within ten meters of hitting the *Cuda* again. The narrow miss had all eyes watching, helpless to avoid what was to come. To everyone's relief, the separation between the two ships grew, and the collision was narrowly avoided.

Beaumont said, "Captain, we're untethered but suffered some damage on the escape. We have no reported casualties but will need repair assistance when we come to a halt."

Cheers on the Bridge overwhelmed Tregevek's microphone. He waited for them to die down before talking. "Captain Eskar, permission to step down as temporary captain."

Eskar smiled and put his hand on Tregevek's back. "Permission granted. Excellent job, Ari."

As Tregevek stepped away, he raised his head and spoke to the crew. "It was an honor to serve with all of you today. Again, excellent work."

CHAPTER FORTY-FOUR

Restless Discovery

Kadon couldn't sleep, her mind swirling with activity. She tried getting up and drinking some water, but anytime she was near the point of resting, another thought would invade her tranquility. Rather than fight it all night, she decided to head to the Med Bay and get some work done.

Wearily, she got dressed and made the way to her office. Most of the lights in the Bay were dimmed, but the hallway leading to the three holding rooms was brightly illuminated. Four occupied gurneys rested in the lit corridor.

A young woman saw her and wearily lifted her hand as she groaned. The noise startled Kadon and she hastened to tend to the patient's needs. , Milla was already caring for her, before the doctor could even ask what was wrong. She sighed deeply and regathered her focus.

"Nightmare?" a familiar voice startled her again. She turned to see Temkin leaning on the wall.

Kadon put her hand over her heart and shook her head. "No. You should watch out, Deke! You're lucky I wasn't carrying a scalpel or something. I might have slashed you right there."

Temkin slowly grinned as he shifted his weight. The

movement brought out a faint grimace. "I'll keep that in mind."

"I couldn't sleep and am compiling a lot in my noggin right now. I figure since I'm up anyway, I might as well come down here and take care of some business. What about you?"

"Well, mine were indeed nightmares."

Kadon smacked her lips. "Oh, I'm sorry. Has that gotten any better?"

"Not for twenty years."

Kadon started walking to her office. "Well, I haven't been able to get around to it with everything on the ship, but I owe you quite a few sessions. Do you want to come in and talk about it?"

"Officially?"

Kadon was irritated at the comment, but she understood where it was coming from once she considered it. Temkin was all alone, and Kadon was among the few people he had discussions with. The revelation calmed her response. "Yes, *officially*. But it could be unofficial if you'd like. Besides, I'd like to check your leg. It should be getting better by now."

Temkin looked down at his leg. "Are you worried, Doc?"

"No, not really. Everyone heals at their own pace. I want to make sure it's healing properly. Just to be safe."

Temkin got a defiant smile. "How could I resist when you put it that way?"

Kadon continued walking. "Come on down, goofball. It'll take me two minutes tops."

Temkin bounced off the wall and firmly planted his cane on the floor as he followed Kadon down the hall. "My leg is doing better."

Kadon nodded. "That's good to hear. Now, let me see for myself."

Eventually, Temkin made his way into Kadon's office. He sat down on the closest chair and took a deep breath. "This isn't going to hurt, is it?"

Kadon snorted. "Why? Are you afraid?"

"Always. What I hate most is when a doctor says something like 'you might feel a little pressure.' You know that's a euphemism for excruciating pain."

Kadon let out a guttural belly laugh. "You know? I've never thought of it before, but I've used the line. I'm sorry if you've experienced that. We try to warn you of what's coming, but you got us on that one!"

"I knew it. It's a conspiracy among all doctors to deceive their patients," Temkin said as he tried to stick his leg out to be examined, with moderate success.

Kadon grabbed a scanner from her desktop and sat down next to him. "Okay. Now sit still. You might feel a little pressure."

Temkin stopped breathing and then smiled. "Good one, Doc. You actually had me there for a second."

"Turnabout is fair play, Deke." Kadon giggled as she examined his leg. When she did, she began to frown. "Oh boy."

Temkin immediately tensed up. "What's wrong?"

"Nothing. Your leg is healing fine. It's a little slower than I'd like, but it's fine. You're just too easy." Kadon looked up and smiled.

Temkin frowned. "Very funny, Doc."

"I thought so." Kadon moved away from Temkin and sat back down. She lifted her tablet off her desk. "So, what would you like to talk about *unofficially*?"

"But you picked up the tablet?"

Kadon looked down at her hand. "Yeah. We can talk, but I

fidget. The tablet helps me stay focused on the topic. I know it sounds funny, but it's true."

Temkin shrugged. "Fair enough. Can I ask you doctor-type questions, but unofficially?"

"Shoot. I'm all ears."

"Is it normal to have memory lapses?"

"Are you asking for a friend?" Kadon snickered.

Temkin frowned. "I wish, but no."

Kadon regretted making her joke, and it showed in her expression. "Oh... Well, you'll have to be more specific than that."

"So, for instance, you remember that fight I got into a few weeks ago? I remember getting hit, then the next thing I remember is sitting on a bench and looking at the poor guy grabbing his neck."

Kadon thought about it. "From what I heard, he hit you pretty hard. Jarring shots like that can cause short-term memory loss. Have you suffered any other side effects like nausea or headaches?"

Temkin slumped in his chair as Kadon observed his body language. "No, not really, but this happens every now and then."

Kadon moved forward in her chair. "How often?"

"I don't know. It happens most often when I'm sleeping. I'll end up in another part of my room."

"So, maybe it's like sleepwalking?"

Temkin took a deep breath. "I suppose it could be that, but honestly, I've another thing that happens too."

"What other thing?"

"Sometimes, I'll have memories of doing things that I don't remember doing."

Kadon looked confused. "You mean like vivid dreams?"

"No, more like vivid memories."

Kadon tried to put together what Temkin was saying. "I've read your records. Is this what they wrote about when you told them you saw your father die?"

Temkin looked surprised. He began to play with the top of his cane. "Umm... Yes, that's precisely what I'm talking about."

Kadon tried to remain unemotional. Though only five years older, she resisted the urge to hug the young man like a mother would hug her child. "The mind is an incredible thing. Sometimes, it'll intentionally blot things from our memory to protect itself. I'm not going to lie, you had a horrific childhood, and I don't know how you turned out so... normal." She hastily added, "No offense."

Temkin shook his head. "No, I understand."

"That normalcy seems to have come at some cost. I think these inserted memories and memory loss are all part of your mind protecting you from your circumstances. Does that make sense?"

"Yeah, it does. But it's not giving me a warm and fuzzy feeling, if you know what I mean."

Kadon studied Temkin closely. The pain in his face resonated with her. She decided it was time to switch gears. "I do. I also saw in your file that you played football in high school."

"I did." Temkin's eyebrows raised.

"Captain, right?"

"Yep. I was made captain in my junior year. I loved playing."

Good! We're off that subject for now, "she thought to herself, then said, "Tell me what you loved so much about playing."

Temkin grinned as he recalled his memories. "Well, there's so much to say about that. My mom let me join the team in junior high..."

As Temkin began to share, Kadon decided to check her mail. She noticed one from Alan Wittle. She looked up from the tablet to assure Temkin she was still listening as she opened the message. In it were the promised video links. *Perfect! Something mindless to look at as Temkin talked,* she thought as she clicked on the first link.

Temkin continued speaking. "... so, I started playing linebacker..."

Kadon watched the first feed; nothing stuck out. She moved on to the second link. The video showed the culprit walking away from the camera. She tried to conceal her frustration that the suspect was so clever at hiding his face. Looking up again, she could see Temkin was still monologuing the heck out of his love for football.

She was about to go to the third link when something in her gut told her to watch the second link again. She was about to click the link when she heard Temkin asking. "Did you play any sports when you were young?"

Kadon luckily caught the question. "Yeah. I played volleyball and basketball. I was so-so at both, I loved volleyball and I wanted to be the best, but I wasn't fast enough. It's what pushed me to be a doctor. One day, our best player broke her ankle. Fortunately, one of the fathers was a doctor. I watched him help her and realized I wanted to do that — I wanted to help people."

"That's pretty noble."

"I never thought of it like that. It was my sophomore year, and from then on, I knew what I had to do. I hit the books hard and let the Navy help me become a medic."

"The good old Navy."

"Yes, indeed. What else do you remember that you liked from

high school?"

"Well, I hated most classes. That's for sure."

Kadon leaned back in her chair. "Did you have any hobbies?"

"I loved playing guitar. My mom said my dad would play, too."

"When did you pick up the guitar?"

Kadon could see that same grin as when Temkin spoke about football. "I found my dad's guitar in the closet…"

Kadon waited a moment, then clicked the second link again. This time, she ran the video at half speed. Something stuck out to her as she studied the feed, and she could feel her heartbeat racing. She tapped the screen to pause the feed.

The man in the video feed had just bent over to pick up something off the floor. When he did, it exposed his lower neck. Kadon leaned in closer to the tablet to make sure of what she was looking at. She briefly glanced up to see if Temkin was still talking, then examined the neckline again to ensure she wasn't just seeing things. Right at the collar line was the tiny point of a dagger tattoo.

Kadon became sick. She looked up to see Temkin still talking about his guitar. *What do I do?* she thought as she considered her options. As calmly as possible, she opened an app to summon Milla. She looked down the list of options and picked heavy sedation, emergency, doctor in danger, and silent alarm. She looked up one last time, sent the request, and closed the dialog.

Temkin had just finished his story about the guitar when his watch alarm beeped. Immediately, he looked down and read the message. The smile on his face turned grim. "Oh, Jill. What have you done?" He looked at the message on his watch as he shook his head.

"Me? What do you mean?" Kadon tried to remain calm.

Before she could say another word, Temkin rose effortlessly from his chair. The cane fell to the ground and made a loud smack on impact. Kadon had never noticed how massive Temkin was until this moment. He walked over without any sign of a limp and grabbed her tablet. He saw the paused picture of himself and sneered. "Damn. I was being so careful too."

"Deke? What's going on?" Kadon pushed back in her chair. Out of the corner of her eye, she could see Milla approaching.

Temkin chuckled. "Deke? I'm afraid Deke has left the building."

Kadon watched a med-bot glide into the room, holding a syringe. "I don't understand." *Thank God, just in time. Wait a minute. That's Irena, not Milla. What the heck is going on?* Her heart raced faster as she tried to grasp what was happening.

Temkin grabbed her arm. "It's a damn shame too. Deke really liked you. I knew you were going to be the problem. But now you'll understand."

Irena walked over and calmly inserted the needle into Kadon's arm. Kadon looked at the med-bot as if her best friend had betrayed her. Tears flowed as she slowly fell unconscious in Temkin's arms.

CHAPTER FORTY-FIVE

Getting To Know You

Kadon could hear voices calling to her, but it was as if someone was shouting at her at the other end of a long tunnel. Slowly, the sound got louder and louder. She had an itch on her forehead, but when she went to scratch it, she realized that her hands were restrained. The shock of the moment forced her eyes wide open.

"Well, look who's back with us." Temkin sat comfortably in a chair, waiting for the rest of Kadon's senses to return to her.

"What's going on?" Kadon struggled to free herself, but her arms and legs were secured to the bed. She felt something heavy and metal attached around her throat like a necklace.

Temkin stood and walked closer to the bed. "Doctor, before you try to scream, I must warn you. I've rigged up a Taser around your neck. It's like a shock collar for a dog, but this one will keep Tasing you until you're knocked out, and I'm the sound meter. I know it's a little ruthless, but it's all I could think of in a pinch. Still, I'd be cautious with how loudly you choose to speak." Temkin held up the switch for Kadon to see.

Kadon followed the cable to the switch and could feel it move when Temkin shook his hand. Her understanding of the situation became crystal clear. She closed her eyes to find some solace, but none came. Finally, she spoke in a low tone, "Why are you doing this, Deke?"

Temkin smiled. "All in good time, Doctor. First, we need to restart our original conversation. Do you remember that?"

Kadon shook her head in disgust. "What?"

Temkin snickered. "You know, the 'tell me a little bit about yourself' conversation."

"Are you playing games with me, Deke?"

Temkin stopped smiling. "Ah, there it is again. No, Jill, I'm not. Ask me the question again... Go ahead." He sat down and scooted his chair much closer to Kadon than she would have liked.

Kadon didn't comprehend and shook her head, but slowly, she understood. She began to speak in a low voice. "Okay. Major Temkin, tell me a little about yourself."

Temkin smiled with pleasure. "There you go. Now, that wasn't so hard, was it? So, yes, I'm Major Temkin, but you can call me Greg." Temkin waited for the statement to have gravity.

Kadon's brow furrowed as she tried to compile the statement. "Greg..." Finally, her eyes brightened. "Split personality. Son of a..."

Temkin cut her off before she could finish. "Now, now, Doctor. No need to use such language. We're friends, after all."

Kadon's eyes grew wild. "Are you going to kill me too?"

Temkin folded his hands and leaned back in his chair. "You know, that's the million-kreda question, isn't it? I don't want to kill anyone, and Deke seems quite fond of you, but you probably figured that much out. The truth is that I'm in a pickle. You see, I'm not a killer."

Kadon was doing everything she could to remain calm. "You

killed the entire crew of the *Hercules.*"

Temkin frowned. "Is that what you think? Actually, most of them killed each other."

Kadon's anger was rising. "You put them in that situation with the virus you put on that ship and then by killing the reactor."

Temkin shook his head. "I didn't place any virus on that ship." He lifted three fingers in the air. "Rider's honor. I probably shouldn't be telling you this, but that was my secret mission."

Kadon didn't know how to respond. "That's bullshit, and you know it."

Temkin laughed. "Careful, Doctor. I wouldn't recommend raising your voice. Please watch your language. No, it's true. I was tasked with finding who smuggled weapons out of Navy depots for us and the Martians."

"You really expect me to believe that?"

"Yes, I do. I've never lied to you once. Lieutenant Terrance McGill was the guy I discovered on the *Hercules*, but it got much worse. I don't know if you looked at the ship's registry, but that was the SOB I was tracking."

Kadon vaguely recalled the name. "He was smuggling weapons."

Temkin adjusted in his seat. "Yes. You're catching on."

Kadon sneered. "No. I'm trapped and being held against my will."

"True, but let's keep going. McGill figured out that Bigsby and I were on to him and told the captain."

"I don't understand."

"Oh, I didn't mention this? The captain was in on the smuggling too. Most of the crew was. Bigsby and our team? Well, we stuck out like punch on a prom dress."

"So why didn't you tell us any of this?"

"You'll know why in a second. There's more."

Kadon tried to adjust in her bed, but there was no way to get comfortable. "Go on."

"Have you ever heard the saying about making deals with the devil?"

"Of course."

"Yeah, well, someone must have tipped off the ring, and they had one of their own on the ship."

Kadon raised her eyebrows. "One of their own?"

"Yeah, not someone being paid to deliver contraband, someone who was in the organization."

"The *organization*? What the hell are you talking about?"

"The smuggling ring. Come on, Jill, stay with me here."

"Okay, I'm following."

Temkin reached over and patted her arm. "I knew you were pretty smart, Doc. I believe this person released the virus and sabotaged the reactor."

"And this person wasn't you?"

Temkin shook his head. "Doctor, I told you. I won't lie to you."

"Could it be Major Ulysses Maric?"

"Captain Eskar asked me about him. Why do you keep mentioning him?"

Kadon adjusted her position. "He was on the *Hercules*."

"That traitor SOB. Yes, Doc, that's probably who did it."

"While we're on the subject of lying, I want to ask you a quick side question. Did you kill your father?"

"Whoa! How did we get there? Yes, I did. I told you I won't lie to you."

Kadon was growing impatient with these games. "But you've

been lying your whole life. I saw that you passed multiple polygraphs. You expect me to believe you magically turned over a new leaf?"

Temkin leaned back in his chair and chuckled. "I didn't pass any polygraphs. Deke did."

Kadon's thoughts recoiled in horror. "Deke didn't know anything about you."

Temkin sneered as he spoke. "That wimp? Heck, when Dad was around and angry, he would wet the bed. I'd have to be in bed all night, breathing in fresh urine. He couldn't hurt a fire ant. I think he'd have memories occasionally, but he thought they were nightmares. Deke was really as good a guy as you suspected."

Kadon tried to look into Temkin's eyes, but she couldn't. "That means you're his bad side?"

"Bad? Nope. I'm the protector. When my dad was beating my mom and me, I snapped and shouted, 'No more!' My mom was already unconscious, and I kept hitting him until he stopped breathing."

"He was so big. How did you move him?"

"One of our neighbors helped me. He called the police many times on my dad, but Mom would never press charges. When he heard this last fight, he came over and helped me move him to an abandoned warehouse. It was his idea to put the rope around his neck. It was our secret. We returned to the house, and Mom was still unconscious. He called 911 for the last time. The EMTs came and took us both to the hospital."

"That's horrible."

"Yeah, but if it were up to Deke, Dad would have killed Mom and me that night. Mom was planning on leaving him, and he found out somehow. Can I get back to my story now?"

Kadon tried to remain calm, but fear was overwhelming her. "You said you think this guy sabotaged the ship."

"Yes... and he is probably the one who killed any survivors. I always wondered why no one came looking for me. In another unexpected twist, I think someone was sent to retrieve McGill from the ship."

"That's kind of expected."

Temkin cocked his head to the side in agreement. "True, but I knew the guy they sent. I served with him for years. Unfortunately, he didn't realize that the virus that crippled the *Hercules* had done its work on his ship too."

Kadon did her best to hide her real emotions and continue the conversation. "Greg, all of this sounds like you're the good guy here. Why don't you turn yourself in and let us figure this out?"

Temkin laughed. "I sound like a good guy? Are you serious? Come on, Doc, has that line ever worked? I told you that these smugglers controlled the ship. When the captain realized the smugglers were planning to kill everyone, he suddenly needed our help."

"Okay..."

"He broke Bigsby and me up. He had me work on the communication array and Bigsby on the reactor. Both of us knew we were dead after we got those things working, so we figured out a way to stay alive... Well, I thought we figured it out. You see, I killed the CO_2 scrubber."

"Deke said that the captain did."

Temkin shook his head. "No, Deke said that they accidentally shut it off. That's all that schmuck knew. I did it, and he had no idea."

"Wouldn't the CO_2 kill everyone?"

"Obviously not everyone. I'm here, after all. The plan was to allow everyone to suffer from hypoxia. It would ensure that we had every advantage when the time came. We had oxygen tanks that we hid in one of the stalls in the bathroom. Flat out, I'm no saint."

Kadon rolled her eyes. "So, you did plan to kill these people."

Temkin bobbed his head left and right. "Well, to be fair, we planned to live. But, hopefully, you can now see why turning myself in isn't on the table."

"I see it worked for you. What happened to Bigsby?"

"Deke's account was accurate. Captain Haynes freaked out and shot him in the back. Deke managed to get out of there like the coward he was. I'd have shot Haynes between the eyes. Again, no saint here."

Kadon shook her head. "I don't understand how you can talk about yourself like that."

Temkin grinned. "It bugs you, doesn't it? Look, we share this body. I'm in charge, but Deke has his uses. No one suspects that guy. He is as good as he's charismatic. Wouldn't you agree?"

Kadon frowned. "Well, that ship has sailed."

"Ouch. Come on, Doc, you know you like the guy."

"Look... Greg... you and Deke are one package. I know you don't think that's true, but it is. It doesn't matter whether I like you or not."

Temkin crossed his arms. "Okay, Doc, whatever you say. All I know is that I'm here to protect Deke. Not just his life but also his lifestyle. I think of myself more as Deke's guardian angel."

Kadon struggled to remain cordial. "Well, you probably realize that your lifestyle is going to change. News flash, buddy, you'll get exhausted running."

Temkin's lips pursed, and he slowly nodded. "Yeah. But it is what it is."

"Did Deke get a vote in this?"

"A vote in what?"

"It looks to me like you've destroyed your life without giving Deke a say-so."

"True. I could have let Deke die because that would've been much better for him, right?"

Kadon sighed. "I don't know what to tell you."

"I guess it's good that I didn't really ask. Now, about you, Doctor Kadon. You're a serious conundrum."

"What does that mean?"

"Well... you've met Greg... which is me."

Kadon was utterly confused. "Yeah... so?"

"No one meets me. That's how this schtick works."

"Well, I've met you."

Temkin leaned forward. "I want you to think about that for a moment."

The revelation made Kadon gasp. "What are you planning on doing?"

Temkin took a deep breath. "I just don't know. You understand the problem, right? You're a loose end. In full disclosure, I've already been setting up your drug addiction and overdose."

Kadon's heart raced. "My what?"

"Doc, I'm Special Operations. I do this stuff all the time. You're so squeaky-clean that you were easy to pepper. A little advice: Believe it or not, having just a little dirt in your profile is better. When folks are that pure, people question the authenticity."

Kadon started to struggle in her restraints. "You've got to be kidding me."

"You see my problem? Up 'til now, everyone I've eliminated had it coming."

"That's really sick." Tears slowly slid from her eyes.

"I told you that I was going to be honest with you, Doc. It's a real pickle."

"Killing me won't help your cause."

Temkin shook his head. "Well, if you're the sole person on the ship who knows Deke's other identity, I think Deke could pull off the doe-in-the-headlights kind of thing. He's pretty good at that."

"You know, if I figured out who took Irena, I'm pretty sure Captain Eskar or Antoni Capalov will figure it out. Also, why did you take Irena? You would probably be free and clear if you didn't."

Temkin stared up at the ceiling. "It's the paranoia in me that made me take Irena. I always have to have contingencies — Irena was a precaution. As for your group figuring this out... that's only three people, including you. I could probably arrange departures for Remy and Antoni."

"Oh my God! Are you serious?"

There was a knock at the door. Temkin leaned over and typed something into his watch. "Yeah... I guess I am. Don't even think about screaming. I need to think about this some more. As usual, Doc, it's always helpful talking to you. I see why Deke likes you so much. But now it's time for you to go night-night. Sweet dreams."

Immediately, Irena turned and came to the bedside. All Kadon could do was curse at him as her eyes slowly closed. Temkin looked over at the med-bot and ordered it to answer the door.

Chapter Forty-Six

Missing

"Well, Remy, thank you for dinner. I'm going to head back to my quarters now." Captain Tregevek stood from his chair as Eskar rose to escort him to the door.

"It was my pleasure, Ari. Perhaps we'll be able to do this again soon," Eskar said while shaking his hand.

"I'd like that. Good night."

Eskar watched his guest leave, then quietly began clearing the dinner table. The irritation of fabricated food was the only negative to an otherwise pleasant evening. He was thankful for his stash of Terran wine.

With all the dishes cleaned and stowed, Eskar decided to walk to the Bridge. Usually, he'd waste no time and use the elevators to traverse the three floors up. Today, he opted to take the longer walking route to the ship's forward section.

The journey allowed him to visit Doctor Kadon in Med Bay. As he turned the corner, he was greeted by Milla. "Hello, Captain Eskar. Is there some way I can be of assistance to you?"

The lack of facial expression always made Eskar uncomfortable. He looked down at its nameplate and then began to speak. "Hello, Milla. I was looking for Doctor Kadon."

"I apologize, Captain Eskar. Doctor Kadon is SIQ today."

Eskar was surprised. In over fifteen years of service, he could never recall her being sick, let alone to the point of quarter confinement. "Sick in quarters? She never takes time off. Is she contagious?"

"I apologize, Captain Eskar, but I cannot discuss her personal information."

Eskar looked around, hoping one of the human attendants would be less informed about the confidentiality laws. To his disappointment, none were there. He breathed a heavy sigh and said, "Okay, Milla, thank you."

"Of course, Captain Eskar. While you are here, I see you are due for your annual physical. Would you like to schedule an appointment right now?"

Eskar tried his best to remain calm. "I'm a little preoccupied at the moment, Milla. When Doctor Kadon returns, you can have her contact me on this matter."

Milla unemotionally but pleasantly responded, "That is entirely understandable, Captain Eskar. I will remind her when she returns to work. In the meantime, I have noticed that your vitals have elevated. Can I give you something to relax you? Perhaps some herbal tea?"

Eskar shook his head. "No, thanks. I'm fine, but thank you. I'll try to go down and visit her."

"I am sure she will appreciate the gesture, Captain Eskar."

Eskar quickly turned and headed down the hallway to Kadon's quarters. It was thirty meters from the Med Bay. When he knocked on the door, only a few seconds before it slid open, and Irena greeted Eskar. "Good evening, Captain Eskar. How may I be of service to you?"

Eskar smiled. Standing close to the med-bots was even more unnerving than talking to them. Their emotionless but solid frames and the gracefulness with which they moved made them seem more like ghosts than humans. "I was hoping to check in on Doctor Kadon to see how she's feeling."

"Yes, Captain Eskar, she is resting right now. I am not at liberty to discuss her situation, but I can tell her you stopped by."

"If you don't mind, that would be wonderful. Thank you."

"Of course, Captain Eskar."

Before Eskar could say anything else, the door began to slide close. Out of the corner of his eye, he noticed a cane leaning on the wall in her quarters. He momentarily closed his eyes, trying to visualize what he saw and ensure he didn't just imagine it. To make certain, he decided to knock on the door again. Irena swiftly answered.

"Hello, Captain Eskar. Did you have another question?"

Eskar realized he had knocked too quickly. In his enthusiasm to confirm what he saw, he forgot to make a reason to knock. He looked where he thought he saw the cane, which was no longer there. "Yes, umm... Milla said I needed to make an appointment for my annual physical. Can you also tell Doctor Kadon to contact me concerning that?"

"I would be happy to when she is active again, Captain Eskar."

"Thank you, Irena."

"You are most welcome, Captain Eskar." The door slid closed again.

Your mind is playing tricks on you, old man. Yet I know I saw a cane in there. It's all too strange, he thought as he turned to leave. He decided to continue walking to the Bridge because he knew Ensign Capalov was on duty.

"Captain Eskar." Lieutenant Polson hailed Eskar from across the hall.

With his head spinning, the distraction was welcome. "Good evening, Lieutenant. I'm heading to the Bridge if you would care to walk with me."

"Yes, sir. I've looked into the security camera in the spare room."

"So, did it turn up anything?"

"It did, but I don't know if it's very useful." Polson picked up her pace to match Eskar's gait.

"I'm interested to hear what you have found."

"Well, whoever took the part from the storeroom understood where the cameras were. They craftily moved so we never got a good image of them."

Eskar frowned. "So, how is this useful?"

"We established when the part was taken, and it was way before the extra ship arrived."

"So, this was done by someone on the inside." Eskar felt anger but couldn't pinpoint the reason why.

"Yes, sir. I'd say the person on the ship worked with our mystery guest."

Eskar raised an eyebrow. "Why would you say that?"

"The corrosion was intentionally done. Whoever did this needed a way to escape. I surmise that would be the best reason for an unknown ship to visit the *Hercules* mid-mission."

"That's plausible. What if this virus infected the visiting ship? It happened with the frigates, right?"

Polson thought for a moment on the questions. "The accomplice pulled their partner into the Venus flytrap... so to speak."

Eskar leaned over as if he were sharing a secret. "I don't know about you, but that might piss me off."

"Me too."

"Great work, Polson. It gives me more to think about."

Polson stiffened slightly as she continued to walk. "Thank you, sir."

Eskar began to think aloud, "I think I need to pay a visit to our favorite refugee."

"Major Temkin?"

"That's the one."

"You know, He visited me yesterday in Engineering."

Eskar's curiosity was piqued. "He did? What was he doing down there?"

"Well, he said he was fixing a circuit board, which was odd. I mean, he has no responsibilities on the ship, right?"

"You're correct. What kind of circuit board was it?"

Polson thought for a moment. "It was a medical board. I could tell because of the white thermal coating. Greg said it was his toaster, and it was behaving intermittently. I figured he was Special Ops and couldn't tell me what it really was."

The hairs on Eskar's neck stood up. "I'm sorry, who did you say came down to Engineering?"

Polson looked confused. "Umm... Major Temkin, but he said to call him Greg."

Eskar had a sinking feeling in his gut. He stopped walking and turned to Polson. "Lieutenant Polson, I'll talk with you later. I just realized that I need to check something out. Great work!"

"Uhh... Yes, sir... Goodbye."

Eskar quickly made his way back to Med Bay. As he walked in again, Milla greeted him, "Were you able to see Doctor Kadon,

Captain Eskar?"

Eskar shook his head. "No, Irena said she was resting."

"Rest is good, Captain Eskar. If there is nothing else, I do have patients to attend to. Hopefully, Doctor Kadon will be back soon."

Eskar's frustration grew. *Why did I come back here? It's not like Jill is here,* he pondered as he looked down, determined to head to Temkin's quarters.

Before he turned to walk out, he happened to gaze into Kadon's office. Her tablet was resting on the floor beside her desk. Without asking, he walked into the room. Milla followed him, citing objections to his entry into Kadon's private space. Eskar ignored the med-bot.

Eskar knelt to pick up the tablet. The screen was cracked, but when he touched it, it turned on. *I'd say something to her about a lock screen, but I'm glad she doesn't have one right now.*

The device came to life. On the tablet was a paused frame of a man in a cap and black clothes leaning down. Eskar minimized the image and realized this was from security footage concerning who had abducted Irena. He decided to watch the entire video.

Nothing stuck out to him as odd, so he found the spot where Kadon had paused and studied it further. He couldn't see anything that was telling. He decided to move on and minimize the mail system. That's when he noticed the emergency order to Milla earlier that evening.

Milla continued to remind him of his intrusion into Kadon's office.

"Milla, first of all, I'm the ship's captain, and I can look anywhere on this ship at any time. Secondly, did Doctor Kadon send you this emergency message earlier this evening?"

Milla stopped warning Eskar that he was violating the doctor's privacy and looked at the tablet. "Yes, Captain Eskar. I received that message at 1834."

"Did you come in here then?"

"No, Captain Eskar, Irena came in for me."

Eskar nodded and put his hands up, stopping Milla from continuing to hurry its answer along. "And what happened?"

"I apologize, Captain Eskar, I do not understand the question."

"Milla, what was the emergency?"

"It turned out to be nothing, Captain Eskar. Irena ordered Doctor Kadon to retire to her quarters."

Eskar slowly looked at the tablet again. "So you saw Doctor Kadon leave for her quarters?"

"No, Captain Eskar, I was told that Irena escorted her to her room."

Eskar's patience was tested with each question. "Milla, please quit saying my name; I know who I am, and you and I are the only ones in this room. Did Irena carry her or escort her?"

"I do not know. But the SIQ petition was approved at 1839."

As Milla spoke, Eskar's mind began racing. He lifted the tablet and pulled the paused image back up. After a few moments, he turned to Milla. "Milla, when Major Temkin was brought in from the *Hercules*, did the rescue team take pictures of his body?"

"Many pictures were taken."

"I don't want to compromise anyone's privacy, but may I look at any picture you have of his back? It doesn't have to show any injuries. I'd just like to see a picture of his back."

"Yes, I believe I can comply with that." Milla walked over to a console, touched it, and displayed an image of Temkin's back. "This was one of the first pictures taken of Major Temkin."

Eskar studied Irena's picture and saw what he was looking for: A large dagger tattoo that started between his shoulder blades and pointed to the small of his neck. His stomach churned as he looked back at the tablet and saw why Doctor Kadon paused the video.

chapter forty-seven

Hunted

Eskar jogged toward Doctor Kadon's room as he spoke through his communicator. "Mason, I need two security details. One at Doctor Kadon's quarters, and one at the VOQ. We need to apprehend Major Temkin. I suspect he's armed and dangerous and holding Doctor Kadon."

Mason responded without delay, "Yes, sir. We're on our way."

Eskar arrived at the door of Kadon's quarters and waited for the security detail. To his delight, he could hear the team coming down the hall. He stood by the door, resisting the urge to storm in.

A senior officer immediately approached Eskar. "Sir, we got here as quickly as possible. If you don't mind standing back, we'll scan the room for signs of life and traps."

Eskar obliged as he watched with anticipation. One of the security detail said, "The room is clear. We're ready to open it."

Two men walked to the door with a device designed to open it. Before they tried to pry it, the senior officer scanned his ID, which caused it to slide open, to his surprise. "Clear! Go! Go! Go!"

Eskar obliged as he watched the four officers storm into the room. "All clear."

The senior officer returned. "No signs of them, sir."

Eskar pulled his cap off and scratched his head. "Damn, they were just there fifteen minutes ago. They can't be far."

Eskar's communicator beeped. It was Mason. "Sir, the VOQ is clear. No signs of Temkin or Doctor Kadon."

"Thanks, Mason. Doctor Kadon's room is also empty. Let's begin sweeping the ship."

"Yes, sir. I'll get surveillance involved, too."

Eskar could hear Mason on the security officers' lines. The officers moved quickly as they began looking for suspects from room to room. He decided to communicate with Capalov. "Antoni, we lost Temkin, and we believe he's taken Doctor Kadon. Can you run their trackers to see where they are?"

"Yes, sir. Give me a minute." Eskar could hear the blip of Capalov's computer. "This says they're both in Doctor Kadon's quarters."

Eskar walked back into the doctor's room. He looked around and noticed two small devices on the bathroom counter. Though cleaned, they still had small traces of blood on them. "It looks like the trackers were cut out."

Capalov stated, "Only Milla or Irena could do that, sir."

"My guess is it was Irena. It answered the door when I came by earlier. Dammit, I could have prevented this whole thing if I had been more on top of it."

"We'll find them, Captain. I won't stop until I figure something out."

"I know you will, Antoni. Thank you."

Eskar started thinking about what he'd do in this situation. He made a quick call. "Hey, Mason. Get some folks down to the auxiliaries. There aren't a lot of places to hide on the ship. My money is that he'll try to escape on one of the Mantis ships."

"Good call, Captain. I'm on it, sir."

This guy seems to be one step ahead of us every time. Eskar thought about Temkin's countermove, knowing the ships would probably be guarded.

The next fifteen minutes seemed like an eternity for Eskar. He constantly checked his communicator for the possibility of a dropped message. To his disappointment, no message came.

Commander Mason walked calmly to him as Eskar stood in the hall waiting for news. "I don't know where the hell they are, but we haven't come across them. I've placed guards around all the Mantis ships, and we'll continue our watch. And we'll keep searching."

Eskar pulled his cap off and threw it at the wall, rubbing his hand through his thinning hair. His communicator grabbed his attention. It was Capalov. "Sir, Admiral Shoapa has returned. She's hailing you."

Eskar gritted his teeth as he picked up his cap from the floor. "I'll be up there in a minute."

CHAPTER FORTY-EIGHT

Abduction

Kadon felt the sharp pain of a bolt head pushing into the small of her back. Slowly, she began to come to her senses. She scanned around and realized she was no longer in her room. Looking down, she could still feel the Taser necklace around her. She tried to adjust to provide some relief. Her efforts were rewarded, and a grateful sigh exited her mouth.

"Ah, Doc, welcome back. You were right. The captain is on to me."

Kadon nodded. "I figured. At least I'm not dead. I thought for sure you were going to kill me."

"About that, sorry. I just had to make sure you were silent. I don't think killing you is in my cards. That doesn't mean I won't. You're now my last bartering chip."

Kadon wiggled, trying to make herself more comfortable. "That makes me feel so much better."

Temkin frowned. "Don't make me regret my decision, Doc."

Kadon stayed silent for a few minutes. She looked around and didn't recognize the surroundings. "Where are we?"

Temkin looked up from what he was doing. "We're in an escape pod."

She tried to look out the window, but the pods were still attached to the ship. "Apparently, we haven't escaped yet."

Temkin shook his head. "No, not yet. I've rigged some things to help with that. When we get near a port, I've got a plan."

"Assuming no one will find you first."

"No one's going to find us in here."

Kadon's senses were returning. She could feel her temples throbbing, along with shooting pain up both sides of her neck. "You sound so sure."

Temkin went back to preparing something. "Did you fight in the Martian Secession, Doc?"

"Fight? No. Help the wounded? Most assuredly."

"Were you in the battle for Crystal Valley?"

"No. I was on the other side of Mars at that time."

"Did you ever hear about what happened there?"

Kadon bobbed her head. "I've heard many stories of its brutality."

"I was on the IPFS *Kincade*. We were part of the advance group that initially engaged the Martian fleet."

"I read that in your profile. The captain of your ship ended up a rear admiral."

"Yep. Captain Oskaweitz. He was a fantastic man. Our first engagement was devastating. We took out three ships in less than five minutes. We sustained some damage but were still in fighting condition."

"Didn't we lose a battleship in that conflict?"

"Yes. We lost the IPFS *Yamm*. The battle was going well in the air and on the ground, but the *Yamm* took three direct hits, and the hull became comprised."

Kadon was curious. "What did they do?"

"They put out a distress call, and we and the *Leopard* responded. We could see they had already launched their escape pods as we approached the battleship. There were hundreds of them heading toward the Martian surface."

"Oh, I do kind of remember this story now, but please remind me."

"Well, one of the Martian captains was so upset that they were losing the battle that he ordered his fighters to scan the pods and shoot any with living people in them."

"That's terrible."

"It's not a first. In World War II, for instance, the commanders in the Luftwaffe ordered their pilots to shoot down enemy personnel who ejected from their planes. The idea was that they would never be able to reenter the war if they were dead. The men were sitting ducks floating with their parachutes. At Crystal Valley, it's estimated that we lost about nine hundred men and women in those escape pods."

Kadon could only shake her head. "Again, that's so horrible. This is why we wanted a few men brought up for war crimes after the conflict."

Temkin agreed. "Without question. After that battle, the escape pods were redesigned with significant changes. They're now double-hulled and impervious to scans. They have an automatic defensive cannon. Also, the beacon must be started manually, or it kicks in when the person's vitals drop below a certain level."

"How does that help?"

"A fighter or drone couldn't determine if a pod was just ejected or had occupants. If their tracking system targets the pod, it'll fire return shots. All of these changes were designed to deter the enemy from trying to make short work of helpless vessels."

Kadon's brow furrowed. "I don't see how this story is relevant here."

"Come on, Doc, use your imagination. How are they trying to find us? They're using their scanners. With our door closed like this, no one can see or scan us."

Kadon wasn't as confident. "But they can walk in here and see that the door is closed."

Temkin chuckled. "You're sharp, but I thought of that too. I've closed all the doors in this row of pods. No one will notice, and the doors won't automatically open. Security has already been by. When the doors didn't open, they tried to scan the pod and found nothing."

Kadon sat quietly and listened. Finally, she spoke again. "What are you going to do with me?"

Temkin laughed a little louder. "Right now, you know my plan, so you're stuck with me for the time being. I may let you go... or kill you... I haven't decided."

Kadon closed her eyes as her head and neck continued to hurt. "You think that's funny?"

"Doc, if you haven't figured it out yet, that was a joke. I'll grant you it was in poor taste, but it was a joke nonetheless. I'll find a way to let you go after I've escaped."

Kadon couldn't control her tears. "Why are you screwing with me like this?"

"I don't mean anything by it. It's not like you haven't already come to that yourself."

"Please stop with the jokes."

"I'll try, Doc, but I can't make any promises. They just kind of flow out."

CHAPTER FORTY-NINE

Guess Who's Back?

"**A**dmiral Shoapa, it's great to have you back." Eskar stood at attention as he spoke to her.

Shoapa smiled and nodded. "I brought the cavalry with me, Captain. I see you've successfully separated the *Wraith* from the *Cuda*. We're prepared to offload our people from your ship."

Eskar's smile faded. "Sir, we have a situation that we're trying to handle on the ship. I hope you'll respectfully understand that once this situation is dealt with, we'll open our pads to transfer your personnel."

Shoapa frowned. "A situation, Captain? Have our officers caused problems?"

Eskar shook his head. "We've had a few minor scuffles, but nothing that amounted to charges on either side. For the most part, everyone has been on good behavior."

"So, what's going on?"

Eskar paused for a moment. "Sir, we believe we have found the person responsible for our virus and the death of the crew of the *Hercules*."

"Let me guess. Was it the person you saved?"

"Yes, sir. It was. We're on shutdown at this moment. There's nowhere for this person to go. I'm worried that he might try to escape in the confusion of retrieving your crew. We're trying to close down all opportunities for him to get away."

Shoapa paused for a moment before answering. "I appreciate the predicament, but you can understand my desire to get our crew back. I'd offer to bring some additional security, but I don't believe that would help matters."

"No, sir. It wouldn't. I'd like Captain Tregevek to keep you updated on our progress. We're hoping to resolve this in the next few hours."

Admiral Shoapa cautiously smiled. "That would be acceptable for the time being, Captain. Though I can empathize with your dilemma, I hope you can understand and appreciate mine."

"I do, Admiral. We're not at war, so I hope you can extend us grace on this. I'll keep Captain Tregevek up to speed on our progress so he can relay information to you, if that's acceptable."

"It is, Captain. I pray that you apprehend this suspect quickly and without casualties."

"Thank you, Admiral. I'll reach out to Captain Tregevek and have him contact you."

"I'd greatly appreciate it, Captain. Shoapa out."

The line went blank, and Eskar at once addressed Capalov. "Antoni, will you hail Captain Tregevek and have him meet me in my quarters?"

"Of course, Captain."

"Also, please keep me informed of how our manhunt is going."

Capalov straightened up. "Yes, sir. I don't think it's going to be long. There aren't many places to hide on this ship."

Eskar's eyes lit up. "Places to hide... Antoni, I think I know where he might be. Rather than telling Captain Tregevek to meet me in my quarters, inform him I'll come to him as soon as I resolve a pressing matter."

"Yes, sir. Where do you think they might be?"

"In one of the safest places on the ship."

CHAPTER FIFTY

In Hiding

Kadon felt boldness growing inside of her, pushing her to press Temkin. "You say Deke hasn't lied to me."

"That's right."

"Explain to me how you can walk without a limp. It doesn't even look like you were injured, but Deke could barely take a step."

Temkin looked down at his ankle. "He never lied to you. It's just pain. I can deal with that, and Deke lets it get the best of him."

Kadon continued to wiggle in her restraints. "So what are we going to do now? Just sit here?"

Temkin looked at her with a smug smile. "Yeah, pretty much. We have enough food for a few weeks. It'll get a little fresh with no shower here, but we can live."

She stared indignantly at her captor. "Isn't that grand? Well, I need to use the bathroom."

Temkin rolled his eyes. "Hold on a second." He walked over and effortlessly picked her up. In a few quick motions, Kadon's arms and legs were untied. "The stall is behind that door."

"You aren't going to watch me?"

Temkin shook his head. "Why? Where are you going to go? There isn't even a window in there. Start moving, Doc."

Kadon rubbed her arms for a moment, staring unfavorably at Temkin. She then stumbled into the small service closet. The walls were so tight she wondered if Temkin could even sit.

Kadon looked around the small chamber. There was nothing to weaponize. She flushed the toilet and cleaned her hands in the small faucet. Using the opportunity, she doused her face and neck with cool water. The fluid gave her momentary comfort, but the reality of her situation quickly overshadowed any relaxation.

"Time's up, Doc. Don't make me come in there and get you."

Kadon scowled at the comment and forcefully opened the door. The accordion-style door expanded and slammed together.

The noise startled Temkin. "Careful, Doc. That's the only stall we got. Now, come on over here and let me have your arms."

Kadon slowly complied. "You're not a killer. I can tell."

Temkin chuckled.

Kadon's head tilted as she tried to understand his reaction. "What's so funny?"

"You probably should talk to the many men I've killed in my career. I will say this, Doc, you're much braver than most of them."

Kadon was in no place to receive a compliment, but she let those words sink in. "You're not a bad man, Greg. Do you know why that story about Crystal Valley sticks so vividly in your mind?"

"Because it's a great example of evil?"

"Well, that's also true. But it sticks because those lives were senselessly taken. You witnessed the most horrific act someone could do by slaughtering those helpless officers."

Temkin shook his head. "It's not the most horrific act."

Kadon decided to keep him engaged in conversation. "Really? What would you say could be worse?"

"When a person kills four or five people, they're called mass murderers, but when they kill thousands or millions, they're called dictators. The worst kind of killing is when you systematically take out each plank of hope that someone has. And when they have nothing left, you kill them while staring into their empty, hopeless eyes."

Kadon's mind spun at what she heard. "Um... I don't know what to say to that. That's about as horrific a description as I've ever heard."

Temkin's face grew cold. "That's where my mom and I were, with my dad. I was born out of that hopelessness. No one wakes up, looks in the mirror and says, 'Hey, I'm going to do some bad today.' Almost nobody thinks they're wicked. Most say they're just dealing with the cards they've been dealt. But I've looked evil in the face, and I assure you it exists. I've looked in the mirror and have seen good, but not when I'm in charge." Temkin began resecuring Kadon's arms and legs. In seconds, she was tied up and placed back in the chair.

Kadon watched Temkin's eyes. She recognized the signs of his desperation. "Greg, up until now, your good is wrapped in keeping Deke safe."

Temkin shook his head. "Not good enough, Doc. Not good enough. I had one job, Doc. One job! I've failed at the one thing I was created for."

"You didn't fail."

Temkin's eyes darted at the comment. "Really? How do you

think I protected Deke in this situation? I screwed everything up. I mean, you said it yourself: If I wouldn't have messed with Irena, we would have gotten away with this."

Kadon paused before speaking. "Did you do what you thought was best?"

Temkin frowned as he answered. "My best was failure, Jill. There's no way to get around that."

"I don't know. There are times when a protector sounds pretty…"

Temkin put his hand on Kadon's leg and shushed her. She heard the sound of the emergency panel doors rolling open on the other side of the escape pod deck. He looked at Kadon, and she could see that his desperation had turned to despair.

Temkin reached into his pocket and pulled out a mini recorder. "Doc, I know you don't like me, but you must do me this courtesy, if not favor. I've recorded all of our conversations. It's my testimony, and it tells what happened on the *Hercules*. No matter what happens, please make sure Captain Eskar gets this."

Kadon nodded as Temkin placed the device in her chest pocket. "I promise he'll get it. Greg, listen to me. You don't have to do this. Please, just turn yourself in. If you really want to protect Deke, that's the best thing to do."

Temkin pursed his lips. "The way I see it, I've given Deke more than twenty extra years of life. He trusted you, Doc, and I promise I'd have never harmed you because of that. I'm really sorry for all of this."

Temkin lifted his hand, holding the small switch, and pressed the button. Kadon braced for the worst shock of her life, but nothing happened. "See, Doc, I couldn't even wire this up. You were safe all the time."

His eyes grew wide and wild as he heard Eskar giving orders. He turned back one more time and looked at Kadon. "It has been a pleasure getting to know you, Doc. Now you stay in here and keep quiet."

Kadon watched in silent horror as Temkin manually rolled up the pod's exit hatch door.

CHAPTER FIFTY-ONE

One Way

Eskar slowly walked onto the escape pod deck with two armed Marines at his side. "Major Temkin, we know you're in there. Please release Doctor Kadon and come out."

The captain looked at the eight pods on this deck. Rather than having their ports open for entry, all of them were closed. Finally, he heard the sound of one of the doors opening. The two Marines focused their guns on the pod while four other Marines spread around the deck.

It took about a minute for the pod door to open fully. Temkin put his hand out of the entry, holding a gray box with a large red button. "Captain, I hope you understand that if I let go of this switch, bad things will happen."

Eskar studied the switch for a moment, then yelled, "He's holding a dead man's switch!" He turned to the guards beside him and ordered them to stand down. The two Marines complied and lowered their guns. "Okay, Temkin. I've ordered these Marines to stand down."

Temkin chuckled. "What about the other five or six around our position?"

Eskar rolled his eyes. "How exactly do you think this will turn out, Deke?"

Temkin stayed in the pod, using it for cover. "Well, I'd like a Mantis ship and an assurance of safe passage. I'll tell you right now that I didn't kill all those people on the *Hercules*."

Eskar moved slightly so he could see Temkin's face. What he saw was not a man in control but a man at the end of his rope. "Maybe so, but all of this looks pretty bad for you, wouldn't you say? Why don't you turn yourself in, and we can sort it all out. I promise you'll get your opportunity to tell us what really happened over there."

Temkin tried switching subjects. "How did you know where I was?"

Eskar simply responded, "Crystal Valley."

Temkin's eyes lit up. "Yep. I forgot that we spoke about that."

"So... whataya say, Deke? Turn yourself in, let the doctor go, and call it a day."

Temkin slowly shook his head. "I think you know I can't do that."

Eskar could sense the panic rising in Temkin. "Hey, man, I don't want anyone to get hurt here. Just undo the dead man switch and walk over here. No one is going to hurt you."

"You mean if I do that... Right?

Tread lightly, old man. He's on the edge, and I have no idea what that trigger is hooked to, Eskar thought as he considered the question. "Work with me here, Deke. I'm trying to make sure nothing else happens."

"It's Greg."

Eskar didn't understand where this was going. "Okay. Do you want to go by Greg? You want me to call you Greg?"

Temkin answered coldly, "I'd prefer that, yes."

Eskar crossed his arms as he spoke. "Well, Greg, we're at a bit of an impasse here."

Temkin cocked his head. "Are we? It seems to me like you're holding most of the cards."

"Yeah... umm... Greg, I think it's in your interest to surrender before this escalates further."

"I don't think it's that easy."

Eskar took off his cap and scratched his head. "Why not? No one wants any more death here."

Temkin nervously smiled as he shook his head. "Yeah, I just don't want to go to prison. That's not a life. That's just death waiting to happen."

"I'm not going to lie to you, Greg. You know that's probably gonna happen." Eskar took a closer look at Temkin's face. Tears flowed, and he wiped his nose with his other arm.

"Captain, you've been very kind to Deke. I appreciate your hospitality. I've mentioned my mother and how much I cared for her. Before you talk to her, please listen to all the evidence and tell her I love her dearly."

Eskar knew what was coming. He took a step forward and raised his hands. "Greg? Why don't you surrender, and you can tell her yourself? It would mean so much more coming from you—"

Before Eskar could finish, Temkin spoke. "Captain, you and I both know this can't end well. I don't think I can come down from here." Perhaps unconsciously, he quickly raised the hand with the trigger in the air. Two shots cracked through the air, and Temkin slumped to the ground, letting out one last gasp.

Eskar watched in horror. He saw that the switch wasn't activated, then shouted at the top of his lungs, "Stand down!

Stand down!" As the two Marines charged past him into the escape pod to secure the hostage. He looked down at the lifeless body at his feet.

Doctor Kadon came out and saw Temkin lying on the deck. She stopped for a moment as her eyes welled up with tears. A Marine placed a blanket around her as she was escorted past the fallen officer. A medic rushed over to check Temkin's vitals. She looked up at Eskar. "He's deceased, Captain."

Kadon stopped and returned to Eskar. "Captain, Greg wanted me to give this to you. It's his confession and account of what occurred on the *Hercules*." She reached into her pocket and handed over the small recording device.

Eskar studied it for a second. "Jill, he left us no choice."

Kadon slowly nodded as tears dropped from her cheeks. "I know. Temkin forced you to make that choice. This mess was his fault, not yours."

Eskar put his cap back on and received the recorder. He turned away from Temkin and began to walk. "I need to inform Captain Tregevek, then write the longest report I've ever written."

Epilogue

The staff prepared the captain's dining table. Each place carried the adornment used for dignitaries. Admiral Shoapa was the first to enter and was pleased with the setting. "This is impressive, Captain."

Eskar smiled at the admiral's pleasure. "I decided to have our chef prepare the meal tonight rather than me trying to do it."

Captains Tregevek and Beaumont followed behind the admiral.

Tregevek chimed in, "I don't think I've ever felt so honored. This is quite a setup."

Eskar looked around at his guests and smiled. "We expect one more, but they just informed me they're running late. If everyone would take a seat, we can start."

Everyone took their seat with the aid of a personal attendant. The first course was arriving when the last attendee entered.

Eskar saw her walk in and stood out of respect for his friend. "Doctor Kadon, I'm so honored you could make it."

Kadon's long black dress complemented her figure, gold necklace and matching earrings spoke to her taste. "I apologize for my tardiness. I was attending to a patient."

"That's most understandable, Doctor," Admiral Shoapa said, attempting to put Kadon at ease. "We're just thankful that you're safe."

Kadon's smile dimmed slightly. "Yes. It has been good to come back to active duty. These last three days in my room have been difficult."

Tregevek said, "I'm sure it hasn't been easy. You should jump back in and try to return to what defines your life as normal."

Kadon nodded slowly. "I like how you put that, Captain. I might have to borrow that in the future." Kadon took her place just in time to receive a hot towel to clean her hands. "I thought I got away from this when I left Med Bay."

Everyone politely laughed.

Shoapa turned to Eskar. "I read your report, Captain. This whole situation is indeed a tragedy. Like you, I believe Major Temkin exposed this massive smuggling ring that has been plaguing both of our fleets. In a strange way, he really is a hero in this situation... It's most unfortunate."

Eskar frowned. "The whole thing is tragic beyond measure. It was one of the hardest things I've ever had to write. I won't lie, I've shed some tears while compiling
this report."

Shoapa continued. "I know it won't say this in the report, but what was your conclusion on whether this was a suicide or a mistake by your security team?"

Eskar lost all emotion from his face. He quickly glanced over at Kadon, who nodded. "I've watched the footage many times now, and I just can't tell if it was a deliberate act or not. Protocol says that my security team made the right call. When I was there, it felt right, but watching the footage, it's just impossible to say. The switch wasn't connected to anything, though he made Doctor Kadon think it was. I believe he was at a breaking point."

"I'm sorry for the difficulties this has caused," Shoapa said, "I believe you've put the best light on the situation. Some things are just better left open. His actions, whether intentional or not, dictated counteraction, and your team behaved accordingly."

"Thank you, Admiral."

Tregevek spoke. "Captain Eskar? Sorry to change the subject, but we were speaking on our way here. We noticed your mention of Crystal Valley in your report."

Eskar stiffened at the reference. "Yes, it was part of how I figured out where he was hiding. I assure you that I didn't put it there to offend."

Tregevek quickly shook his head. "No, we didn't take it that way at all. What you presented made it very understandable, but we felt like there's something that you should know about Crystal Valley."

Eskar raised his eyebrows. "Oh?"

Tregevek looked at his other comrades. Shoapa nodded as if to encourage him to complete his thought. "Yes, sir. Crystal Valley was the darkest battle of the war, but there are standards that no person should ever cross."

"Okay. I think we agree on that." Eskar was treading cautiously.

"We thought it was important that you know. We saw what was done, and it disgusted us. Captain Nguyen and his XO, who made that decision, were demoted the day after that battle. Later that year, they both were court-martialed. I know it's not the war crimes your politicians called for, but we recognize it was an atrocity and embarrassment to our country. They'll at least live with that shame the rest of their days."

Eskar felt emotional, but he tried to remain stoic. He looked over to see that the words struck a soothing chord with Kadon. "Captain, that means more to us than you could possibly know. I hope you don't mind if I share that information with some of our other commanders."

Tregevek nodded. "Most certainly. We welcome it."

"Thank you so much for that. On that note, I'd like to propose a toast." Eskar stood and raised his glass. "Here's to a long peace between our two great nations. May we never meet in battle again."

Acknowledgments

I would love to give some tremendous love to some individuals who helped me make this book a reality. If you want to know some amazing people, look no further than this list:

- To my family (**Laura, Emily, and Elizabeth**), who gave me the time and freedom to create this creepy tale.

- To **Mike Bennett**, who endured my blow-by-blow as I wrote this book and filled my mind with great suggestions.

- To my kind but thorough Beta Reader/Copy Editor, **Danny Raye** (https://writerdannyraye.com/), who helped me believe this was worth publishing and also filled my mind with great suggestions. (If you are writing a book, hire this lady... you won't regret it).

- To **Chris Richcreek**, for his wonderful and brilliant color commentary and editing. I still laugh as I read some of your notes.

(Continued)

- To my designer and extraordinary artist, **Leraynne S.**, who turned my vague descriptions into an amazing book cover.

- To my kind and vibrant narrator, **Chynna T.**, who brought these words to life.

- To **Garret Gordon**, for finding my narrator in the most unlikely of places. :)

About the author

Growing up, Doug was surrounded by technology and science fiction, and the concept of outer space captured his imagination. However, bad vision and excessive height ensured him that being an astronaut wasn't in his future. He quickly changed his focus from being a pilot to an engineer. Forty years later, he is a happily married owner of a small aerospace engineering company that makes components for flight simulation.

As a lover of the arts, his main outlet is music (primarily guitar). He has appeared on multiple albums and was even a music critic for four international publications, producing over 300 articles.

As the father of two delightful girls, he often made up stories that would propel them past their agreed-to bedtimes. This annoyed his patient wife, but he managed to survive, allowing their girls to dream in wide-eyed wonder.

This is his first endeavor in publishing a fictional novel.

Also by

Always come by and check out my website:
www.DougRJoseph.com

Current books:
Practical Evangelism:
A Yankee Christian in King David's Court

Lessons learned about sharing my faith and
walking faithfully while in Israel.

www.ingramcontent.com/pod-product-compliance
Lightning Source LLC
Chambersburg PA
CBHW022308310726
48973CB00001B/271